THE CHAMELEON MAN

&

OTHER TERRORS

DAVID WILLIAMSON

PARALLEL UNIVERSE PUBLICATIONS

Parallel Universe Publications
First Published in the UK in 2016
Copyright © 2016 David Williamson
Introduction © 2016 Charles Black
Cover design © 2016

ISBN: 978-0-9935742-8-3
Parallel Universe Publications, 130 Union Road,
Oswaldtwistle, Lancashire, BB5 3DR, UK

CONTENTS

INTRODUCTION

The popular opinion of the *Pan Book of Horror Stories* is that the quality went down as more volumes were published. And if you've ever read anything about the Pans you'll have probably seen Ramsey Campbell's thoughts on them. For instance: "I did like the first one when I was thirteen years old, but I thought the series became increasingly illiterate and disgusting and meritless", or "...the typical stuff became increasingly offensive and pornographic..."

In particular, the volumes edited by Clarence Paget are the ones that are usually considered the worst. But there is much that is good in those final five books: tales by Craig Herbertson, Philip Lorimer, Jonathon Cruise, Christopher Fowler, and Alan Temperley to mention just a few, and indeed one of the best stories in the entire series, J.P. Dixon's 'The Surgeon's Tale' appears in volume 29. Personally, I love them all, highs and lows; and what's wrong with disgusting, offensive, and pornographic anyway?!

Another writer who appeared towards the end of the series was the author of this collection: David Williamson. Of whom, *the* expert on the *Pan Horrors*, Johnny Mains wrote in 2008:

"The lead tale – 'Lawnmower Man' by Stephen King should never have been the first story in the series, that honour should have gone to the Samaritan stories by David Williamson (William Davidson...who WAS this guy???). Out of the pair, 'The Not So Good Samaritan' is by far the nastiest of 30 - and comes in for being one of the funniest of the series."

As I'm writing this, frankly rubbish, introduction, and have published several of David's stories over the past few years, you'll have probably realised that I'm a fan of his fiction too. In fact, why are you wasting your time reading my words when you could be reading the horrors conjured up by David Williamson?

Go read of marriages that are falling apart, and so are the spouses, squabbling siblings, children who either loathe their parents, or love them too much, murderers, madmen, ghosts, and ghouls... Go read some proper HORROR and grin in ghoulish delight or shudder in terror!

Charles Black
November 2016

THE PROCEDURE

"It's just a simple procedure Mr. McNab, it will take less than an hour to complete. You are a fit, healthy young man and there is nothing at all for you to worry about. I promise you, you won't know anything about it until you come round. You'll be fine, trust me."

Shaun McNab looked at the consultant's confident, smiling face and could only feel a cold dread in the pit of his stomach. He idly touched at the small, round lump to the lower right of his navel, a hernia according to the diagnosis, and deeply rued the day that he had offered to help his friend move that pile of old steel girders a couple of months earlier.

"It's...well, it's just that I have this terrible phobia of hospitals," he replied, quietly.

The consultant surgeon laughed softly and nodded his head, with his mane of dark, slightly grey-tinged hair and his finely chiselled features, he looked as though he had every confidence in his own abilities with a scalpel. Shaun realised that he was actually very lucky to have Mr. King carry out this relatively minor procedure, but that in no way reduced the terror he was experiencing at that moment.

"Mr. McNab, *everybody* has a fear of hospitals, including, I might add, many of us working in the medical profession! It's completely normal, I assure you. After all, nobody in their right mind wants to be cut open and messed about with, but it's the only way for you to get well again, I'm afraid."

Shaun visibly paled at the phrase 'cut open and messed about with', but he understood that the surgeon was, of course, right. And he *had* been suffering with the constant, nagging pain for weeks now.

"Please don't worry, Mr. McNab. Trust me, I'm a doctor!" smiled the medical man.

*

He was swimming. Swimming slowly upwards, up towards the light. His head felt as though it had been crammed full of cotton wool as he experienced the sensation of being lifted sideways onto a steel trolley, before he was wheeled out of the brightly lit operating theatre and into the recovery room.

"There, Mr. McNab, how are you feeling now...are you back with us?" asked a kindly faced Asian nurse as she checked his pulse, before shining a small torch into his eyes, checking the reaction of his pupils.

Shaun was still feeling very groggy as he struggled to form words with which to reply. His throat felt really sore and his mouth was as dry as the Sahara, prompting the nurse to give him a sip of water via a straw from a plastic beaker.

The water helped to ease his burning throat a little and he tried to speak once more.

"Fuzzy...I feel fuzzy...here," he managed to say, pointing at his own head before indicating that he wanted some more water.

"Of course you feel fuzzy, Mr. McNab! I would feel fuzzy too if I'd been pumped full of anaesthetic for over four hours!"

Shaun's dulled brain try to grasp the words 'four hours'. What had happened to the 'simple procedure' that was supposed to take no more than an hour?

"Whaaa...I...?" he tried to speak but the cotton wool pressing inside his brain wanted to block out all his efforts at thinking and he quickly lapsed back into a deep sleep.

The next morning, his head felt much clearer.

"Nurse...how did it go yesterday? Was everything okay?" he asked. The nurse looked at his medical chart and smiled thinly.

"The surgeon, Mr. King, will be here to see you shortly. Until then, Mr. McNab, please just try and relax?" And she bustled out of the room before he could ask her any further questions.

As he lay there quietly as the nurse had instructed, Shaun noticed for the first time that he appeared to be the sole occupant of the ward. There were five other beds, three opposite and one either side of him, but none of them were even so much as made up, let alone occupied by other patients.

Almost an hour later, Mr. King and a staff nurse, together with a couple of junior doctors came in to see him.

"Ah, Mr. McNab, so you're back with us again?" asked the surgeon, jovially, as he idly flipped through his patient's chart, before handing it over to his juniors for them to study.

"Yes, I'm back in the land of the living, thank you. But tell me, how did the operation go? Was everything okay?"

The surgeon looked from the sister to his junior doctors and, retrieving the chart from one of them, briefly glanced through it once more before placing it back where he'd found it.

"Ah...well..." he began, and Shaun's heart began to sink quickly towards his stomach.

"When we opened you up yesterday, I'm afraid we discovered that things were much worse than they had appeared to be on the scan we did of your injury."

Shaun looked horrified. His mouth felt dry and his head was suddenly spinning, but he managed to ask.

"*How* much worse?" he asked, weakly, his face now ashen and shocked looking.

"I won't beat about the bush, Mr. McNab; I'm afraid that we found it necessary to remove one of your kidneys, the right one to be more accurate, which, unfortunately, we discovered was quite badly diseased. I'm very sorry to have to break it to you like this…"

If Shaun was pale before, he was now whiter than the hospital linen and he found himself trembling badly after the sudden traumatic news.

"A diseased kidney…but…but…?" he petered out, no longer able to think straight.

"I appreciate that this is a terrible shock for you, Mr. McNab, but on the bright side, the other kidney was in perfect health, and, as I am sure you are aware, it's completely possible to live a full and healthy life with just the one. Many people across the world do, you know."

Shaun was now in a cold sweat and he was shaking worse than ever.

"Bu…bu…" he spluttered, but could manage to say no more.

"Sister," said the surgeon, "I think Mr. McNab could do with a little something to help settle him down, perhaps."

And before Shaun could utter another word, he felt the sharp prick of a hypodermic needle entering his arm and the world started to swim before his eyes. Down, down, down…nothing.

*

The next thing he knew, he was swimming back up towards the light once more, followed by the now almost familiar sensation of being lifted sideways onto a trolley, before he passed out again.

"Hello, Mr. McNab…are you back with us again?" It was the kindly Asian nurse once more and Shaun began to wonder whether this was just a really bad dream or some kind of hideous Déjà Vu experience as he struggled hard to croak some kind of a response.

"Just lie still, please, and I'll get you some water," offered the nurse, before she held a plastic straw to his mouth.

"Whaaat's happenin…where am I…?" he managed to mumble between small sips of water.

The nurse smiled. "You're alright…you are just in the recovery room at the moment. You'll soon be right as rain, Mr. McNab."

*

Shaun had no idea how long he had been out, but he awoke back in the ward some time later and looked around at the five other empty beds and wondered again whether he was dreaming it all. He had heard how anaesthetics can sometimes lead to all manner of problems with certain people and he guessed, or rather *hoped* that was what was causing his confused state of mind.

Then his befuddled brain slowly realised that he was now hooked up to a ventilator machine and he also had a couple of drips plugged into his right arm, his chest covered with monitoring devices.

He groped around for the call button above his head and pressed it weakly. Moments later, a nurse appeared at his bed side and he pointed to all the medical contraptions attached to him, unable to speak with the breathing mask which covered his mouth.

The nurse consulted his charts before speaking.

"Mr. King will be along shortly to see you, Mr. McNab. You've had a very lucky escape, it would seem," she said, before leaving him lying there with a thousand unanswered questions spinning around in his dazed head.

*

"Mr. McNab…can you hear me alright? Mr. McNab…?" It was Mr. King, the surgeon with his usual entourage by his side.

Shaun nodded weakly and tried to sit up.

"Whoa, Mr. McNab! Lie still…please! You've had a serious operation and have to take things extremely easy for a while!"

His patient tried to pull the face mask off and speak, but he was far too weak, and his arm flopped back uselessly by his side, twitching on the bed like a freshly landed fish.

"I realise that you must have a hundred questions, but, please, try to remain calm while I explain what has happened," said the surgeon. "When we sent the kidney we had previously removed off for further analysis, the results which came back were not at all promising. They gave us every indication that the disease may well have spread further than we had at first anticipated, and we were forced to investigate the situation."

Shaun could only stare dumbly at the surgeon, tears forming in his rheumy eyes as he listened.

"What we found was…er…not good. I'm afraid, Mr. McNab, that your right lung had become seriously infected and we had…we had to remove it to stop the infection spreading further throughout your body. I'm terribly sorry."

Shaun was now shaking his head from side to side. All this because of a hernia!? Surely, this had to be some kind of a nightmare…it *had* to be?

"Mr. McNab is becoming distressed, Sister."

He once again felt the sharp prick of the hypodermic needle in his arm and the world rapidly started to go black. Just before he went completely under, he could have sworn that he heard music playing somewhere, way off in the distance. He recognised the tune as an old Eagles song, but didn't have the time to recall which one…

*

The next time Shaun woke up, he discovered, through a mist of pain, that he could now only see through one of his eyes. He was still connected to the ventilator, yet there seemed to be even more lines in his arm and a whole maze of wiring now led from his chest area to a series of monitoring devices standing beside his bed.

Groggily, he tried to reach out for the call button, but as he groped about the headboard of his bed, he thought he heard a voice, a voice which seemed to be coming from a million miles away.

"He's coming round."

Shaun tried to focus on the three faces wavering above him, without success.

"Mr. McNab? Mr. McNab…?"

The patient groaned slightly by way of a reply.

"Ah, Mr. McNab…you've come back to us." The voice sounded vaguely familiar to Shaun, though for the life of him, he couldn't recall the speaker's name.

"I'm sorry to tell you that you've been in the wars again, I'm afraid, Mr. McNab. More bad news for you, alas," said the distant voice. Shaun was trying, unsuccessfully, to fix his eyes on the ethereal face speaking to him, and groaned again in his frustration.

"The infection has spread, I have to inform you. We…erm…we've had to remove half of your liver as well as your right eye in an attempt to stop the disease encroaching further…"

Shaun could only slowly shake his head in terror. He tried to speak, to sit up and focus on the surgeon, but he was too ill and too heavily drugged to move. He felt completely numb with the horror of his situation. Through his one remaining eye, he could just make out the white swathe of bandages covering his torso from the top of his chest downwards towards his waist and an anguished sob escaped from his throat, muffled by the ventilator mask fastened across his mouth.

The surgeon, who had been carefully studying his patient's notes, handed the clipboard back to a nurse.

"We'll speak again later, Mr. McNab…when you're feeling up to it. I know that all this is very hard for you to take in, but we really are doing our very best for you, you know." And with that, he and the other medical staff left the room.

Shaun tried desperately to think. He tried to summon up enough drug-free brain cells to focus his attention on his predicament, he tried to work out what had…what *was* happening to him, but it was a losing fight. He was too doped up to string even the simplest of thoughts into any kind of logical reasoning.

He lapsed once more into a deep, dreamless sleep.

When he awoke, what felt like several hours later, he was able to focus a little more clearly and, although still heavily sedated, he managed to glance slowly around the room. The still empty room, apart from himself and the five vacant beds.

That half-remembered Eagles' tune was playing softly once more, somewhere outside in the corridor, and he struggled in vain to recall the song's name.

As he glanced towards the brightly lit reception area beyond his room, he noticed for the first time a sign attached to the half open ward door.

With the last of his remaining strength, he put every ounce of his effort into trying to read what it said.

The red, block capital letters swam before his one remaining eye, and then slowly came into sharp focus. It read:

MEDICAL DONORS INC.
STAFF ONLY.
KEEP OUT!

At that moment, the smiling Asian nurse quietly came into the room carrying a small stainless steel tray with a large hypodermic placed upon it.

Shaun's horrified brain suddenly remembered the name of the Eagle's song, and one verse in particular.

He struggled to rise up from the bed, to get out of there before it was too late, but the needle slid sharply into his arm, the hypodermic's contents flowing slowly into his artery, and almost immediately he was slipping once more into unconsciousness.

The song was *Hotel California*.

The verse was;

"You can check out anytime you want, but you can never leave…"

THE SCRYER

"Mr. Kelly? Mr. Daniel Kelly?"

The visitor was a short, thin weasel of a man in his mid to late 60s with a Bobby Charlton style comb-over the like of which Dan hadn't seen in many a year and a small, neat black moustache. He carried a battered leather briefcase in his left hand and proffered a laminated business card with his right.

Dan gave the card a cursory look, but sensed that this unwelcome caller was from either the council calling about the rent arrears or from the social services regarding his latest incapacity benefit claim. Either way, the creep wasn't getting into his flat…not unless he had a warrant!

"Well…*are* you Mr. Kelly or not?" asked the stranger, a somewhat peeved tone in his voice. Dan held the door ajar just wide enough to speak through the gap.

"Who wants to know?"

The visitor thrust the card forward, so that it was directly in front of Dan's eyes.

"My name is Mitchell Pink. I'm from Plunkett, Pink and Wareham, probate solicitors…?"

At the mention of the word 'solicitor', Dan slammed the door of his council flat in the face of the stranger and set the dead lock. Almost immediately, the letter box flap opened.

"I'm here as the bearer of possibly very good news, Mr. Kelly! I'm not after money…rather the complete opposite, in fact!"

The shabby door to the flat remained closed for all of ten seconds, before its occupant opened it wide and ushered Mitchell Pink into the hallway.

"Okay, you've got my attention. What's this 'very good news' you mentioned?"

Pink glanced around the tatty hallway, noticing the large pile of unopened final demands stacked on a side table, the pealing wallpaper, and the row of battered shoes carelessly lined up along the skirting. The place smelt of un-emptied garbage, grease and a general airless mustiness. The solicitor tucked his briefcase firmly beneath his arm.

"Is there somewhere…er…more *comfortable* we could speak?" he asked. Dan smiled tightly and shook his head in disbelief.

"Nowhere *you* would think of as 'comfortable', but the front room has seating, if that's what you mean?"

"That would be admirable, Mr. Kelly…please, lead the way…?"

Dan picked up the assorted scattered detritus littering the settee and dumped it over the back, out of sight.

"Take a pew." He couldn't help but smile as he saw Pink's nose visibly wrinkle before he settled himself, uncomfortably, at one end of the settee, place the briefcase across his lap and undo the clip holding it shut.

"Please…take a seat yourself, Mr. Kelly? This could take some time…"

Dan Kelly sighed aloud, shook his head and sat in the armchair beside his unbidden visitor.

"So…what's this all about, Mr…?"

"Pink…Mitchell Pink."

"Okay, Mr. Mitchell Pink…I'm all ears."

The little solicitor cleared his throat, removed a buff coloured folder from his battered case, took out the wad of papers contained within, placed a pair of wire rimmed glasses on his prominent nose, and began.

"Right, Mr. Kelly…just a few formalities firstly; can you please tell me your date and place of birth?"

"Why? What's this all about?"

Pink shook his head and part of his careful comb-over fell across his brow making him resemble a balding Hitler look-a-like. Dan almost laughed out loud as the solicitor carefully eased his hair back into place.

"Please, Mr. Kelly. I assure you that if you are the *right* Mr. Daniel Kelly, this meeting will benefit you greatly. However, I need to confirm that I have the correct person."

Dan frowned.

"Okay, okay. I was born on the 31st of January 1969 in Isleworth, Greater London."

The solicitor looked at his notes, nodded and gave the briefest of smiles.

"And your parents' names, please?"

"Thomas Arthur and Mary Janet…Kelly, obviously. Both of them now pushing up the daisies, alas."

Pink smiled tightly once more and scribbled something on the paper before him.

"And just to confirm: do you have any siblings…brothers or sisters? Any other relatives?"

Dan shook his head.

"Nope. I'm an only child and both my parents were only children as well. Not big breeders in our family!"

The solicitor nodded, removed his glasses and folded his hands across the papers on his lap, smiling excitedly.

"Well, Mr. Kelly…I am pleased to say that it would seem that I have traced the right man!"

Dan frowned and then shrugged.

"Oh, goody-good. So now what…have I won the lottery or has someone donated their kidneys to me?" he asked, sarcastically.

Pink smiled broadly.

"In a manner of speaking, *yes*, you have won the lottery, though you will have to sort out the kidney donation for yourself, I'm afraid." And he chuckled dryly.

Dan raised an eyebrow and studied the little man seated opposite him.

"This is your lucky day, Mr. Kelly. A *very* lucky day, indeed!"

Kelly sat forward on his chair and nodded encouragingly.

"Right; I have to tell you that a distant relation of yours, your *only* relation so far as we can detect, passed away some months ago leaving a property as well as a not insubstantial amount of money."

Dan was now *very* interested in what his visitor had to say, and nodded enthusiastically for the man to continue. The solicitor consulted his notes and then added:

"The property, I have not seen it myself I might add, is in Essex. And you, as the only surviving member of the family, are in the fortunate position to have inherited everything."

Dan looked in a state of shock. His eyes had grown wide and his mouth trembled slightly as the news began to sink in. Finally, he found his voice.

"*Essex*? I've never been north of the Thames in my life! *Essex*?" he repeated, still unable to fully comprehend the information he had just been given.

"I understand that it's quite a substantial property," continued the solicitor, as he looked around the grungy, cluttered lounge of the flat. "Certainly, it's rather larger than your...er...current accommodation..."

As Dan Kelly sat there, shaking his head in disbelief, the front door to the flat opened and then slammed shut and two raised female voices could be heard arguing out in the hallway.

"Don't speak to me like that, you rude little cow! I'm your bleedin' mother, not one of your scummy mates!"

"My mates ain't scummy...*you're* the scummy one!"

The women were still bickering as they burst into the living room, and both stopped mid-sentence as they noticed the diminutive figure of Mitchell Pink seated uncomfortably on the settee.

"Who the bleeding 'ell is this? Not another bailiff...I *told* you not to let anyone in!" screeched the older of the women.

Pink and Dan got to their feet at the same time, Dan clearly attempting to silence his wife with a telling glare and a shake of his head.

"It's nothing like that, Irene. This is Mr. Pink...he's brought us some unbelievably good news..."

The solicitor smiled thinly and held out a dainty hand.

"Pleased to meet you...erm...?"

"Sorry, Mr. Pink. This is Irene, my wife, and this is our daughter, Kelly..."

Pink looked a little baffled.

"Yeah, that's right Mister...Kelly Kelly...how bleedin' stupid is that, eh?" explained the girl, shaking her head furiously and glaring from mother to father as if they were the most stupid people on the planet.

Pink looked both dumfounded and a little embarrassed, and decided to gather up his paperwork, which he replaced inside his tatty briefcase, latching the lid shut once more.

"Well then, Mr. Kelly, I'll leave you to relate the good news to your family, and I'll be in touch within the next few days with all the details regarding the property etc."

"Property? *What* property?" demanded Irene, as Pink edged his way between the two women and out into the hall, only pausing to hand Dan one of his business cards before opening the front door.

"I'll be in touch shortly. Mr. Kelly...ladies..." and with that, he was gone.

Dan closed the door and leant against it, not knowing whether to faint, scream or laugh hysterically. The suspicious faces of the women in his life bought him back to earth with a thud.

"Daniel Kelly...what the bleedin' hell have you been up to, and what was that weird looking bloke on about?"

*

A little over a week later, Dan, Irene, Kelly and Mitchell Pink were being driven in a hired car to a relatively remote area of Essex close to the border with Suffolk. The driver, with some difficulty, located the property now owned by Dan and his family and pulled up outside a set of large, wrought iron gates with sturdy-looking brick pillars supporting their weight. Each pillar had a strange, gremlin-like character upon its top and a paint-flaking sign attached to one of the gates announced that they had arrived at 'The Old Manor House'.

"This appears to be the place," said Pink, with more than a touch of awe in his voice.

"Bloody hell!" replied Kelly.

Dan let out a long whistle as his wife merely sat there in dumbstruck silence. The driver hopped out and opened the double gates wide, before easing his car through and proceeding along the overgrown gravel drive towards the Old Manor House. Even Kelly remained silent as they travelled for some five hundred yards before being greeted with the sight of a very large, timber framed building which clearly dated back to Tudor times, possibly even older.

They drove around the circular driveway and pulled up beside a set of great oaken doors, obviously the main entrance to the property, before the driver jumped out of the car and ran around to open the passenger doors.

Slowly, the occupants clambered out of the car and stood in awed silence, simply staring up at the huge old building in complete disbelief.

Finally, Kelly broke the silence.

"Yuk! What's that horrible *smell*?" she asked, and everyone sniffed the air and turned to look at the girl.

"I think you'll find that's the smell of the countryside, Miss Kelly," suggested the solicitor, somehow managing to maintain a straight face as he spoke.

"Pwoar! It's *disgusting*!"

Mitchell Pink shook his head in disbelief and then fished in his briefcase for the keys to the building, selecting the largest of the bunch, before stepping forward and unlocking the large double front doors. As they entered the building, they were greeted by the smell of an old house which had clearly not been aired for quite some time. A similar smell to the Kelly's old flat, thought the solicitor. They should feel completely at home here, he mused.

The wide hallway was panelled in finely detailed oak, the floor paved in its original thick, heavy local stone. Overhead, the ceiling was formed from beautifully ornate and detailed plasterwork, which seemed to be in amazingly good condition considering its age. Candle sconces, now converted to electricity, lined the panelling every few yards, and Pink flicked a light switch near the door turning them on to give a weak, pale yellow glow to the hallway.

Ahead of them, stood a huge wooden staircase, with thick handrails and bulbous, heavily carved balusters sweeping up to the floors above. The hallway itself extended for some sixty feet or so and finely carved doors, set into the panelling, obviously led off to a selection of living rooms. The hall alone was probably twice the size of their entire flat back in south London.

Dan was completely stunned by the place.

"And...all this is *ours*?" he asked, incredulously.

The solicitor smiled. "Yes, Mr. Kelly. I can assure you that there has been no mistake...the whole house is yours, lock, stock and barrel, to do with what you will."

Dan let out a low whistle.

"Blimey! But how much does it cost to run a house like this? And all the grounds out there to look after, too...?" he marvelled.

Mitchell Pink rummaged in his battered old briefcase once more and produced an envelope, which he handed to Dan.

"These are the full details of your inheritance, Mr. Kelly. I think once you've studied the figures, you'll be more than happy to realise that you can live here in comfort...providing that you do so using a certain amount of prudence?"

"Prudence?" asked Kelly. "Who the hell is she?"

The solicitor smiled patiently.

"I mean, so long as you don't blow the lot on race horses, fast motor cars, helicopters and other such frivolous items, you will have enough to live very comfortably in this wonderful old house for the rest of your days."

"Oh!" she replied, simply.

*

The house was fully furnished and most of the antique furniture was worth a small fortune in its own right, so the only items they needed to buy to allow them to move straight in were some more up to date appliances for the kitchen and a few other mod cons. Irene, perhaps understandably, insisted on all new bedding throughout.

"We don't know who this relation of yours was, what he died of, or even *where* he died. So, I'm taking no chances on catching something!" Which was probably fair enough, all things considered.

Kelly demanded the biggest flat screen television they could find, but other than that, and the occasional complaint about missing her mates back on the estate…oh, and the regular debate on whether all that fresh, country air was actually good for you or not, she seemed reasonably satisfied. At least, as satisfied as any seventeen-year-old would ever be.

Dan's distant relation, evidently a cousin several times removed by the name of Quentin Kelly, had employed a woman from the nearest village, which was some three miles distant, as a house keeper, and she was soon re-employed to 'do' for the new residents of The Old Manor House.

Despite Dan's careful questioning regarding his late departed relative, the old woman had very little to say about him, other than the fact that he had kept himself to himself, was a very quiet sort of gentleman and had always paid her wages on time. He had had few friends that she was aware of, although, she added, as she only worked until mid-afternoon, she had no idea what went on when she wasn't there.

*

Their new life quickly settled into a routine, and oddly, even though their previous existence had been a constant battle of trying to make ends meet with the odd bit of wheeling and dealing, never quite knowing where the next penny was coming from, Dan found himself becoming bored. Now that he could do anything he wanted to and had the money to enable him not to have to worry about bills, he soon discovered, somewhat ironically, that he didn't really know *what* to do with himself.

He had explored the majority of the house since they'd moved in almost six weeks earlier, but decided on a whim that he would have a poke around in the vast cellars which spread the full length and width of

18

the manor house. The housekeeper had told him that the Old Manor House had been built on the site of a much older, medieval building dating back to the fourteenth century and he considered it worth a poke around to see what was down there.

Oddly, there was no lighting in the vast cellar, so, after a brief investigation with a small torch, he rigged up a series of portable lights so as to better see what secrets, if any, the place held. For such a cavernous cellar, it seemed strangely empty. There were a few old tea chests scattered around near the bottom of the stairs, various bits of broken old furniture, a few suitcases mainly packed with mouldering, ancient clothes, but very little else of any real interest.

The vaulted ceiling was supported by thick stone pillars and there were several arched storage niches throughout, mostly empty. But at the far end, covered with a ragged, moth eaten old blanket, he discovered a small, worked-leather trunk with a large ornate lock on its front. Dan tried to lift the trunk, but it was heavier than it looked, so he dragged it the length of the cellar, back towards the lights and set about trying to open the thing. It was locked, obviously. Nothing interesting could possibly be that simple to open, now could it?

Then he remembered the bunch of keys which Pink had given him and headed back upstairs to fetch them. No luck at all; none of the keys on the bunch looked even remotely as though they would fit the lock on the trunk.

Plan B was called for, and although the leather trunk was clearly several hundred years old and no doubt worth a small fortune, needs must, so he took a heavy screwdriver to the intricate brass lock and jemmied the thing open. It took a considerable effort, and Dan mused that they certainly knew how to make things that would last way back then.

Oddly, although the trunk was heavy, there was very little inside it. There were a couple of musty old leather-bound books, one of which was wrapped in some sort of oilskin, a pair of what appeared to be silver candle sticks, some kind of strange hat, and lastly, buried beneath a mouldering cloth right at the bottom, a piece of badly tarnished metal with an ornate stand which would enable the thing to be stood upright.

There was also a handful of old, probably silver coins, the like of which he had never seen before. But that was all; no hidden treasure, no bars of gold or diamond necklaces. Dan sighed aloud. He unwrapped the book which had been protected by the oilskin and idly flipped through the pages, which were not made of paper but rather some kind of skin. Vellum, possibly?

The pages were covered in a spider-like scrawl and there were strange diagrams painstakingly drawn in the margins. The writing was completely unintelligible, at least as far as he was concerned. It was neither English nor any other language he had ever seen, not that he was any kind of an expert of course, but he had thumbed through some of the old Tudor-era books kept in the library upstairs, and this scribble wasn't remotely like any of those.

He re-wrapped the book and shoved it his back pocket, when the light caught the piece of metal with the ornate stand and he spotted for the first time that it too had been etched with symbols and writing similar to those in the book, and he picked it up to study it more closely. It was far heavier than it looked and he almost dropped the thing until he grasped it firmly with both hands.

It was badly tarnished, but by adjusting the angle and the lighting, he could definitely make out the scratched symbols and strange writing. He decided that it might be worth cleaning up and, as he had nothing better to do with his time, he hefted the thing against his chest, kicked the lid of the chest closed with his foot and headed back upstairs.

*

"What the hell is *that* thing?" asked Irene, her face resembling someone who'd been sucking on a particularly sour lemon.

Dan placed the last wad of Brasso back into its tin and looked at the result of his two hours of labour. The whatever-it-was was now gleaming brightly and he could pick out far more detail on its carefully etched surface. The stand was even more ornate looking now that he had cleaned it up, and he noticed that it had been moulded with the faces of goblins, or possibly demons? Whatever they were, they looked positively *evil* but he found them completely fascinating and studied them for quite some time.

"I asked you what the hell *that* thing is? I'm not sure I even want it in my house!" repeated his wife.

Dan noticed his reflection in the now highly polished surface of the metal and realised for the first time that it was obviously an ancient mirror. He had to force himself to look away as it seemed to have a hypnotic effect on him, somehow drawing him into its depths.

Dan turned to his wife.

"'*Your*' house? Since when did you have a rich relative who died and left *you* a mansion?" he asked, bitterly.

Irene was not a woman who was easily flustered, but the odd look in his eyes unsettled her and rather than confront him further, she turned on her heal and stormed out of the kitchen. Dan smiled to himself and returned to look at his find from the cellar.

Yes, it was definitely a mirror. And a very *fine* mirror at that. It made him look...what? *Different* in some way? He appeared...what was the word? More *handsome*? No...not that. *Dignified* perhaps? Hmm, possibly? *Knowing*...yes, that was it; he looked more *knowledgeable* somehow. A man who knew what he wanted from life and how to go about getting it.

He *really* liked this mirror.

He was still seated at the kitchen table, which was covered in newspaper and scraps of wading, when Kelly came home after visiting her old friends from the estate.

"What's that bit of old crap? You been out car booting again?" she asked, sniggering at her own wit.

Dan turned suddenly and stared at his daughter, a dark look in his eyes which shut her up immediately.

"You would be the one to know about crap, young lady. You have no idea of the finer things in life…just like your mother!" and with that, he snatched up his mirror and left the room, heading upstairs leaving his daughter lost for a witty retort for once.

*

Dinner that night was a very quiet affair, with Irene and Kelly casting one another questioning glances as Dan sat at the head of the large oak dining table, looking for all the world like a medieval lord waiting to be served by his wenches. He didn't say a word throughout the meal, other than to ask why they were living in such a grand old house, yet still eating rubbish like pizza and chips.

"You always *liked* pizza and chips before we moved here and you started getting all high and mighty!" retorted his wife, but he merely raised his hand to silence her and said.

"That was when we didn't have the money for the finer things in life and didn't know any better. Things have to change now that we're here…and change for the better."

The two women looked at one another and said nothing.

*

Shortly afterwards, the dreams started.

Night after night, Dan would dream the strangest things, always about a bearded man who wore a high ruff collar and had the most piercing, dark eyes at the forefront of each of them. He could hear muffled chanting in the background, voices speaking in some unintelligible language, words that Dan could not even begin to imagine the meaning of. And the dreams always took place in what looked like the vast cellar beneath the house, poorly lit by thick, fat candles which gave off a pungent, acrid odour.

For some reason, which he could not explain, Dan felt a connection with the man in those dreams, almost as though he knew him somehow, as if there were some kind of a *bond* between them, a bond which extended throughout time and space. In fact, the dreams/nightmares, call them what you will, were so vivid that Irene had insisted that he move into one of the spare rooms so that she could get a decent night's sleep without him moaning and thrashing about in their bed.

He had agreed, rather too quickly she thought, and he now had the mirror in pride of place on his bedside cabinet and seemed more than happy not to be sharing the matrimonial bed with his wife.

*

Three days later, Mitchell Pink arrived out of the blue along with his partners Alistair Plunkett and Gordon Wareham.

"Hello, Mrs. Kelly," said Pink, cheerily as though they were old friends.

"We were in the vicinity and decided to pop in and see how things are going with your new life? How are you settling in, my dear lady?"

If Irene Kelly thought that it was at all odd that these three men just happened to be 'in the vicinity', she said nothing as she ushered them into the drawing room and summoned the housekeeper to organise some tea and whatever else was going for her unexpected guests.

"Well," she began by way of a reply, "it's certainly different from our old place, that's for sure! Not sure that Dan is enjoying it that much though…he seems a bit…er…tense these days?"

Mr. Plunkett spoke for the other two.

"'Tense', in what way is your husband 'tense', Mrs. Kelly?" he asked.

Irene looked at the solicitors perched on the edge of a large sofa and decided that they seemed more like three old fashioned undertakers than men of the law, and she repressed an almost overwhelming urge to laugh out loud.

"I don't know how to describe it really. He was fine until he started rummaging about down in the cellar… He's been a bit odd ever since then."

She couldn't help but notice the look which passed between the men, which, although fleeting, worried her for some inexplicable reason.

Wareham was the next to speak.

"Would it be possible to speak with your husband, Mrs. Kelly…if it's not at all inconvenient, of course?" And the solicitors sat there, each with identical expressions on their faces, and Mitchell Pink carefully fussing with a wayward lock of his comb-over.

Just at that moment, there was a light knock on the door and the housekeeper wheeled in a trolley containing the tea things. The woman smiled and nodded at the men, almost as though she had met them before, but there was no acknowledgement from any of the solicitors. After tea, Irene went and found her husband who was, as was often the case these days, to be found in his room staring blankly into the mirror beside his bed.

"Pink is here with his two mates. They want to speak to you…don't

22

ask me what about. They give me the creeps!"

Dan snapped out of his reverie immediately.

"Tell them I'll be right down," he replied, dismissively, and she left the room without another word.

"Ah, Daniel!" said Pink. "Allow me to introduce you to my partners in crime. This is Alistair Plunkett and my other colleague, Gordon Wareham; gentlemen, *this* is Mr. Daniel Kelly."

A smile sprang to the lips of both men, and they thrust out their hands in greeting. They looked very pleased to make Dan's acquaintance, almost as though they were in the presence of minor royalty or at the very least a celebrity of some sort.

"Well then gentlemen, to what do I owe this honour? You lot, out here in the middle of nowhere? What can I do for you?"

It was Plunkett who spoke, clearly the senior partner of the three solicitors.

"A-hem...well, it's not what you can do for us, Mr. Kelly...it's really more a question of what we can do for you!"

Dan smiled warmly. "I would say that you gentlemen have done *more* than enough for me, already. Just look at this place for a start...I'd have still been living in that filthy hovel on a dreadful housing estate if it wasn't for you!"

Plunkett waved his hand dismissively and continued.

"Ah, but that was our duty...to find the last surviving heir to Quentin's estate. The very last of the bloodline, so to speak."

Their host looked puzzled. "Am I missing something here? I really can't imagine what more you could possibly do for me..."

Mitchell Pink spoke now.

"Your wife tells us that you have been investigating the cellar. Might I enquire as to whether you've found anything of interest down there? It's a very old house, as you know...there must have been something worth discovering..."

Dan could detect a faint nervousness between the men, an uneasiness in their manner which led him to believe that there was far more going on than he was able to grasp.

"Well, aside from several heaps of cra...rubbish and a load of broken furniture, there was this old trunk..."

The look which darted between the three older men was too obvious to hide and Dan quickly seized the opportunity to cut to the chase.

"So...what exactly, interests you gents in my cellar? Is it the book...or the mirror?"

Plunkett, who had risen to his feet, sat down again heavily, and taking a clean white handkerchief from his jacket pocket, dabbed nervously at his brow. Gordon Wareham spoke for the first time.

"It would seem that you have seen through our little deception, Mr. Kelly. We have, as they used to say, been undone!"

"Wait here, please…I have something to show you all."

Five minutes later, Dan had the mirror and the book placed on the coffee table in front of his guests, and they sat staring at them in undisguised admiration…and more than that perhaps. There was an aura of fear mixed with anticipation hanging in the room and an almost fanatical gleam in the lawyers' eyes, particularly as they studied the metal mirror.

"Is *this* what you've come here to see?" asked Dan, simply.

The visitors nodded dumbly, barely able to tear their eyes away from the mirror, just as Dan himself had found it so difficult to do when he'd first cleaned it.

"Mr. Kelly…there are certain details that I feel we have omitted in our dealings with you. Important details which I feel we should enlighten you with…and more so, now that you have discovered the Scrying glass."

"The *whating* glass?"

"This is no mere mirror. Please, let me start from the beginning and everything will make sense, I hope."

Dan settled himself down into a chair opposite his guests.

"Please…tell all," he said.

"Have you ever heard of Doctor John Dee, by any chance?"

Dan shook his head.

"Well, he was a famous, perhaps *infamous*, gentleman way back in the reign of Queen Elizabeth 1st. He was, at some time, her personal tutor in astrology as well as other arts. But, there was a darker side to the man. It was said that he was involved in necromancy, alchemy and 'other' black arts, the full extent of which we will probably never know."

Wareham paused to take a sip of his cold tea, before continuing.

"Doctor Dee, though clearly a very forward thinking and highly intelligent man…way ahead of his time, alas, had one flaw in his character. Although he was deeply involved in occult matters, he was unable to…er, shall we say 'communicate' with the other side. For this, he needed an expert in that field. A Scryer as they were known. And the best of those Scryers was a man named Edward or Ned Kelley…"

A frown passed across Dan's face.

"Yes, Mr. Kelly…Edward Kelley is your direct ancestor. We haven't tried to work out exactly how many 'greats' are involved, but please take it from me, that you are indeed his descendant. His only *surviving* male descendant, I might add."

The younger man looked nonplussed. Although he had never heard of this man Edward Kelley, he somehow felt, deep in the back of his mind, that he *knew* the man.

"What did he look like…this ancestor of mine?" he asked.

"Ah, that's easy," replied Mitchell Pink, smiling and delving into his ever-present briefcase. "Here is a drawing of him from the time," and he handed the likeness to Dan.

Dan took the drawing and knew before he even set eyes on it that this was the man in his dreams. Although he was half expecting to recognise the face, the reality shot through him like an electric charge and he found himself shaking, a cold sweat erupting across his brow. The three solicitors were studying his face intently as he looked at the old drawing of Edward Kelley. Mitchell Pink smiled tightly and said, "You've seen this man before somewhere, I gather...?"

Dan closed his eyes, and nodded, handing the illustration back to Pink.

The older men looked at one another, satisfaction clearly evident in their expressions as they waited for Dan to reply.

"Mr. Kelly...?" pressed Wareham.

Dan rubbed his face with both hands as though trying to wake himself.

"Yes...I've seen him before. In my dreams. He's been appearing every night in my dreams..."

"He's made a *connection!*" whispered Plunkett, triumphantly, to the others.

Their host suddenly opened his eyes and studied the older men, noticing their look of triumph and undisguised excitement.

"Connection? What do you mean...I've made a connection?" he asked.

The solicitors were staring at Dan and smiling excitedly.

"I mean," replied Plunkett, "that you have made a connection with your ancestor...Edward Kelley. Edward Kelley, the original owner of the Scrying glass which you discovered in the cellar. *This* Scrying glass," he added, reverentially touching the metal mirror placed on the table before them.

Dan shook his head.

"What the hell are you talking about? The man's been dead for what...four hundred years or so? How can I have made a 'connection' with a dead man?"

"Four hundred and fifteen years, to be precise," interrupted Mitchell Pink, continuing, "Ned Kelley was a very mysterious character, Daniel. It was said that he could, amongst other talents, turn base metals into gold. Indeed, it was this ability which ultimately lead to his downfall, as he was imprisoned by Rudolf II of Bohemia who refused to release Ned until he had supplied the king with enough gold!"

"But what does all that have to do with him appearing in my dreams, for God's sake?"

"I'm coming to that, Daniel," continued Pink. "As has already been mentioned, Kelley was involved in 'other' practices...especially when he worked with Dee. Necromancy was a very great interest of those men. The practice of communicating with the dead for purposes of foretelling future events, and discovering hidden knowledge…witchcraft, as it was often called by the uneducated."

Dan let out a low whistle.

"So old Ned was a witch then?"

Pink smiled tightly.

"You *could* say that, I suppose. But he was also so much more than that; so much more than the typical depiction of witches in popular mythology. While others were healing the sick with their remedies and casting petty curses on those they disliked, Kelley was doing great works! And undoubtedly, via his Scrying glass, he is, even now, trying to contact you…his last surviving relative. As…er…as we hoped would be the case, before we managed to track you down…"

Dan's eyes narrowed and he fixed Mitchell Pink with a piercing stare.

"So you *knew* all this stuff even before you met me?" he asked, incredulously.

The solicitors looked sheepishly at one another, and nodded in unison.

"I'm afraid we did…yes," responded Pink. "The man you inherited this property from, Quentin Kelly, knew the whole story, but unlike you, he simply didn't have the 'gift'. Although we tried for many years to make contact with Edward Kelley, it never happened. Oh, we've tried many other so-called mediums, naturally, but we realised that it had to be a descendant…a *direct* descendant of Kelley himself. Fortunately, not only are you the last of the line, but you also possess 'the gift'!"

Dan's eyes narrowed again, but there was a certain look of dawning knowledge in his face now.

"I thought you told me that you'd never so much as seen this house before the day you brought me here?" he said to Pink, who had the decency to flush a deep red, before shrugging his shoulders.

"I'm sorry, Daniel. It seemed a harmless enough ruse at the time…"

Dan pursed his lips and considered his position briefly.

"So, what are *you* lot after? Gold, I guess? You want me to contact old Ned to discovery his secrets, then?"

"*No!*" shouted Pink. "There is so much *more* to be discovered than just gold, Daniel! Ned Kelley had 'other gifts' which concern us more. Certain *connections* of his own…links to a much higher power, a power worth more than all the gold in the world to us and to… other people!"

Dan was quick to spot the reference.

"Which *other* people?" he demanded.

Pink realised that he had said too much and looked nervously between the other two men. They were both glaring at him angrily, but the damage had already been done.

"If you expect my assistance, gentlemen, and you obviously *need* it, I want to know everything…and I mean, *everything!*"

Plunkett shrugged, resignedly, and said, "Well, Mitchell…you had better finish what you've started."

Pink nervously patted at his comb-over before speaking. He cleared his throat and continued.

"We…that is the three of us, are part of a group. There are nine others within the group…your great uncle was the tenth before his demise. The group is made up of a variety of powerful men; businessmen, politicians, a police commissioner, a bishop…twelve in all. You would naturally become the thirteenth member of our…er…coven, and would also, obviously, be the most important member, as you are the one with the 'gift'." Pink paused to let Dan digest the information, before continuing.

"We are all convinced that, with your assistance of course, we can communicate with Edward Kelley and hopefully learn all that he is willing to share with us…or rather, share with you. Knowledge that has been lost in time…things that will help to make our group become the most powerful men on the planet! You included."

*

The dream that night was the most vivid to date.

Dan was a bystander down in the cellar of the house, which was lit by guttering torches fixed to the stone walls. There was a group of men, each dressed in black robes, their hoods raised so that he could not see their faces. They were gathered in a circle surrounding a man seated at what looked like a stone altar with tall, black candles placed upon it at either end. The seated man was Edward Kelley, and he was staring intently at his Scrying glass, his brow etched with concentration, his dark eyes focused upon something which Dan couldn't see from where he was 'standing', beside one of the thick pillars which supported the vaulted stone ceiling.

Then the circle of hooded men began chanting in a tongue which Dan could not understand. They appeared to be repeating the same phrase over, and over, a phrase which started in low voices and which grew in volume until the whole cellar reverberated with the ancient words and Dan had to cover his ears to block out the cacophony.

"*Nigrum Dominus, nos precor ostende te!*"
"*Nigrum Dominus, nos precor ostende te!*"
"*Nigrum Dominus, nos precor ostende te!*"

Suddenly, in his dream state, Dan found himself standing directly behind his ancestor, Edward Kelley, and he was looking into the Scrying mirror, seeing what *he* could see. The surface of the mirror appeared to be cloudy, but the cloudiness slowly cleared and a face appeared on its surface. A man's face. Dan almost screamed aloud as he recognised the image in the Scrying mirror.

It was *his* face!

The strangest thing, if things could become any stranger, was the fact that his image in the mirror showed him to be asleep and in his own bed. His face was contorted and twitching, his eyes beneath his eyelids were rolling from side to side, proving that he was in a very deep sleep.

Then he realised, with dawning horror, that Edward Kelley had now turned to face him from his seated position at the altar. Indeed, *everyone* present in the cellar was now staring at him silently. The faceless, hooded 'congregation' had now ceased their chanting, but Dan found the sudden, total silence far scarier than the alien sounding words.

"Ah...he *sees* us!" said Kelley, triumphantly, rising slowly from his seat.

"We have made the *connection!*"

*

The screams had woken both Irene and her daughter, and they stood trembling and clutching one another on the threshold of Dan's bedroom, staring at him as he thrashed wildly about in his bed. Suddenly, he sat bolt upright, sweat dripping down his terrified face, his hair matted and damp, the duvet wrapped about his body holding him in an anaconda-like grip. He sat there, trembling and gasping for air like a semi-drowned man, his eyes staring, his lips twitching.

"What the hell is going on here, Dan?" asked Irene, nervously. "What's happening to you? You've never had so much as a bad dream in all the years I've known you, until we moved into this place!"

Dan shook his head, sweat flying from his hair and splattering his daughter's face, who wiped it off without thinking, too scared to speak or complain in her usual manner. Her father's chin dropped to his chest and it appeared as though he had passed out, when he suddenly took a deep breath, releasing it slowly before speaking for the first time.

"I...I...don't know what's wrong with me. I just keep getting these really vivid dreams...*horrible* dreams about a lot of men in robes and Edward Kelley...you know, my so-called ancestor, is always in them ...calling to me..." A wracking sob escaped from his mouth and he collapsed back onto the bed, exhausted. Irene and Kelly looked at one another, a puzzled expression on both their faces. Irene shook her head and said, "Well, I think you need to see a doctor...get some help. You're in a terrible state and you're making us nervous wrecks seeing you like this. I don't know how much more we can take!"

Dan rubbed a hand across his face, propped himself up on one elbow, and looked at his wife.

"Okay...you're right. I'll get it sorted," he said, before collapsing back onto his pillows as his wife and daughter turned and silently left his room.

*

Two weeks later, and Dan still hadn't been to seek help. His wife was now staying at her sister's house in Kent and Kelly meanwhile had left in a teenage huff and gone to stay with friends back on the estate in south London, leaving their respective husband/father to his own devices. Irene said that she would only return if or when Dan finally made the effort to get himself sorted out. And who could blame her?

Dan was now a shadow of his former self. He had lost over a stone and a half in weight and looked sallow skinned and gaunt. He had never been one to take any great pride in his appearance, but was now unkempt, dirty and unshaven, his hair greasy and plastered across his scalp. He also had a permanently haunted look about him, his eyes red and constantly darting nervously from side to side as though he could hear or see things which no one else could.

He had been on his own like this for over a week, when suddenly the doorbell began to ring persistently, giving him no alternative but to either rip the thing off the wall or answer its shrill and demanding call. He chose the latter of the options and discovered the three elderly solicitors waiting patiently on his ample doorstep. Behind them, he could see several expensive cars parked around the circle of his driveway. Oddly, although he was on the surface surprised to see these callers, he had somehow been half expecting a further visit from them.

As he opened the double oak doors wide and ushered the solicitors into the hallway, he couldn't help but notice how they stared at his appearance.

"Daniel..." began Mitchell Pink, falteringly, "you look *dreadful*! Is everything alright?"

Dan smiled sardonically at Pink. "Does is *look* like everything is alright? Well...*does* it? I haven't slept for days...every time I *do* manage to doze off, I see *him*!" He was visibly shaking, and suddenly slumped down onto one of the hall chairs as though the very life had been drained from his body.

Pink put a gnarled old hand on the younger man's shoulder.

"That is why we have come, Daniel. We...the rest of the coven and ourselves, have felt the call to come here and help you in any way we can."

Dan sat bolt upright in the chair and stared from one solicitor to the other.

"*Help* me? 'Felt the call'? What the fuck are you talking about? It's because of *you*," he pointed to each man in turn, "that I'm in this mess! I was fine before I heard from you lot and came to live in this ...this shit hole!"

Mitchell Pink took a step back, unsettled by the sudden outburst. Alistair Plunkett spoke next.

"We are aware that we have deceived you somewhat, Mr. Kelly..." he began.

"'*Deceived*' me? I should bloody well say you've deceived me! You've led me into something that's ruined my life! This…this *business* is killing me!"

Plunkett was unruffled, and continued.

"However…and I am sincere when I say this, we *are* here to assist you in any way we can. I can only imagine what you must have been experiencing over the last few weeks, but we know much about such things, having studied what is now laughingly referred to as 'The Black Arts' for many years between us. To put it bluntly, Mr. Kelly…we are your only hope…"

Dan ran his dirty fingers through his equally dirty hair and smiled mirthlessly at Alistair Plunkett.

"Well…all I can say is, if you lot are my only hope, then I am well and truly fucked!"

*

The coven of thirteen men, including Dan, were assembled down in the cellar. It was almost exactly as Dan had dreamt it over the weeks; all the men were dressed in black, hooded gowns with no one, not even the elderly solicitors' faces revealed, so he had no notion as to who was who. Dan himself was also wearing one of the gowns, which had been supplied by Gordon Wareham, and he was seated, just as in the dreams, at a table (this was the only difference to the altar in his nightmares) with the Scrying mirror placed before him.

He felt very strange. He had no recollection of coming down into the cellar, nor of the other twelve men joining him, or of him getting changed into his donated robes, but another part of him seemed to know and understand *why* he was there and *what* was required of him. Yet another portion of his brain told him that this must be another of his hideous dreams. The line between reality and insanity was becoming increasingly blurred.

Then the chanting began, the same words, or so they sounded, as the chanting in his nightmares. The rest of the coven surrounded him forming a perfect circle, and they chanted as he sat at the table with the Scrying mirror set before him.

"Nigrum Dominus, nos precor ostende te!"

"Nigrum Dominus, nos precor ostende te!"

"*Nigrum Dominus, nos precor ostende te!*"

Was this another nightmare? *Could* this be reality?

As the chanting reached a crescendo, the Scrying mirror took on the now familiar misty appearance upon its surface and he was horribly aware that a face was appearing from the hazy depths. Dan tried to avert his gaze, but some force kept him focused on the mirror and he was unable to move or even so much as close his eyes or blink.

Then a voice, an ancient, deep, booming voice filled the room, followed by a terrifying, maniacal laughter which reverberated throughout the vast cellar, echoing from the stone pillars and arched ceiling, filling his brain with the hideous noise until he felt as though his head might explode.

The chanting immediately stopped as soon as the laughter started, the hooded figures looking at one another anxiously, uncertainty clearly visible in their body language, as they slowly backed away from the desk and the Scrying mirror.

"DANIEL...DANIEL KELLEY..." said the voice from the mirror. The voice of Edward Kelley. The voice of a man supposedly dead these last four hundred or so years.

The coven now cowered in one corner of the huge cellar, congregated beneath one of the large stone arches. Dan could only stare back at the image in the mirror, the image which stared back at him with deep black eyes and a terrifying expression. The image of a long dead yet *not* dead relative who had long ago discovered the secrets of the ages, the mysteries of life after death.

"DANIEL KELLEY...THESE MEN ARE FOOLS! THEY SEEK TO USE YOU AND YOUR INHERITED POWER FOR THEIR OWN GAIN, TO ENHANCE THEIR PUNY LIVES AND TO RULE OVER OTHERS. BUT THEY ARE UNWORTHY DOGS!"

As the voice boomed around the stone walls, the coven whimpered like whipped curs and they shivered in their terror as they began to realise exactly what they had unleashed upon themselves. First one, then each and every one of them knelt on the hard, stone cellar floor, heads bowed in supine surrender.

"LOOK AT THEM, DANIEL. ARE THEY NOT THE MOST UNWORTHY OF MEN?" And Dan did indeed look at the once powerful men as they wailed and hugged one another in their fright.

Slowly, the Scrying mirror began to glow with a faint yellow light, which gradually grew in intensity until it was blindingly white, filling the immense cellar with its brightness. Then something seemed to emerge from the mirror, the shape of a head at first, then shoulders, torso. Within the space of a minute, the person of Edward Kelley, Scryer to Doctor John Dee, alchemist and necromancer, stood in the room beside his only living relative.

Kelley extended his arms wide and smiled.

"Come to me, Daniel. Let us embrace and unite!" And as Dan stepped automatically forward, as though in a deep state of trance, the two men appeared to merge into one entity, Edward Kelley absorbing the life force and substance of his distant relation, so that eventually only one being remained.

The ancient, now re-born Scryer turned back to the still glowing Scrying mirror and spoke.

"You see, my Lords? *This* is how it is done, as I have vowed to you throughout the long years. Please, come forth and help yourself to a life renewed through these cowering curs!"

As the Scrying mirror glowed brightly once more, and the would-be necromancers finally found the courage to try and make a desperate break for life and freedom, they were overwhelmed by a far older and much more experienced band of twelve men who were truly versed in the black arts.

When, finally, the screaming had abated, Edward Kelley addressed his faithful followers.

"We are come, my Lords, to a new world! Look ye not at the tired old bodies which some of you now inhabit, for there will be more suitable persons for us all. Whenever or whoever we so choose. This is the beginning, a *new* beginning for each and every one of us. A beginning without an end, my Lords!"

As a mighty cheer echoed around the cellar, the door at the top of the stairs opened.

"Dad, are you down there? Hope you don't mind, but I've brought a few mates back with me..."

"Ah...fresh meat, so soon!" whispered Edward Kelley, as he and his disciples slowly made their way up the stone stairs.

NO ROOM AT THE FLAT

"Look...I've told you...he's *not* coming, and that's final!"

Sarah stared with pleading, spaniel eyes at her husband although she knew in her heart that he was right. Unfortunately, her heart knew, but her head was in command at that moment!

"But the *kids*...what about *them*? And he's been with us for so long! It's...it's *inhuman*, that's what it is!" and she fled from the room, avoiding the packing cases which were scattered about the lounge and hallway, the tears welling in her eyes, already red and puffy from a morning spent crying and begging for a stay of execution.

Barry too had a lump the size of a billiard ball in his throat. He hated to play the heavy, but *someone* had to and Sarah certainly wouldn't do it! The sound of barking from the back garden reminded him of the unpleasant task that lay ahead, and Barry let out a long, hopeless sigh of resignation.

He crossed to the patio doors, slid them open and called the Alsatian over to him.

"Come on, Shep...we've got to go see a man about a dog," he said sadly, roughing the animal's thick fur as it panted and slobbered affectionately in his face.

The appointment at the Vet's had been for eleven-fifteen. It was now twelve-ten and Barry was still sitting in his car in the lonely lay-by, looking out across the vast expanse of moorland spread out below him.

He had actually made it as far as the surgery door, but that was all. Shep had somehow sensed what was about to happen to him. He had known in the way that only animals seem to have of knowing, that he was about to die.

He hadn't tried to struggle, although he was powerful enough to have escaped if he had wanted to. No, he had simply stood there, looking up at Barry with those brown trusting eyes, and the lump in Barry's throat had grown to the size of a football, threatening to choke him, to burst his windpipe.

Then he had driven away, fast and furiously; ignoring the hoots and angry shouts of fellow drivers as he had cut them up, crossing through red lights as he fought back the tears and tried hard to swallow the impossibly large blockage in his throat.

Now, here he was, staring out across mile upon mile of open grassland, clumps of purple heather and distant thickets of pine trees.

Shep was seated next to him on the passenger's seat, his great tongue lolling as he panted with the anticipation of being allowed to roam the wilderness, just on the other side of the glass.

Barry wiped his eyes with the back of his hand and took a deep breath. It was better this way, he was sure of that. At least the poor bloody animal had a chance now. A chance to be free, to wander the countryside at will, to eat and sleep when he wanted to instead of having his life dictated by the whims of his human keepers! At least he had life, the choice to live as he wanted to, and it had to be better than ending up in a black plastic bag at the vet's, waiting for the dustmen to take him to the rubbish tip.

Barry hugged the dog so suddenly that it yelped with surprise.

"Come on, old son...time for your walkies!" and he leant across the car and opened the passenger door. Shep barked in gratitude and leapt from the Volvo, tearing off into a patch of tall bracken to chase imaginary rabbits.

Barry pulled the door shut, tasting the salt from the tears that streamed down his face.

"Goodbye, Shep!" was all he could manage to say before he choked on a sob.

He started the car's engine, took one final look at the Alsatian as it bounded across the moor and then drove off, back to what would soon be his old home, back to where the removal men would, even now, be placing the final few items of furniture into the back of their van, ready to take Barry and his family to a new life in London, two hundred miles away.

The dog had charged about for the better part of an hour, sniffing, urinating, barking at birds and trying to catch rabbits that were far faster than he, before he noticed that something was wrong.

Although he obviously had no concept of time as would a human, he sensed that he had been alone for far longer than was usual.

There had been none of the normal interference, no 'Here Boy!', no yanking on his leash, no scolding as he barked for no apparent reason when really he was just shouting for joy.

Shep had traced his own scent back to his people's car, but his man wasn't there! He had circled about the whole area, casting about for the man's scent and calling for him, but no one had come to take him back to the place where they all lived; the man, the woman and the two youngsters whom he had grown up with.

The dog had remained by the scent of his man's car for the rest of that day and night, whimpering hopelessly, hungry and tired, but too afraid to sleep in case he should miss the man's return.

When finally, after forty-eight hours of loneliness and terror he fell into a troubled and restless sleep, he knew that the man and his family would not be coming to fetch him. If he wanted them, he would have to find them!

"I said, 'I hate this place!' It's so bloody *small*…just look at it!" Sarah spread her arms wide as if she could touch all four wall of their newly built flat. Barry had to admit that it was a lot smaller than their three-bedroomed semi had been, but this was London and this was all they could afford until his new job took off. *Then* they would be able to get something better, maybe a two-bedded semi?

"Well you knew what it was going to be like before we came here! Trust you to moan when it's already too late! And *you* wanted the dog to live here as well. Christ…I give up with you!"

Sarah pouted at the mention of Shep. Barry had not had the heart to tell her the truth about him releasing the animal. He knew that she would have been up there searching those moors, day and night until she found the dog, with no consideration for what she would do with it afterwards.

The kids had been inconsolable when he had finally returned that terrible day. They had cried, then shouted, then refused even to speak or look at him. He had tried to explain that there simply was not the room for Shep in the flat, and that it would have been cruel to keep such a big dog in a place without a garden. The nearest park was more than a mile away, and that was hardly larger than a handkerchief!

Slowly, *very* slowly, the children began to speak, albeit grudgingly, to him. He had almost blown it again when he had foolishly promised them a new pup whenever they could eventually afford a house with a garden.

"It won't be the same, will it? It won't be *Shep*…you *killed* Shep, didn't you?" screamed Tania, his nine-year-old daughter, and he had not mentioned the idea again.

Life began to settle down to some sort of normality over the following weeks, and, after three months, even Sarah had stopped belly-aching quite so much as before. There were advantages to living in the Capital, although she still considered them to be outweighed by their cramped living conditions and the incessant traffic noise that seemed to surround them.

Even the children had settled into their new school without much upset, although they were still barely on speaking terms with their 'horrid' father.

So, it was with great surprise that six-year-old James and his sister came dashing into the kitchen one afternoon to tell their mother that there was something scratching at the front door, trying to get in!

Sarah fastened the heavy chain and slowly inched the door open. Although the landing was poorly lit, she could just make out what looked like a tatty old fur coat lying at the foot of the door. It was only when the 'coat' made a weak whimpering sound that she realised whatever it was, the 'thing' was still alive.

"What is it, Mum? What's up?" asked Tania, trying to push her way past her mother.

"I don't know. Look, stand back and I'll open the door so we can all see!"

James was the first to recognise Shep, although Sarah thought later that he might have been guessing.

The once powerfully built Alsatian was now emaciated almost beyond recognition, his fur filthy and matted, with a large patch of dried blood from what looked like a nasty wound on his flank.

As the three of them carried him into the hallway, Sarah could see that the poor animal was almost at death's door and she ran to fetch him a dish of water which she had to ladle out with her hand into the animal's mouth.

Later, when they had made Shep as comfortable as they could, Sarah turned to her children and said:

"Your father has got some explaining to do when he gets home and it had better be damned good!" Tania and James nodded in silent agreement.

It was almost eight o'clock before Barry eventually rolled up, clearly the worse for wear with drink.

The children had been sent to bed early in preparation for the war that lay ahead and Sarah made no attempt to open the door as she listened to her husband fumbling with his keys outside. She listened patiently as he dropped them, swore, dropped them again before finally opening the door and lurching into the lounge.

"You could've opened the piggin' door, 'stead of jus' sittin' there! I've 'ad an 'ard day you know, not jus' slouchin' aroun' the 'ouse all day, doing nowt...!" Barry belched loudly and slumped into his armchair where he tried, unsuccessfully, to kick off his shoes.

"Wasferdinner then, eh?"

Sarah was staring at him with ill-disguised loathing.

"What did you do with Shep, you bastard?" she almost snarled at him. Barry hiccupped and tried to focus on his wife's pinched face. A tiny alarm bell was starting to ring in the depths of his brain, but he was far too gone to pay it any heed.

"Whatyeronabout woman? 'E's dead...the vet gave 'im a jab and sscchhwiip…!" Barry indicated the end result by drawing his index finger across his throat. He tried to grin but Sarah could see that he was lying through his teeth. Strangely, she could also see that there was a great sadness in his eyes; he might be a lying swine, but he really did miss that dog.

Sarah fixed him with a withering stare. "You lying sod!" she spat so viciously that Barry fell backwards in his chair, mouth open and eyes staring. He flinched as Sarah stood abruptly, thinking she might hit him, but she stormed over to the living room door and tugged it with such force that the handle came off in her hand.

"Come with me!" she shouted and, drunk as he was, Barry knew that she meant business. He stumbled to his feet and followed her obediently towards the kitchen.

Sarah pushed the door gently open and stood back so that Barry could see the damage he had caused. He stopped dead in his tracks as he realised that the scrawny bundle of fur and bones was Shep; lovely old Shep who he had deserted weeks earlier. Abandoned to starve almost to death. The tears, this time of joy, were already springing to his eyes as he rushed forward to embrace his faithful old friend once more.

Shep opened first one eye and then the other.

The rest and the small amount of food he'd been able to eat had made him feel a little better; better than he had felt for weeks.

His eyes slowly focused on the two people standing by the kitchen door and he recognised both immediately.

At the very instant that Barry bent to hug his dog, Shep summoned up his last vestige of strength and hurled himself at the man who had abandoned him.

Before either Barry or Sarah could react, the Alsatian had ripped the man's windpipe from his throat and left him dying in a rapidly expanding pool of his own blood.

As Barry lay twitching on the floor in the final throes of his death, Shep wagged his tail weakly and collapsed back onto the blanket where he had been sleeping.

The children, aroused by the uproar in the kitchen, looked on dispassionately as their father gave one last spasm before dying with a horrible rattling sound that bubbled from his torn windpipe.

The mother and her two children stared at the grisly, blood-stained sight on the floor as though it were something from another world. Shep remained still yet breathing heavily on the blanket, alive, but only just so.

Tania looked at her mother, a puzzled frown creasing her brow.

"Mummy, can Shep stay now that *he's* gone?" she asked, primly.

THE SANDMAN

The pain was incredible!

He had never realized that such agony could exist. The *really* worrying thing, though, was that he could feel nothing from his chest downwards, although he knew that both his legs had to be shattered.

His spine must be damaged. It had to be.

He would be crippled for the rest of his days if he didn't get out of this bloody mess, and quickly!

It was a beautiful day, one of the best of the year so far. That was why he had roused himself extra early, attracted by the deep, clear blue sky and the gentle heat, that even at that early hour was filtering through the curtains of his hotel room window and warming the pillow on which he had lain.

Carol, his girlfriend, was still fast asleep beside him. Still, as Mr. and Mrs. Smith they had had a very late night at one of the local hot spots. She would be asleep for quite a while yet and would only be in a filthy mood for the rest of the day if he tried to wake her now.

He had showered and dressed quickly and quietly, and crept from their room to head out along the rugged coastline towards the magnificent clifftop views that he knew awaited him a mile or so further on.

He loved Cornwall; simply adored the place.

There was nowhere in the world, so far as he was concerned, that could touch the beautiful countryside of this area, and he would cheerfully spend the rest of his days in such a tranquil setting, if he were lucky enough to be allowed to do so.

Then he had gone too close to the edge of the cliff. The crumbling sandstone had given way, and he had plunged the sixty feet or so on to the beach below, closely followed by a small avalanche of debris that threatened to engulf him, to bury him alive!

He still could not understand *why* he was alive. It was a hell of a drop from the clifftop, far above, and it could only be the relative softness of the sand which had saved him from death.

Saved him?

As he struggled to look about him, his body buried up to the neck in sand, fallen sandstone and loose earth, he began to wonder just how *safe* he was.

There was no one else on the crescent-shaped sliver of golden sand. It was far too early for that. He could see that the tide was coming slowly in, but it would be a long time before that would pose any sort of threat to him. His more immediate problem was how he was going to get himself out of this predicament, with no one around to help him.

Right then...*concentrate*! He put every ounce of his strength into trying to move one or other of his arms. Then the pain hit him. He didn't have to be a trained medical man to realize that both his arms had been smashed in the fall. The agony seared up through them like a thousand tiny blow-torches, tearing up his arms and ripping into his groggy brain, which was ill-prepared for such a terrible shock.

He blacked out.

When he came to his senses again, his world was one of mind-numbing hell. There had been nothing more than a dull, aching throb until he had tried to move. He must have done himself more harm, and the pain was a constant and spiteful reminder that he should not try anything so reckless again.

He must have been out for some time because he could see that the tide had crept further up the beach towards him, having moved closer by several yards. Sweeping slowly, deliberately closer to the place where he lay trapped, almost *entombed* by the debris that pinned him to the ground.

The agony which consumed his body was now joined by a deep terror as he watched the sea move ever closer.

He became aware of a sound, somewhere further up the beach. It was the sound of children playing, shouting to one another. And they were coming closer; coming his way. He would be *saved*, if only he could attract their attention, call them over to him? Then he could be out of this mess and on his way to hospital.

The light laughter of the twin five-year-old boys drifted across the sands towards the rocks where he lay trapped. The boys, together with their mother, were the only other people on the beach, preferring to arrive early before the crowds came.

James and William bounded over the dry sand on their way to the water's edge, where they intended to build sandcastles and try to collect as many different shells as they could find.

William was also a boy who loved to climb, although he had been warned, in no uncertain terms, of the dangers of climbing on these loose and crumbling cliffs. Nevertheless, his first reaction was to head off to the large pile of rocks and rubble that he had spotted lying at the base of the towering cliff.

He was also, therefore, the first of the two boys to hear the faint and pathetic call for help from the man buried there.

The boys stood and stared in open-mouthed astonishment at the bloodied, sand streaked face of the man, as his dry throat, barely able to speak because of the enormous weight on his chest, tried to make himself understood.

It was a miracle that anyone had heard him at all over the sound of the pounding surf, now only scant feet away from his trapped and shattered legs. He had summoned every remaining ounce of his flagging strength to call to them, fighting against the terrible and ever present urge to pass out from the pain which screamed through his entire body.

The end result had been a high-pitched, reedy little voice that sounded more like something from a cartoon than from a fully grown twenty-two-year-old man.

But they *had* heard him! Thank God, they *had* heard him!

"Please...please, help...get help!" he whispered through cracked and parched lips.

The two boys merely stood watching him with stoic, unmoving faces. Although not exactly frightened by the strange-looking creature buried in the sand, neither of them could quite understand what *it* was trying to say to them.

It really was a funny looking thing. It looked like a man, but it didn't have any body or legs!

The man could feel the blood rising in his throat, as the steady pressure from the rocks and debris upon his chest had snapped some of his ribs, puncturing one of his lungs.

His mind reeled in desperation as he croaked another plea for the boys to go and get help before it was too late.

There was a sudden shower of dust and the twins looked up to the cliff just in time to see a small rock come plummeting down and strike the man-thing on the back of its head.

It even *bled* like a real person!

The man was unconscious now; stunned by the rock that had hit him, no doubt loosened when he had fallen from the clifftop.

The two boys inched closer. They knew what to do now. They had found a dead fish on the beach only the other day, and their mother had told them to bury the poor thing. They did just that with the man-thing's head, piling a neat row of rocks all around it, and then filling in the cracks with wet sand, until nothing, not even a single hair could be seen.

Their mother was yelling from her position on the travelling rug, spread out beside the car. It was lunchtime already!

They shot off across the sand, little legs pumping, throwing great gouts of sand into the air as they went.

After lunch, William turned to his mother, a familiar look on his tiny upturned face, which she knew meant another question was on its way.

She smiled and prepared herself.

"Mummy...what does the Sandman look like?" he asked in that long drawn-out way that young children have of speaking.

His mother sighed patiently. "I don't know, Will. Why do you ask?" she replied.

"Because we've just *seen* him...over *there*!" chipped in the other twin.

Oh, it was one of *those* games, was it? She would play along with them. Anything for a quiet life!

"Oh yes...and what was the Sandman *doing* on the beach?" she asked, hoping to catch them out.

"He was *sleeping*, of course!" came the stereophonic reply from the two shrill little voices.

The tide was now well past the spot where the man lay.

His head would be under almost two feet of water.

"Any more cake, boys?" asked the mother.

THE TOO GOOD SAMARITAN

It was late. 3:30 a.m. to be more accurate.

Still four hours until the end of Cathy's shift. The evening had been a fairly quiet one; surprisingly so considering the time of year. But then tomorrow night would be different...*very* different. Christmas Eve, together with New Year's Eve, were always their busiest times of all, and understandably so.

In a world that advocated that the spirit of Christmas be a shared, family experience, full of goodwill and love to all men, it was no wonder that the friendless, the despairing and the ill should feel left out of it all. Lonely people, men and women, young and old, perhaps trapped through illness or their own phobias in dingy bedsits, depressed, afraid...suicidal?

Yes, without doubt, tomorrow night would be a busy one, all right. This was just the lull before the storm broke.

Cathy was almost dozing off when the phone shattered the silence of the cramped little office. She shook her head, trying to clear the fog of sleep and lifted the handset, silencing the clammering bell in mid-ring.

"Hello, Samaritans...how can I help you?" she asked as cheerfully as possible for that hour of the morning.

Several moments passed without reply. Cathy could hear the caller breathing steadily at the other end of the line. Maybe they were undecided how to begin the conversation, perhaps even uncertain of their reason for calling. It was a common reaction and one which Cathy had encountered several times in her three short weeks as a Samaritan.

"It's all right...please, take your time. Just tell me what the problem is and I'll see what I can do to help...okay?" she prompted gently, realising just how difficult it must be to pour out your troubles over a telephone to a complete stranger.

There was a sudden sob of despair. A lonely, chilling gasp which sent the fine hairs on the nape of Cathy's neck standing on end.

"Please...?" she implored softly. "Please tell me what's wrong? It might help to share whatever it is..."

Another long period of silence followed as the caller...it sounded as though it was a young woman...battled with her emotions, forcing herself to calm down, to try to speak.

Eventually, after a period of some two minutes, the caller had composed herself enough to say something for the first time.

"Lonely...so lonely..."

Cathy sighed inwardly. They were making progress, slowly, but it was a start at least. Now she had started to talk, it was Cathy's task to make sure that she continued to do so. She had to get the girl to discuss her problem, real or imagined, in the hope that between them, they might come to some sort of solution, be it through the church, social services or some other agency.

"Please...tell me more...?" she began, but the caller interrupted her.

"Alone...so *alone* now...I can't go on any longer...No one left...*no one*...all gone...all gone away now..." The girl's voice sounded so distant, so sad, almost *spectral* in its lightness. She didn't seem to be speaking to Cathy, more as though she was talking to herself or thinking aloud: bearing her soul to a total stranger over an open telephone line.

Cathy glanced around the cluttered office.

Normally, there would have been two of them on duty at any one time, but Peter, her colleague, had called in to say that he had been suffering from a bad migraine and would be unable to make it that night. That meant that she would have no one else to ask advice of until her shift ended at around 7:00...still three and a half hours or so away.

Cathy remembered her training sessions and recalled how the other Samaritans had responded to callers when she had sat in on their shifts.

"There must be *someone* who cares for you? You're never as alone as you might think, you know? However bad you might feel right now; tomorrow is another day...a new start..." but even Cathy felt her words sounded trite and shallow. She could almost hear herself saying something like 'Keep smiling through!' or something equally as crass and feeble.

Whatever she had said so far, it seemed to be having little or no effect on the girl caller.

"No one...all dead...*dead*...all dead...everyone gone...mother... father ...brother...dead...all gone...no one left but me now...can't go on anymore...can't stand another night like *this*..." The disjointed rambling came to another abrupt end as the girl broke down, a heartrending sob bursting from her mouth.

"Poor kid!" thought Cathy. "And she sounds so *young* too."

It was just so hard to think of anything to say to someone who had obviously suffered such a terrible loss. She sounded so desperately lonely and was clearly emotionally disturbed.

Cathy was supposed to be cheering her up, if at all possible; to try and make things seem brighter at least, even if that was only a temporary stop gap until real help could be organised in the morning.

Cathy recalled her training once more. 'Try not to become too personally involved, no matter how hard and heartless it may feel to your natural instincts. Be helpful, be compassionate and above all *listen*, but if you become too wrapped up in their problems on a personal level, you'll be no good to the client or yourself!' That basic rule was very sound advice to anyone, and it had been drummed into her head during the probationary period of her work, just weeks earlier.

The Samaritan tried again.

"Are there no friends...neighbours, who could sit with you for a while? Is there nobody I could call for you?" she probed as gently as possible, not expecting any real response.

"*No!* No friends...I have no friends...never have had any. Mother didn't approve..." There was a long silence, then: "Would *you* be my friend? Please...? I'm so alone...never thought I could be so alone ...*please*? I *beg* you."

The tears were stinging Cathy's eyes as she swallowed hard and struggled to reply. This young girl, so friendless and forsaken, that even a complete stranger like herself was preferable to her all-consuming loneliness.

"Why...of *course* I'll be your friend! I'd like nothing better, Miss...?" It could be important to get the caller's name. Not only did it put things on a friendlier footing, it could be vital in the event of an emergency.

"Sarah...please, just call me Sarah."

"Hi, Sarah...I'm Cathy...Cath to my friends," she hinted cheerfully.

"Cathy and Sarah...Cath...Cathy...?" the disturbed girl repeated the two names over and over again, then:

"Can I see you, Cath? Please...? Can I see you *now*?"

It was a very good sign and Cathy jumped at the opportunity.

"Of *course* you can, Sarah! You know where the office is? In the High Street...number 26...?"

"NO...NO...NO!" screamed Sarah, so suddenly that Cathy almost dropped her handset.

"I can't leave *here*! I can't go *out*! NO...you must come and see *me*! *Please*? Cathy...oh, *please, you must!*"

Cathy was quite shocked by Sarah's outburst. She had seemed pretty calm, almost rational just a moment earlier, and now this? It was her own fault of course...Cathy had tried to rush things along too fast with *this* as a result.

It was out of the question for her to visit a client; against all the rules of both The Samaritans and common sense. She was there to offer a kindly word, to listen, and where feasible, pass on details to the appropriate authorities, the professionals, whoever they might be.

But one thing was patently clear; never, *ever* get involved yourself ...no matter what!

All this flashed through Cathy's mind in an instant as she listened to Sarah whimpering at the other end of the connection. It made sense to her and she respected the reasoning behind the theory. But there was something about this particular caller, something which cried out for attention, for affection and understanding. After all, the sweet child had no one in the world. Christmas was just around the corner, and not a solitary soul to share even a moment of it with her.

Cathy began to consider, against all the advice and her own better judgement. Maybe a five-minute visit...? A quick cup of tea and a chat?

It could make all the difference to Sarah. Possibly even the difference between a Christmas spent inside a psychiatric hospital or, worse still, the city morgue!

At least, if she *did* pop in for a while, it would show the girl that *someone* cared, that *someone* could take the trouble to go and see her.

A gesture of hope for the future, that was all she needed, ten minutes of her own time to save a young girl's life. How could she possibly refuse such a request and still call herself a Christian?

Damn the stupid rules! And anyway, who would ever know about it?

"Look, Sarah...I'm not supposed to make personal calls to people's homes..."

A wail of anguish cut through her head like a machete and she continued quickly, not wishing to upset the girl any further with her own dilly-dallying.

"*BUT*...please listen...I'd *love* to come and see you. Especially as we're now such good friends. It'll be our little secret...just you and I will know of it. OK?"

Cathy could almost *hear* Sarah smiling at the other end of the phone line and she was so pleased that she had agreed to visit the girl.

"When can you come...*now*? Oh, please come soon!" Sarah spoke with almost childish delight. Cathy glanced at the dusty electric clock hanging on the wall, and was surprised to see that it showed 3:55. She would dearly have loved to have gone straight home to her comfortable bed after work, but this could be a matter of life or death.

"Look, I finish here around seven. Give me your address and I'll be there as soon afterwards as possible."

There was a moment's hesitation, an instant of mistrust as Sarah weighed up the possibilities of the Samaritan betraying her to the authorities.

Cathy seemed to sense this and said, "It's all right...you really can trust me to keep quiet...honestly!"

It was all the girl needed. She gave Cathy her address, which turned out to be on the other side of town, and the Samaritan vowed to be there as soon as she could.

"You *will* come...you promise me, Cath?" implored the desperate girl.

"I'll be there...I won't let you down, Sarah!"

It was a part of the town unfamiliar to Cathy. The area had a general rundown air about it. The old houses, although once owned by wealthy merchants and money lenders, were now seedy and suffering from disrepair. No doubt awaiting the developers to move in to make a quick and handsome profit.

Sarah's house was every bit as seedy-looking as the others in that street. The paint on the front door was cracked and flaking. The windows looked dusty, the frames rotting, with putty missing from every pane. A leaky gutter had stained the upper two floors on the front of the house, leaving a horrid green-coloured streak of moss to add to the general unkempt look of the place.

Litter blew in small flurries, stirred by the early morning breeze as tiny eddies of dust danced at the kerbside, the whole scene lit by what must have been one of the very first electric street lamps ever to have been installed in the town. Cathy felt surprised that the thing was still working in this down-at-heel area and she was thankful for the illumination that it offered, even though a grey dawn was just beginning to break over the rooftops.

It certainly was an eerie-looking part of town, with none of the usual early morning activity that one would expect.

Cathy pulled her flimsy jacket tightly about her throat and shuddered in the chill morning air. She glanced up at the drab and empty looking old house and started up the steps which led to the front door. It was only when she caught a brief glimpse of a moving curtain in the corner of her eye that she realised she had indeed come to the right address.

She pulled at the old-fashioned bell and heard a distant tinkle in reply. Seconds later, Cathy heard the shuffle of slippered feet moving over linoleum. There followed the sound of a huge bolt being drawn and a chain being released. Finally, the door swung open to reveal a petite young woman, with matted fair hair and a very pallid-looking face. She looked about sixteen years of age, although her eyes somehow gave the impression of her being much older.

"Sarah?" asked Cathy, offering a tentative hand in greeting. Cathy noticed that, although it was a freezing December morning, the girl was wearing only a thin housecoat, with clearly nothing beneath it. Sarah rushed forward and circled her thin arms around Cathy's neck, pressing her greasy head next to the Samaritan's face so that she could hardly breathe.

There was an earthy smell about the girl that made Cathy's nose wrinkle in disgust and it was all she could do to prevent herself from pushing Sarah away. The girl must have sensed this as she released Cathy from her grip and stood back to look at her one and only friend.

"I'm sorry, Cath. It's just that I'm so pleased to see someone…you don't know how lonely it gets in this big old house all by myself!"

The very thought of spending more than a few minutes in that mausoleum of a house sent an uncontrollable shudder through Cathy's body. She could see now quite why the girl was so desperate for companionship. Cathy fought down her natural repugnance and took Sarah's grimy hand in her own.

"I'm very pleased to meet you, Sarah. Even at *this* hour of the morning!" she added, and both women laughed nervously.

Sarah led the way through to a surprisingly cosy-looking kitchen at the rear of the ramshackle old house, where she made tea with condensed milk (which was declined by Cathy). They sat and chatted almost like old friends, and as they did so, Cathy was surprised to discover that Sarah was a lot more stable than she had first thought. The girl had a wisdom which seemed to belie her age.

Finally, and much though the notion grieved her, Cathy broached the subject of Sarah's parents' death. It must surely have been a tragic accident for them both to have been wiped out so suddenly, and hadn't she mentioned something about a brother as well...?

"I'm sorry to bring this up...you don't have to talk about it if it's too painful..." Sarah suddenly sat rigidly on the kitchen stool, a pained expression crossing her face at the mention, however oblique, of her parents' demise.

"It's all right, Sarah...we don't have to talk about that," interjected Cathy, quickly noticing the younger woman's distress. Sarah waved her apologies aside and stood up, gripping the edge of the table as she did so.

"No...no...I'd like to talk about them...really I would! Let's go to the lounge. We can talk better there." Sarah held open the kitchen door and motioned Cathy through into the long dark hallway.

As they walked along the corridor, Sarah placed her hand on the Samaritan's shoulder and squeezed it affectionately.

"You've no idea how pleased I am to see you, Cathy. I've been so alone, but now you are here, everything is all right again."

"I'm glad to be of help. Loneliness is a terrible thing; I know that much!" Cathy saw a door on her right and felt for the handle.

"This is the room...go in," invited the girl.

Cathy turned the handle and pushed the door open. The question was still demanding a reply inside her head and she put it to Sarah as they entered the lounge.

"How long since...how long have you been 'on your own'?"

There was a pause as Sarah groped for the light switch and flipped it on.

"Oh...only since yesterday morning," replied Sarah, brightly.

Cathy stared in open-mouthed horror at the scene in the room.

There were three recently killed people seated as a family group on the sofa.

A man, a woman and a young boy who would have been about six years old or so. All three had their throats cut and all three had been terribly mutilated.

Cathy reeled under the horror of what she was witnessing, and only vaguely heard Sarah say:

"*They* didn't want me to have any friends...said I was too *dangerous*,

47

but now I have a *real* friend. And *you'll* never leave me, will you Cath?"

The last thing Cathy the Samaritan ever saw was the flash of a butcher's carving knife before it ripped out her windpipe, even before she could release the scream that had formed itself in her throat.

Later, Sarah placed Cathy, her friend, at the head of the dining table, in pride of place. There were sandwiches for everyone and a big bottle of lemonade in the centre of the tablecloth.

Sarah smiled proudly and caressed Cathy's mangled arm.

"Shall I be mum?" she asked of no one in particular.

THE NOT SO GOOD
SAMARITAN

"Samaritans…how can I help you?"

"Hello…The Samaritans?" confirmed the caller, needlessly.

Roger sighed. "Yes, that's right. How can I help you?"

"I'm going to kill myself," the caller stated simply, almost as a challenge. When it was clear that the man wasn't going to add anything to this statement, Roger felt duty bound to ask questions.

"Oh? And why do you feel this way? Surely, nothing could really be as bad as all that?" he offered as a token argument. If the man had really intended to do away with himself, it was highly unlikely that he would have taken the trouble to telephone the Samaritans first.

"Oh no? If *you* had to sit in this bloody house all day, every day, month after month, I reckon *you'd* want to kill *yourself*! I've got no work, no friends and I can't afford any female company. You just tell me what the point of it all is? Go on, give me one good reason for not ending it all!"

The gauntlet had been thrown; it was Roger's job to pick it up.

"Have you tried joining an association? There are hundreds of other people in your situation, you know, but they are trying to better themselves with Job Clubs, self-help schemes, that sort of thing."

The caller laughed sardonically.

"A waste of bloody time, the whole lot of it! A load of old cobblers if you ask me! No…I've had enough of this lot! I'm off out of it…punching me card, clocking off for the last time, going to the only place I can think of where there's one hundred percent full time employment and no unions to bugger it up for everyone!"

Roger shook his head sadly.

It was a reflection of the times in which we live. A sad but inescapable fact that there were the haves and the have-nots and the latter were getting decidedly browned off by it all. This man seemed adamant enough, although Roger could not find himself agreeing with his drastic solution. The very idea of someone taking their own life made him feel sick to his stomach.

"Surely there's another way? When God put us on this…"

"*God!*" screamed the caller. "Don't you give me that *God* crap! If there *is* such a being, do you really think that He would let us suffer like we do? *Eh*? Now the *other* fella, I could believe in *him*. No problem. I mean, there's plenty of nasty little evil people about the place: murderers, rapists, muggers, child molesters, the list is endless and who're they all working for? Why, Old Nick himself, of course! The Prince of Darkness and his Evil Hordes!"

Roger couldn't help thinking that maybe the caller was right. He was putting up such a damned good argument, that the Samaritan was at a loss to contest it.

"You could have a point there," he conceded, aloud.

Then: "Look...why don't we meet up somewhere after I've finished here? We could have a good chat and maybe find a way of helping you out of this patch of misfortune? Well...what do you say, hmmm?"

The caller fell silent for a moment, wary of this sudden turn of events. It was the very last thing that he had expected. He had just wanted to have a damn good argument with someone, and as he had no friends of his own, the Samaritans had seemed as good a place as any to have a go at.

It wasn't the first time he'd called them, but on other occasions, they had bent over backwards to talk him out of his threat. This was, well...*weird*, was the only word that sprang to mind.

"I thought that you people weren't supposed to visit clients outside of the office? I thought it was against your code of conduct to get too involved?"

Roger smiled. "Well...to tell you the truth, you're absolutely right. But I'm pretty new to this lark and I made a vow to myself that I'd never allow a person to take their own life, if there was anything I could do to prevent that happening. You are just my second caller threatening to end it all, and I'd like to offer you this personal service, over and above the usual confidential consultation!"

The caller, ever with an eye for the main chance, licked his thin lips and thought the proposal over. Maybe, just *maybe* there was a way to extract a few quid from this do-bloody-gooder! They were always an easy touch for a few bob, why not use the idiot if he wanted to be parted from his ill-gotten money?

"All right, you're on! But I don't talk too good with a dry throat, and *water* isn't what I had in mind. Understand?"

Roger grinned even wider. He understood perfectly.

"How about a drop of whisky, is that alright?" he suggested.

"Does a pig fart? Of *course* it's alright, but only so long as it's twelve-year-old malt...I can't stomach that cheap firewater!"

"Only the best for you, Mr...?" enquired the Samaritan, his pen poised over a notepad.

"Benton...Arthur Benton, redundant refuse collector!"

"Right then, Mr. Benton, if you would like to furnish me with your address, I'll be there as soon as I can get away from this place, with a drop of the hard stuff and two glasses. Is that fair enough?"

Benton laughed, sounding like a cracked 78 record.

"That is perfectly fair, old son. Very fair indeed!"

23, Viaduct Lane probably wasn't the most desirable address in town.

In fact, as Roger's sleek black Lotus glided over the pot-hole strewn roadway, he imagined that this place would fall somewhere between a doss-house and the old Newgate Prison on a list of ideal homes.

Arthur Benton's hovel was the last in a terrace of similar dilapidated hovels, and was without doubt, the tattiest of the lot. The grey-brown things in the windows were either ancient net curtains or accumulated grime and filth adhering to Victorian spider webs.

The front garden was little more than Arthur's private rubbish tip, where he evidently disposed of all his old tin cans and half empty milk bottles. There was no sign of life from any of the other houses as Roger stepped from his car, and carefully avoiding as much of the litter as he could, he made his way to Benton's front door.

Even before he could raise his hand to knock, the rotting door creaked open and a frightening, balding head was thrust through the aperture, closely followed by the worst stink that Roger had ever smelt in his entire life.

"You the bloke from the Samaritans?" asked the apparition, still with the door only half open.

Roger nodded dumbly, trying his best not to breathe in as he did so. He couldn't help but stare at Arthur's face. It seemed to be covered in a layer of dust and grime several years old, almost as though the man had worked in a coal mine and had forgotten to wash for most of his life. The little which remained of his hair was matted and sticking to his grim, encrusted scalp. A blackened hole made up his mouth which had no sign of teeth, either real or artificial, and a shaggy and deeply stained beard which was obviously 'alive', completed the picture.

Roger swallowed hard.

"Hello, Arthur? I'm Roger...this is my friend Chivas Regal!" he said, holding the bottle of expensive whisky aloft and thanking God that he had brought a pair of his own glasses in which to drink the stuff.

A light of pure greed flashed into Arthur's eyes and he motioned his visitor into the front room of the two-up, two-down cottage-cum-slum.

The smell was even worse inside, if that were at all possible.

Everywhere there were half empty plates containing mouldy food, stained glasses and cups with horrible things apparently living inside them. Bottles full of God knows what were scattered across the table top and filled a battered sideboard. The unmistakable stench of urine wafted from an almost overflowing pot standing next to the fireplace.

Benton snatched the bottle from Roger's hand and proceeded to wipe one of his own scummy glasses with a revolting handkerchief.

"No! I...er, I mean, it's alright, Arthur, I've brought us some proper whisky glasses...look, here they are!" Roger quickly produced them from his overcoat pockets and set them down in the only clear space on the cluttered table.

After some consideration, Benton shrugged his shoulders at his guest's apparent fussiness and poured a full glass for each of them. Arthur downed his in one and was halfway through his next before Roger could speak.

"So, Arthur...what's the problem then?" asked the younger man, sipping at his own drink as he watched Benton pour his third.

Roger's host wiped his mouth on the back of his grimy hand and scratched fiercely at his tatty beard. No doubt the wild-life within it was reacting to the scotch he had dribble into their habitat.

Eventually, he stopped scratching, having presumably quietened the inhabitants, and, after belching loudly, he turned to stare at Roger.

"Ah, nothing really...I just get a bit brassed off livin' all on me lonesome. I go to the call box on the corner and ring someone for a bit of a barney...just to 'ear another human voice, you understand? Well...it passes the time of day you know?" He belched loudly once more and picked up his glass, emptying it.

Roger took another small sip from his own glass and watched as Benton poured and then drank his fourth and fifth in almost as many seconds.

"So all that stuff about you taking your own life, was just so much talk?" asked Roger, eyeing the older man carefully.

Benton laughed loudly, and in person he sounded even more like a cracked record played on an old gramophone.

"Yeah! It was just a load of old guff to get a mug like you to bring me some of this stuff!" He raised his glass and sloshed whisky over his hand.

"Doesn't always work o' course, but there's usually some bloody do-gooder somewhere waiting to dole out a few bob to the needy, like meself!"

A wry smile split Roger's face as he listened to Benton babble on, only pausing to swallow his sixth and seventh whisky. He noticed that Arthur was already lurching as he tried to pour yet another drink.

"Allow me to do that for you, Arthur? That's what I'm here for...to help."

Arthur shrugged his shoulders and belched by way of reply.

Some twenty minutes later the entire bottle of scotch had disappeared and Arthur Benton stared at it stupidly.

"It'sallgawn!" he slurred, tossing the empty container into the grate where it shattered into a thousand pieces.

"Right...yoooo...buggerorf now, you bleedin goody two shoes! *Hic!*"

Roger had the answer to hand. He produced another half bottle of whisky from his inside pocket and Arthur almost snatched his arm off in his haste to get at the liquor. He had by now decided to dispense with his glass and drank the burning liquid straight from the bottle.

"You know, Arthur, I've been thinking," said Roger, casually.

Benton banged the bottle down on the table top, spilling much of its precious contents, and tried to fix on any one of the three swaying images of Roger seated opposite him.

"Yeah…waaat? Waaat yooobin thinkin'?"

"I've been thinking that maybe you *were* right after all. Maybe what you said on the telephone earlier *did* make sense, especially the bit about you ending it all and popping off to visit 'Old Nick', as I think you called him. It sounds like a capital idea and I almost agree with you entirely."

Arthur's tongue was thick and sticky inside his mouth, which in turn was as dry as a good martini. He felt sick and he needed to pee. He really had no idea what this young idiot was going on about and, what's more, he didn't care.

Neither did he notice when Roger, the Good Samaritan, rose quietly from the battered wooden chair and moved with catlike grace across the room, where he stood behind the drunken man.

"There's just one small point, one tiny flaw in your thinking that I simply cannot agree with you on, Arthur old man."

Benton grunted noncommittally, his brain doing a very good impression of a spin dryer.

"I am deeply opposed to anyone taking their own life. Especially …when *I* am here to take it for them!"

Arthur Benton's drink-sodden mind was barely aware of the cheese wire being wrapped around his throat, and before his brain could tell his body to react he was almost dead.

Seconds later, he was.

Roger picked up the two glasses he had brought with him, considered briefly whether to wash them in Arthur's filthy, cluttered sink, and thinking better of it, he wrapped them in his handkerchief and put them in his pocket, along with the remains of the half bottle of whisky.

He felt a warm glow extending throughout his entire body: the feeling he always got after performing such an act of great kindness.

Roger loved his work, the work that God had given him to perform and he carried out that work with an enthusiasm bordering on obsession.

Satisfied that everything was in order, he left the stinking hovel, happy in the knowledge that Arthur had gone on to a better, and most certainly, a *cleaner* place.

As he started the Lotus's engine, he hummed a hymn that was buzzing through his mind:

"Onward Christian soldiers, marching as to war…!"

THE CHAMELEON MAN

The ugly buboes nestling in his armpits were swollen to the size of a hen's egg. They were bloated and angry looking and they burst suddenly with an audible popping sound, sending a trickle of red/grey viscous pus streaming down the man's ribcage.

The rest of his skin was covered in small bleeding spots that quickly turned almost black, giving the disease its terrible name: The Black Death, otherwise known as Bubonic Plague.

The audience oohed and aahed and erupted into spontaneous applause as Charlie Roberts completed his remarkable display. Within seconds, the buboes, horrible black spots and open running sores had completely vanished and his body was once more clear of blemishes and healthy looking.

Professor James Watson stepped forward on the small stage and congratulated Charlie, slapping him heartily on the back with undisguised affection and respect.

"Magnificent, Charlie! Absolutely magnificent! You truly are a wonder to behold!" he shouted above the general uproar in the exhibition chamber. All around the packed circular amphitheatre, more usually employed for demonstrations of surgical procedures, the assembled medical students, doctors, surgeons and dignitaries cheered and applauded as Charlie Roberts smiled wanly. He had given similar displays of his unusual talents at other venues across Europe and America, but never before to such a large and celebrated audience as this one.

The Professor rapped his gavel on the oak podium in an attempt to bring the hall to order. After several tries, the rapturous applause died to a trickle, and finally to a single over-excited medical student who Watson silenced with a withering stare.

"And now, Mr. Roberts will demonstrate the next part of his performance...LEPROSY!" yelled the Professor, not unlike some fairground barker at a dubious side show.

*

Charlie Roberts really was an incredible man. Ever since his childhood, when he had discovered that he could mimic illnesses such as Chickenpox, Measles and the like simply by reading about the symptoms and then concentrating hard with their description in mind.

It had started as a prank, a way of getting out of the classroom, but he soon became a legend amongst his peers and word quickly spread. In the earlier days, he would surely have been burnt as a witch but even in these more enlightened times, he was shunned and feared by some and hated by a few.

Charlie was seventeen when word of this remarkable young man reached the ears of Professor Watson, the world-renowned expert in the field of Tropical Diseases, who was based at The London Institute. Once the Professor had 'discovered' him, Charlie rapidly became the toast of medical science. He was written about in every medical journal and newspaper across the globe, adored and feared now in equal proportions, condemned by the Church as a demon while at the same time being praised by medical men for his amazing insight into illnesses and diseases.

But *today* was something very special for Charlie Roberts.

The greatest medical brains from around the entire globe, together with all the top research scientists plus a handful of particularly brilliant medical students, were all gathered under one roof for an extra special display of his unique talents.

He would replicate, before their very eyes, *thirty-seven* different diseases and severe disfigurements in a three-hour long session, and then take questions at the end of it!

Imagine, being able to see The Black Death from onset to finish, right there in front of you, with no risk of contagion and all over and done with in less than four minutes? Incredible! Or witnessing deadly epidemic Cholera or Typhoid? The list of normally fatal diseases went on and on, with each in plain view from start to finish and every one bringing a further gasp of amazement from the assembled medical men.

It was this incredible ability to mimic these normally murderous afflictions that had given Charlie his 'stage name': The Chameleon Man, for it was the strange Chameleon-like properties within his body which created these fantastic phenomena, with absolutely no actual bacterial infections present.

Even though the display was one hundred percent safe, this hadn't prevented the occasional young medical student from fleeing for his very life as Charlie demonstrated his incredible transformations.

Tonight was the culmination of six years of being prodded and poked, jabbed and examined, together with a thousand other medical tortures devised to get to the bottom of Charlie's unique talents. Tonight was *the big one*; he had been offered a great deal of money for this evening's display and he intended to give them full value, as the cash he'd received would help keep him in grand style well into his old age.

He was a self-made man, celebrated around the world, the likes of whom had never been seen before…and he had done it all *himself*! How his father would laugh on the other side of his face if he were still alive.

'Useless talent' indeed!

As Charlie completed his thirty-sixth disease, the applause in the auditorium was deafening. He had decided before the evening had begun that he would have to end on a 'big one'; something very special that he had been practicing in the peace and quiet of Professor Watson's country house, something which had never been witnessed by a living soul.

The Professor stepped forward on the dais and tried to still the uproar in the hall.

"Please, gentlemen...*PLEASE!*" he implored. After several more minutes, silence finally fell upon the crowd.

"Mr. Roberts...Charlie...will now perform something that nobody, not even myself, has ever been privileged to see before this evening. It is something so *remarkable*, so...*impossible*, that you will, without doubt, disbelieve your own eyes!"

The Professor took a step back, as Charlie, now wearing a long black cape about his shoulders, not so much for theatrical effect as to combat the chill in the old amphitheatre, took his place at the lectern. The room was so still that you truly could have heard the proverbial pin drop as Charlie prepared to speak.

"Ladies and Gentlemen...the things that you have witnessed here this evening have been, I hope you will agree, incredible." A murmur of agreement swept through the audience, together with several hearty 'hear, hears'.

"*But*," continued The Chameleon Man, "all of that is *nothing, nothing* compared to what I will now provide for your entertainment!" Gasps emerged from the stunned audience, and Charlie had to wave them silent before he could continue.

"All the diseases you have seen so far are but mere...shall we say 'surface alterations' to my outer, fleshy layer. *But* I have been working on something that I hope will be the greatest transformation ever performed in any public place!"

Somewhere from the left of the small stage there sounded a theatrical drum-roll as Charlie threw off his cape. All the lights in the auditorium were dimmed, save the brilliant stage spotlight.

"And now...for the first time ever...anywhere in the world...I give you...CURVATURE OF THE SPINE...otherwise known as...HUNCH-BACK!"

The applause was totally deafening. No one, not even the Professor had expected anything quite like this. It was *the* greatest finale to a wonderful evening of medical surprises and chronic illnesses.

The man was a true showman and a genius of the highest order!

Slowly, the room fell into a hushed and expectant silence. Every eye was transfixed on Charlie Roberts as he prepared himself for this latest, wonderful transformation.

The flesh on his back started to stretch and ripple in an alarming manner. The spinal column beneath the skin began to buckle and bend outwards, completely distorting his stance and the entire shape of his ribcage and upper body.

Within the space of two minutes, and, with what seemed to be an amazingly strenuous effort, Charlie stood before the assembled medical brains of the entire world...a *hunchback*!

The other transformations had been miraculous, but *this* was on a whole new level! Was there *nothing*, in terms of bodily disfigurement that this man could not achieve?

He truly was The Chameleon Man!

The applause and cheering was so loud, that the Professor feared the glass roof high above them might shatter with the noise. He covered his ears with his hands, not yet daring to try and stop the crowd's appreciation of what they had just witnessed.

It was nothing short of a miracle, and everybody there knew it.

It took Charlie somewhat longer than usual to revert back to normal. The strain was clearly evident on his face as the Professor guided the younger man towards a chair at the side of the stage. Sweat poured down Charlie's face in tiny rivers and he trembled uncontrollably as he fought to regain his composure.

Watson placed an arm around Charlie's shoulder, his face a mask of concern.

"Are you alright, dear boy; you look so pale?" he asked. The younger man nodded weakly.

After what felt like hours but was in truth no more than a few minutes, the applause still echoing, undiminished, around the hall, Charlie smiled weakly at his friend and mentor and hoisted himself from the chair. He walked unsteadily over to the lectern, holding on tight briefly, before taking a deep bow.

"Encore! Encore! Encore!" the word was shouted by almost every voice in the auditorium. Charlie held up a trembling hand to try to quell the uproar and slowly, row by row, they fell silent. The great man was about to speak and *no one* wanted to miss a single word of what he had to say.

"Thank you! Thank you so much!" he began, shakily. His mentor stepped forward with a glass of water and Charlie took a sip before continuing.

"I hope that you have all enjoyed my little 'exhibition' here, this evening. As you will no doubt be aware, this was my final public appearance. I am now going to study medicine myself in Vienna. I have had enough of being poked and prodded...I feel that it is *my* turn to be the prodder rather than the *prodee*!" Laughter swept briefly through the hall.

There were tears brimming in Charlie's eyes; tears of sadness but also of relief. These demonstrations were starting to take their toll on the young man, and it was time to stop them before they killed him.

The Professor stepped forward and draped Charlie's discarded cape around the younger man's shoulders, smiling warmly at the person he had come to think of as his son. Charlie returned the smile and then turned to face the audience once more.

"I must thank you...every one of you. All of those who have supported me over the years. But especially my friend...my *saviour*, Professor Watson, without whom I would surely have ended up as a freak in a carnival sideshow."

The young man, choked by emotion and with tears streaming down his cheeks, turned and was led away by his friend, to the rapturous cheers and applause from the audience.

Somehow, through all the bedlam, one voice seemed to stand out above all the others and Charlie stopped to see who it was shouting at him. He noticed a young man...a medical student, he guessed, but he couldn't hear what was being said.

Sensing that something was going on, the audience gradually fell silent as Charlie walked towards the young man seated below the stage.

"I'm sorry...what did you say?" asked the star of the show.

The student grinned widely. It appeared for all the world that he had been put up to this, and Charlie had perhaps foolishly taken the bait.

"I said: 'Do you feel that there is no illness or state of health which you cannot recreate?'" The student sat waiting. He had baited the trap, and it was now up to Charlie to avoid it or fall in feet first.

The Chameleon Man was both puzzled and annoyed by the young upstart's pointless question.

"Excuse me...have you just arrived? Or have you been asleep for the last three hours?" he asked, barely able to disguise the contempt in his voice. "Did you not just witness thirty-six diseases, *plus* a severe curvature of the spine, displayed here, on this very stage?" Charlie was clearly furious, made all the worse by the cool, arrogant way the medical student sat staring and smiling from his seat below.

A nervous titter ran through the auditorium as Charlie attempted to put the would-be doctor in his place.

"So," continued the student, "there is no medical or physical state that you cannot recreate. That is what you maintain, is it?" sneered the younger man.

Charlie looked across at the Professor, who shrugged his shoulders helplessly. The showman slammed his fist down hard on the lectern, knocking over the glass of water, which in turn shattered on the floor of the stage.

"Of *course* there isn't, you idiot!" he bellowed at the student.

Another nervous laugh travelled around the hall. The audience was starting to sense that there was something in the air, and once more fell silent.

The cocky young student rose from his seat and stood right next to the stage, where he could be clearly heard by all present.

"Right then, *Mister* Roberts…" The boy paused for maximum effect. "Have you ever tried to mimic the medical state of…DEATH?" he yelled, loud enough for everyone in the hall to hear.

Charlie looked stunned. The Professor looked stunned. In fact, everyone in the entire auditorium, except for the student, looked stunned by the idea, and the place erupted with speculation and chatter.

Charlie looked towards his mentor for support and advice, as the Professor shook his head violently. "*No*, Charlie! It cannot be done. Not even by *you!*" The older man tugged at his ward, trying to usher him away from the stage, but suddenly another voice called out, "Do it!" This followed by another, then another, until the majority of the audience was demanding to know the answer to the young student's question.

For one of the very few times in Charlie Robert's life, he felt scared.

He was scared that he had been challenged to attempt something which couldn't be done. He was scared that he would look foolish in front of all these respected people, and he was scared that if he didn't at least *try* to do it, he would lose every scrap of esteem and appreciation which he'd worked so long and hard for over the years.

He struggled free from the Professor's grip and strode back to the edge of the stage.

"I *repeat*, for the benefit of the deaf and the dense amongst you; there is no medical state that I cannot mimic, given the time and the practice. Not…even…*DEATH!*" He spat the last word and glared at the student, daring him to continue. The younger man merely sat down and crossed his arms, an unpleasant grin spreading across his thin face.

"Then *show* us, Mr. Roberts…*Show* us!" he demanded.

"*Please*, Charlie…this is *madness!*" begged the Professor. "You *know* that it can't be done…you will *kill* yourself!"

Charlie brushed off the Professor's appeals to common sense and ripped off the cape, tossing it into the audience.

He turned to his mentor and whispered fiercely, "Don't you *see* it? It would be the ultimate display of my career…the man who could feign *death!* The greatest trick since Jesus Christ raised Lazarus from the grave! Just *imagine!*"

Watson realised that it was too late.

All because of some childish imbecile in the audience, the most amazing man who had ever lived was about to risk his very life, and there was nothing he could do to prevent it from happening!

He sat down heavily, a beaten man, and waited for the inevitable to happen. He was determined to take no part in what was about to occur.

The next few minutes were taken up with Charlie Roberts directing the stewards in erecting a high table on the stage, so that the whole audience could witness the impossible. At last, everything was ready and The Chameleon Man signalled for the room to be silent. All chatter stopped as he clambered onto the improvised 'death bed'.

He glared at the young student in the front row, and said:

"And now...for the benefit of those amongst you who *disbelieve* me, I shall now mimic the state of...*DEATH!*" For one final time, the theatrical drum roll rang out as Charlie Roberts lay back on the bed, arms folded across his chest like an Egyptian mummy. Utter silence pervaded the auditorium.

At first, his breathing increased and the blood hammered through his veins and arteries as he struggled to imagine what death must *feel* like. Every other illness he had ever mimicked over the years were well documented, but, aside from knowing what a dead person *looked* like, there was of course no *written* description, no first-hand evidence for him to be able to know what it would *feel* like.

He began to wish that he had kept his mouth shut and curbed his temper. That blasted student had this trap in mind for the entire evening and he had blundered into it with his eyes wide open...Fool!

He could hear the odd murmurs in the hall as he tried to concentrate. First one, then another, until there was a general buzz throughout the auditorium.

"Concentrate, Charlie...*concentrate!* You can do this...you can do this...!" he told himself, over and over again.

Gradually, *very* gradually, his heart rate began to slow and his breathing evened out. It felt as though he was drifting into a heavy sleep...the sounds in the hall faded into the background, until he could no longer hear them, and the bright lights were extinguished from his sight...just the slow and steady thud of his heart and the barely noticeable movement of his lungs...he was drifting...drifting on a sea with no horizons...there was no movement...he was just floating it seemed... floating...then, nothing...

The buzz of chatter grew into a roar as the Professor moved quickly to Charlie's side. He felt for a pulse. There was none. He desperately listened for a heartbeat. Nothing! He placed a small mirror over Charlie's mouth to capture any signs of breath escaping. There were none!

Finally, he took a large, steel pin from behind his jacket lapel and jabbed it hard into the muscle of Charlie's right thigh. Not a flicker of movement.

For all intents and purposes, Charlie Roberts was dead. Well and truly dead!

The Professor turned to the audience and shook his head sadly. Even the mouthy student had the good grace to go ashen faced and hung his head in shame.

There would be more tests, naturally. After all, the room was filled to the rafters with the best medical brains in the world. If there were any chance of finding life or reviving The Chameleon Man, these were surely the people to do so? Charlie had simply pressed his luck too far this time.

After an hour had passed not a single person had left the hall. Some were weeping openly, otherwise, the place was unnaturally quiet.

When some three hours had elapsed and, after every possible procedure had been employed in an attempt at resuscitating Charlie Roberts, he was officially declared dead and, given the nature of the audience, talk naturally turned to carrying out an autopsy on the body of the most amazing man who had ever lived. Even though Professor Watson was appalled at the notion, he was, after all, a medical man himself and he only offered a token argument against the idea.

Soon, all was prepared for the investigation into the incredible body of The Chameleon Man and distinguished medics jostled with one another to gain the best view of the proceedings, like children in a playground brawl.

Charlie Roberts lay naked and spread-eagled upon the autopsy table, like a moth on a mount. Professor Watson had been elected as the person to carry out the examination of the strangest case in medical history and, as he stepped forward with scalpel at the ready, his hands were trembling slightly with anticipation.

After hovering briefly above his late friend's abdomen, he vigorously jabbed with the scalpel, drawing it swiftly and expertly upwards and then across, so that all the vital organs were exposed.

"Nothing appears unusual so far," he told the expectant audience.

The examination continued.

Normal procedure would be to remove all organs so that they could be carefully examined, weighed etc. The Professor always started with the heart during autopsies and, after all this was in reality just another one, so that was where he would begin today.

At the very instant he deftly severed the main aorta, the "dead" man's eyes flickered open.

It had taken much longer to get back than he had anticipated, but he had done it! He had lifted the curtain of death and looked beyond, had seen what lie ahead and returned with a knowledge to share with all mankind!

The *wonders* he had witnessed; the *incredible* things he could now relate to these doctors!

"I *TOLD* you I could do it!" he bellowed to the stunned circle of faces surrounding him.

But something seemed to be wrong? *Very* wrong!

Why did they all look at him like that? What had happened while he had been away?

Professor Watson had already severed all the major arteries leading to Charlie's heart, before he realised that his friend had returned from the dead. He had even failed to notice that the once 'dead' organ now held in his hand, had started to beat almost at the moment he had made the first incision, and he now tried desperately to replace the throbbing heart back into the chest cavity, struggling with the haste of the hopeless, already aware that it was far too late to save his former friend.

Charlie Roberts stared with pleading eyes into the face of his mentor. "HELP ME, PROFESSOR...*HELP* ME..."

He emitted a soundless scream and his entire body shook and trembled.

Charlie Roberts returned to the other side.

This time, on a one-way ticket.

THE SWITCH

He couldn't do another stretch inside.

At the age of forty-two, he had spent more than half of his life locked away in one sort of institution or another. Remand school at fifteen, graduating to prison at eighteen. A year here, three years there, wasting away his youth behind bars with only his new criminal 'skills' acquired from other inmates and a deathly white pallor to show for it all.

There was no way he could remain sane and do another term caged up in an overcrowded cell. No way on this earth!

Fifteen years that bastard judge had given him this time. *Fifteen years*! And for what? A couple of credit cards, $200 in cash and a handful of junk jewellery...that's what! All that crap about him being 'a persistent and regular offender and a menace to decent, hardworking folk'. Nothing to do with the fact that the old bag whose house he'd robbed happened to be a Rotarian and a friend of the local sheriff of course...oh no!

But Jesus, he'd been lucky! Someone up there must love him?

Why else would the prison bus have crashed into that tree as it avoided a stray dog? The guard would recover. He'd split the guy's head open with his own baton after the mug had come to check on his prisoner after the accident.

But that was the chance guards took, wasn't it? The schmuck!

Then there had been more good luck as he found the pickup parked with the keys in the ignition outside the burger bar. Okay, so it was a shame the tank was half empty, but it got him out of the city and way out into the countryside before it ran out of gas. More luck when he discovered the old, disused quarry and dumped the truck over the edge, where it smashed into scrap at the bottom.

They would never think to look for him out here, in what to him, was the middle of nowhere. He'd never seen so many trees in his entire life, or so much open space. He was from the big city, and this was *scary*.

But he was *free*! Free as a bird...an ex-jail bird, to be exact! And *that* was the way he intended to remain.

Yep, it sure was the luckiest day of his entire life!

*

He heard the heavy footfalls of someone stumbling through the thick undergrowth, way before he spotted the man. The stranger was blundering noisily through bushes and bracken making as much noise as a stampeding rhino, oblivious as to whether anyone heard him or not.

The man was about the same age, height and build as himself. He even appeared to have similar thickset, dark features and almost identical muscular build.

The convict's mind was whirring like a computer. He quickly estimated that the man's clothes would fit him well enough and he knew that he would have to dump the bright orange prison suit he was wearing as soon as possible. It stood as a Judas testimony to his crimes and profession and it had to go.

The escapee's hand brushed against the hard surface of a partially buried rock in the undergrowth and, without thinking, he dug it out, feeling the weight, estimating the damage it could do.

There was a vacant look in the walker's eyes as the convict sprang from his hiding place and clubbed the man repeatedly with the rock. The stranger made no sound and no effort to either run or defend himself. There was no fear in his expression, no surprise...just, what? Acceptance?

The con knelt at the man's side and felt for signs of a pulse. Nothing. He'd hit the man too hard with the rock. He really hadn't intended to kill the stranger; it was just bad luck. But at least he wouldn't be around to blow the whistle on him.

This wasn't the sort of place where a body could be easily discovered. There were no obvious trails, no picnic site nearby, no tourist attractions.

It could be months before someone found the body, if *ever*.

The resemblance between himself and the blood-spattered face of the dead man was quite remarkable now that he could see him close up. They could well have passed as brothers, or at least close relatives, he thought. This could turn out to be *very* handy if the body had time to rot down for a while before discovery.

The con quickly swapped clothes with the dead man and struggled to re-dress the corpse in his discarded orange coverall.

When he had finished, he looked down at the dead walker at his feet. Yep, give it a few weeks and even his own *mother* wouldn't be able to tell whether it was her only son or not.

The cops would be off his back forever! He would make a new life. A new start somewhere.

The Gods had surely smiled on him today, hadn't they?

It had turned chilly now as the sun was low in the sky, and he was very glad of the brown leather jacket he'd taken from the dead man. It was a good fit, and although somewhat smelly, it was a hell of a lot warmer than his prison clothes had been. Even the man's *shoes* were a perfect fit!

He found himself whistling as he headed out through the dense undergrowth on the lookout for a main road that would take him to his new life. He felt *reborn*, free as the wind, with not a care in the world.

He was still whistling some half-remembered tune as he stepped out from behind a thicket, straight into the path of the speeding white panel truck.

*

He awoke into a world of pain.

There were powerful, bright lights above him and he was stretched out on some kind of hard bed.

"Ah, he's coming to. Stand by, Connors," said a disembodied voice from somewhere on his right.

The convict tried to open his eyes, but the lights were too bright to allow him to see, so he settled for trying to raise himself from the bed, only to discover that he couldn't move a muscle.

"Please, Marco...don't try to get up. You are firmly secured to the table and there is no point in upsetting yourself further," said the disembodied voice.

The con forced his eyes open, regardless of the pain, and he squinted as best he could around the room.

A man wearing a white medic's coat stood over him. He seemed to be in a white tiled hospital examination room. The man who had spoken was standing by the convict's head, holding a hypodermic syringe in one hand.

"What the hell is going on here? Where am I and who the hell are you guys?"

The man with the syringe took a step closer and roughly grasped the convict's face with his latex gloved hand.

The captor studied his prisoner's face intently for several moments, before stepping back from the examination table.

"Connors!" he snapped at the other man in the room. "Who exactly *is* this person, and where did you find him?" Connors, who had been busy looking at his cell phone, strolled across and looked at the captive on the table.

"Why, it's Marco, Doctor. I told you, he walked straight out in front of the truck and..." The senior man held up his gloved hand and silenced Connors, mid-sentence.

"Can you explain just how come Marco, a mute from birth, has managed to find his voice after forty-odd years?" asked the doctor.

"But...but...bu..." spluttered Connors, when, as if to highlight his error, the man on the table spoke again.

"Look...who the fuck is this Marco character? Whoever you people are, there's been some terrible mistake. My name's Carter, Joe Carter..." his voice trailed off as the two men, suddenly joined by a third, stood above him, each staring at him in a very unnerving fashion.

"Holy shit!" exclaimed the third man, shaking his head. "Holy shit!"

"Holy shit , indeed," added the doctor, who was also shaking his head in astonishment.

"Will you guys let me offa this fucking table!" erupted the man, Carter, as he struggled uselessly against the thick webbing pinning him down.

"Let me the fuck*off*!"

The two assistants looked to the doctor for guidance.

"Here, give him a shot. Shut him up while I think," he ordered, simply.

Carter struggled as much as the webbing would allow as the needle was jabbed unceremoniously into his arm. Within seconds, his tongue felt too big for his mouth and his head filled with cotton wool, as he sank down...down...down...out...

*

"So," reiterated the doctor to his two shamefaced assistants. "Let me get this right. You let Marco escape two days before he's due to keep his 'special appointment', and then you bring *this* man back here, wearing the very clothes which Marco stole from the guard he'd just murdered, and *neither* of you noticed that it wasn't Marco? Is *that* about the size of things?" he asked, sneeringly.

Connors and his colleague looked briefly at each other and then turned their gaze to the floor. There wasn't much they could say to justify the almighty fuck-up, a fuck-up compounded by them bringing back a Marco look-alike. However, Connors wasn't the kind of guy to take a beating lying on his back.

"He had us *all* fooled, *you included*, Doctor!" he retaliated, sounding much braver than he actually felt. Then a thought crossed his mind.

"If he fooled *us*, then why not use him? Who's to know the difference?"

The doctor, who'd been rising from his seat behind his desk, sat back down again, abruptly. He stared at Connors for some time before replying.

"There's one small problem that may have escaped your attention, Connors."

The smug smile that had started in the corners of Connors' tight little mouth suddenly stopped.

"Marco was a mute, or did you forget that? How do we explain when our boy out there starts gabbing?" Another frown crossed Connors' face. Yes, he *had* forgotten that small detail.

"We *make* him a mute!" the third man chipped in without a moment's hesitation. His turn to grin now.

Both the doctor and Connors looked at him with the same puzzled expression on their faces.

"We *what*?" asked Connors, annoyed that his thunder had been stolen by his junior.

"I said we make him a mute," repeated the third man. "The Doctor here is a doctor, after all? Should be simple enough?" he concluded, looking to the Doctor for support.

The senior man tented his hands in front of him and pursed his lips in thought. The room fell silent and Connors looked daggers at his colleague.

Finally, the Doctor slammed both hands on his desk top and stood up.

"Right. That's what we'll do then! You've managed to lose the real Marco, who, judging by the clothes our new boy's wearing, is presumably feeding the coyotes out there somewhere. We need to have Marco, or as it turns out, Marco's double ready for the 'special appointment' tomorrow. We have very little choice in the matter if we all intend to remain employed, or, worst case scenario, end up as inmates in the very establishment which employs us!"

The Doctor looked from Connors to the third man and back again, while the two men looked nervously from the Doctor to the floor at the mention of ending up as inmates in their own special unit.

"The United States Government pays us a mighty big fee to keep this private facility running. Which one of you would like to inform them that you've fucked-up? And in an *election* year!"

The two men studied their shoes with meticulous care.

"Okay, Connors, go and prepare the room for surgery. And *you*, just make sure that we're not disturbed!" he said to the third man.

*

Joe Carter awoke to a world of pain once again.

At first, he wondered where the hell he was. That turned into the vain hope that he had experienced a very bad dream, but the terrible pain in his throat assured him that this was no dream. That, and the fact that he was strapped down onto a hospital gurney.

He tried to call out, but only a strange, strangled mewing noise escaped him. He ran his swollen tongue around the inside of his mouth. It felt normal enough, so why couldn't he speak?

Carter tried again. "Heeeeeeewmmmmmph!" was all he could manage.

"We really must stop meeting like this...Mr...er...well, Marco will do for now? You always seem to be coming out of a deep sleep when I meet you?" joked the Doctor, who was standing somewhere to Carter's right, out of his line of sight.

"And just in the nick of time, too. Your big moment has arrived. It's time for your 'special appointment'!"

A large wooden door slid open directly in front of Carter and the gurney started to trundle towards it. He struggled like a madman and mewed like a ram being castrated, but no one expected anything less, given the circumstances.

Carter watched helplessly as he was removed from the gurney and strapped into a wooden chair by two men in uniform. Uniforms he recognised all too well. *Prison guard uniforms.*

Moments later, he was securely held in place by thick leather straps, manacles clamping his arms to the wooden arms of the chair.

Drool oozed from his frantically working mouth as one of the guards attached something to the metal skull cap clamped to his head.

The guard, Connors, stepped forward and spoke from a card held in his hand.

"Raphael Marco de Silva, you have been found guilty by a court of law, of the murder, rape and torture of fourteen women and young girls, in this and other counties, and you have been sentenced to die by electricity being passed through your body. Do you have anything to say before sentence is passed upon you?"

Carter's eyes bulged from their sockets and his wrists bled as he tried to work his hands free from the manacles binding him to the electric chair.

All the witnesses present knew the man couldn't speak. Everyone knew of Marco the Silent Slayer, and everyone present was there to happily see him fry in the chair before he hopefully spent the rest of eternity frying in hell.

Connors stepped back from the chair and nodded towards a window to his left.

"HEEEEELLLLLLPPPPPPPHHHHH!" was the last sound Joe Carter ever made before his eyeballs melted and ran down his cheeks, and his hair started to smoulder as the massive electric shock ripped through his body, to a unanimous cheer from the assembled witnesses and relatives in the audience.

*

Several miles to the east, in a deep forest area well off the beaten track, a bloodstained man wearing orange coveralls, was bathing his battered and bruised face in a stream, and relishing the sweet taste of freedom. A freedom he had never hoped to feel again.

REST IN PIECES

The idea came to him as he was applying the final touches of rouge to the cheeks of the corpse lying on the table before him.

The woman would have been in her early twenties and Harry Jones was doing his best to make her look presentable, prior to her relatives viewing their late departed, before her one-way journey to the cemetery the next morning.

The notion was so stunningly simple that Harry wondered why he had never thought of it before. He was in the ideal situation. It was absolutely brilliant!

"Is she ready yet, Harry? The parents are waiting outside."

The assistant undertaker almost jumped with surprise. He'd been so engrossed with his own thoughts that he hadn't heard old Jackson open the door and creep in behind him.

"Sorry, Mr. Jackson. Yes, just finished with her." Harry replaced the lid on the tub of makeup and quickly gathered up the other cosmetics scattered about the stainless-steel trolley, shoving them all into a small box.

"Pull yerself together, man! We've got a busy day ahead of us!" added Jackson, before sweeping majestically out and into the mortuary viewing room to the waiting mourners, a well-practised, empathetic smile springing to his thin lips.

Harry adjusted the black crepe sheet and carefully fluffed the dead girl's long blonde hair, so that she appeared to be more asleep than deceased. He then left the room via another door so that the girl would be the only occupant when her parents came in for their final farewell.

His earlier thoughts drifted to the back of his mind as the day's business demanded more of his attention. They had three funerals that day, so there was little time for his private day dreams.

However, as he walked into his house and hung his coat on the rack behind the door, his earlier idea came leaping very much to the fore once more.

"You're late! *Again!* That's the second time this week and it's only Tuesday!" screamed his wife, Valerie, from her armchair in the sitting room.

"Your dinner's ruined and it's in the bin!" she continued, going on and on until he could take no more and he stormed out of the house into the back garden for the first of his three allotted cigarettes of the day.

His hands began that familiar unpleasant twitching, and he knew that if he remained within tongue-lashing distance of Valerie his hands would do far more than just twitch!

His wife refused to try and understand him. She simply could not acknowledge that a man in *his* line of business, dealing with death and misery each day, *needed* the occasional drink or two on their way home from work each day. It helped him unwind, that was all.

"And how many distraught relatives have *you* had to console today? How many of their battered loved ones have *you* had to try and make halfway decent looking before they were viewed?" he had asked her one evening, as he'd prodded with little enthusiasm at the now cold grilled trout, staring back at him from an equally cold plate.

Valerie was incapable of displaying the slightest iota of empathy towards him.

"It's *your* job! *You* chose it, so you can bloody well get on with it!" she spat, before snatching the grim looking trout and depositing it into the bin.

There was no point in arguing with her. He hadn't 'chosen' the job. God forbid, it was the very last thing he'd have wanted to do to earn a living. But, after two years on the dole following being made redundant as chief clerk at an engineering firm; two years of Job Club and all the form filling and general humiliation of being unemployed, he had gladly taken the first *real* job offered to him.

Times were bloody hard, and needs must and all that crap. It would at least help pay off the mortgage.

But of course, Valerie couldn't care less about any of that. He'd spoilt her when he was earning decent money. She only seemed to be concerned over whether she would have enough chocolates and other luxuries to maintain her enormous bulk in the manner to which it had become accustomed.

It had begun to drizzle, so Harry moved into his favourite refuge; his beloved greenhouse. A haven of sanity in the sea of life's daily tempest that was his wife.

Of course, matters had become a lot worse since Valerie had found out about his little indiscretion with Maggie Robinson, who lived just along the lane from their small bungalow. Valerie certainly wasn't the forgiving type and, as the weeks had passed, her animosity and loathing towards him had grown and grown, to the extent that now life was nothing more than a one-sided slanging match every time they were in one another's company.

He picked up his spray bottle and idly began to squirt at his tomato plants, imagining the tiny black flies covering the leaves to be miniature Valeries. If only he could get rid of *her* so easily!

His earlier thoughts came flooding back into his mind as he dispatched the tiny insects. The notion grew as more ideas came together, slotting neatly into place until he had the bare bones of a plan in his head.

It would take a lot of planning. Every conceivable eventuality would have to be thought through. But it was possible...*very* possible.

"Harry Jones, boy from the valleys, you're a bloody *genius!*" he whispered, as he stretched up to close the greenhouse louvres against the chilled night air.

*

He was at work very early the next morning. He was usually the first to arrive, but this morning he needed extra time to go through the Day Planner and check on that week's list of burials and cremations. It looked like a pretty full schedule luckily, so everything should run smoothly so long as there were no unexpected delays.

Twenty minutes later, he had it fully sorted in his own mind. It was all in the planning, and Harry liked nothing more than planning stuff.

It would happen on Thursday, he decided, with phase two taking place on the Friday.

"Tidy!" he said aloud, to an empty chapel of rest.

As an extra bonus, old Jackson announced that he would be leaving early on Friday for one of his Masonic meetings, and Harry took that as a sign from the Gods that all was well and they were on his side.

At six o'clock, he strolled across to his battered old Toyota, and, after checking that all his purchases of the day were still in the passenger footwell, he drove home for his nightly confrontation with Valerie.

*

Things had gone far better than he could ever have hoped for.

Valerie had started her usual tirade the moment he'd opened the front door.

Harry let her have her say for about five minutes, watching as she grew redder and redder, all the while a strange little smile playing across his lips.

Then, just as she bent over the waste bin to carry out the nightly ritual of scraping his food into its depths, Harry did what he had been longing to do for years.

The heavy, cast iron milk pan landed on the back of her skull with a sickening squelchy thud, sending a crimson spray of blood squirting onto the tiled work surface and across the cushion flooring below.

Oddly, she didn't collapse like a sack of turnips as he'd imagined, instead she stood there, staring dumbly at her husband, her fleshy mouth working but no sound coming from it.

Then, she just crumpled slowly onto the floor, knocking over her much-beloved waste bin before lying like a beached whale next to the washing machine.

Harry left her where she lay and went out to the car to collect his shopping. There were only two bags, and as he came back into the house and closed the front door, he could hear a faint moaning sound coming from the kitchen.

Valerie was trying to sit up, staring stupidly at the thick blood covering her hands through, misty, pain-filled eyes and, as was her wont, she was moaning, but this time with good cause.

Harry tut-tutted loudly and promptly gave her another whack with the cast iron milk pan, and then another for good measure. *Now* she was dead!

He strolled into the lounge and drew the curtains. It would still be light for a while yet, and he didn't want any prying eyes at this stage of the game. He moved the coffee table and pushed the sofa to the far end of the room, giving himself space to spread out the newly purchased rubber groundsheet across the patterned Axminster carpet.

Perfect! Just the job, he decided.

He then unrolled the shiny new, and very expensive set of butcher's knives and marvelled as they twinkled like a line of deadly stainless steel soldiers on the groundsheet.

The actual manhandling of Valerie's gross body into their bathroom, is something possibly best left to the imagination, but Harry was eternally grateful that she had nagged him into buying a bungalow rather than a house. Humping her carcass upstairs would have been almost impossible!

They had one of those old-fashioned clothes drying racks suspended from the ceiling above the bath and Harry had the foresight to strengthen it the night before. But, even with new four inch screws in place, the pulley and the joist it was attached to both groaned their protest as he began to haul his wife's dead body by her ankles until she was suspended a foot or so above the plughole of the enamelled bath.

He was now shattered by his efforts and had to sit on the laundry basket for several minutes to regain his composure. He watched in fascination as Valerie's corpse swung gently to and fro, the blood from her wounds making almost perfect circles on the white enamel. Very artistic, he thought.

Revitalised, he raised the boning knife to her throat and with one swift slice, he severed her neck down to the spine. The gaping wound now poured rather than dripped her bodily fluids into the bath and Harry was forced to run the taps to help thin the sticky gore into a more manageable consistency.

He left her hanging like that for the next two hours while he mopped up the mess in the kitchen and made himself a nice supper of sausages with beans on toast. He even smoked *four* cigarettes, throwing all caution to the wind.

He was no expert, but Harry thought that she carved beautifully. Just like finest fillet steak, her fatty meat coming clean from the bone with the help of his new knives.

He wasn't too sure about what effect the meat cleaver was having on the Axminster beneath the groundsheet, but he wielded it with great deliberation and no small amount of skill, he thought.

In a little more than two hours, Valerie had been chopped up and carved into more manageable segments. She was parcelled up into either black bin liners or covered with Clingfilm, sometimes both, and she was spread neatly across the large rubber sheet.

It had been surprisingly messy, even though he had taken all that trouble to drain her of blood first. But then, he thought, converting twenty-odd stones of human being into handy joint-sized pieces was always going to be a tad mucky. After all, his *usual* customers had blood which had clotted and hardened inside lifeless arteries.

He found the worst part by far was finding something to contain the organs and general viscera. Something which wouldn't leak yet would be easy to carry and dispose of. What better than Valerie's much loved kitchen waste bin. And how ironic, too?

The whole process, from the initial bash on the head to the final mopping up operation had taken him almost four and a half hours. All he had to do now, was wait until it was late enough for passers-by not to be passing by, and he could then load his car with his 'passenger'.

He had always been grateful that they lived in such a quiet little lane overlooking the River Thames, but never so much as he was right now. There would be no nosy neighbours or twitching net curtains to worry about.

There had been one heart-stopping moment when a dog walker had called out, "Fine evening for a stroll?" and his bloody Spaniel had come sniffing around the boot of the car, but a swift kick up the backside had soon sent the thing yelping into the night, to be comforted by its stupid owner.

*

Harry drove the last three hundred yards to work with the car lights off, and he glided silently into the staff carpark. He let himself in via the side door, and, as quietly as possible, he slid open the large double doors which led to what they called 'the unloading bay'; the place where private ambulances arrived with the dead.

He backed his car in and then slid the doors closed once more. So far, so good. Now the *main* business of the night.

Harry had selected his 'victims' with great care. He had taken into account their size and weight, and he had also allowed for anyone who might wish to see their dear departed one last time. To that end, he selected anyone considered too disfigured to be in an open casket. Those, together with a few elderly men and women who, he had gleaned from Jackson's meticulous records, had no living relatives likely to pop in unexpectedly.

The only anomaly was a man in his early forties who died of a massive stroke the week before. However, Harry had dealt with the man's widow and he knew from experience that she was one woman who wouldn't be grieving for very long! She was far too attractive for that…and there was something in her eyes…?

It took him almost as long to locate and unscrew all the coffin lids, place Valerie's bits and pieces in with the occupants, and then re-fit the lids, but he was mightily relieved when at last it was all over. Pity he'd run out of bin liners by the time he'd remembered her head, but some Clingfilm and a strong elastic band around the stump of her neck would prevent any unfortunate secretions.

Though seeing her battered, horror stricken face glaring at him as he placed her in the final coffin had really shaken him.

Thank God, it was all over!

*

All the funerals went without a hitch. He had been given twenty quid by the 'grieving widow' who had tried her utmost to weep behind her thick veil, but the younger man in his mid-twenties who had slipped his arm around her waist on the way back to the car, and then pinched her bum as she climbed into the front seat, gave the game away. They drove out from the cemetery smiling happily.

The set of shiny new knives was now at the bottom of the Thames, several miles from Harry's bungalow, together with a bloodstained milk pan. The groundsheet was buried under tons of landfill and a suitcase full of Valerie's clothes, her passport and personal effects had been tossed into a huge bonfire on a building site.

He left it for almost a week before paying a visit to his local police station to report his wife as a missing person. Harry explained about the note she had left him, saying that she intended visiting some long-lost aunt's house. He also mentioned that some of her clothes were missing along with personal items and a suitcase. He added that he was out of his mind with worrying about her.

The officer at the desk was very sympathetic and understanding, but he held out little hope that a forty-six-year-old woman, who clearly didn't want to be traced, would turn up again unless she wanted to. He would go through the motions, of course, but said that there was every likelihood of her returning under her own steam, with her tail between her legs and a bag full of apologies for being so daft.

*

A few days later, Harry bumped into Maggie Robinson and told her that

Valerie had finally left him after another blazing row, vowing never to return again.

Maggie soon became a regular nocturnal visitor to his bed, every time that her long-distance lorry driver husband was away on a foreign trip.

Everything in Harry's garden was now looking rosy. Even the *black fly* had finally been sprayed into submission!

*

"Ah, Harry, glad you're in early! We have important visitors today," crowed Jackson. Harry had wondered who owned the strange cars cluttering up the carpark. And so *early*, too?

"What's happening, Mr. Jackson? Has someone important died?" asked a bemused Harry as he took off his jacket and slipped on his working apron.

Jackson smiled like a cat who'd had the cream.

"It's better than that, Harry!" he beamed. "We've been chosen by the Coroner's Office because of our facilities here. They're absolutely full up at the County Mortuary, what with this summer flu epidemic, so we've been selected by the Coroner to help carry out a very special post mortem!" Jackson couldn't have been happier if he'd been voted into the final two of X Factor, as Harry still fumbled to tie his apron.

"What's so urgent about this autopsy then?" he asked, rolling up his shirt sleeves and following Jackson as he headed through the plastic swing doors that led into the mortuary.

Jackson's smile was wider than ever.

"It's an *exhumation*, the first you've witnessed, I believe, Harry."

The pathologist and his assistant were just removing the lid from the coffin as the two undertakers entered the room.

"Jesus Christ!" screamed the assistant, falling back from the open casket with a look of undiluted horror on her face.

Harry spotted it immediately, while old Jackson, unperturbed, prattled away beside him.

"Yes, it's a suspected *poisoning*, Harry. A man in his forties who was possibly murdered by his wife, and *we* actually planted him! What a coincidence, eh?"

Harry wasn't listening.

He was staring at the extra head in the open coffin,

His eyes bulged alarmingly, and his face went a deep purple hue as a strangled sob escaped from his constricted throat and he reeled away from the coffin.

It was far more than the horrible shock of seeing Valerie's decomposing face.

It was the fact that she was...God help him...she was actually *smiling*! A broad, cheery smile which stretched her green, mouldering lips...a

75

smug "I told you so!" sort of a smile that he had hated so much when she'd been alive, and which was now even more hideous in death.

An intense pain shot down his left arm, as Harry's heart finally gave out from the shock and horror and he slumped to the cold mortuary floor. His last thought was of the look in that widow's eyes as she had walked away on the arm of her young lover.

He recognised it as the same look *he* had worn after killing *his* unwanted partner.

ASHES TO ASHES

Water had been running almost non-stop for over forty minutes, as the woman hammered on the bathroom door. Thump, thump, thump!

"How much bloody longer are you gonna be in there? I have to get to work *too*, you know!"

Moments later, Steve Clarke slid back the bolt on the bathroom door and emerged from the steam-filled room, clad in his dressing gown, his head swathed in a large white towel, before Ann Clarke brushed roughly past him, muttering, "'bout bleedin' time too!" and slammed the door noisily behind her.

When she returned to their bedroom, some fifteen minutes later, Steve was seated on their double bed, still wearing his gown, with the towel draped over his head like a prize fighter.

"You're gonna be late!" snapped Ann, doing up her bra before stepping into her underwear. In fact, she was completely dressed and starting her morning makeup ritual before she realised that her husband hadn't replied or stirred from his position on the edge of the bed.

"You alright?" she finally relented.

Steve Clarke replied by way of removing the white towel covering his head, and as he did so, a shower of white flaky material fluttered from the towel and wafted gently, before settling on the duvet.

Ann let out a low whistle. "Bloody hell, Steve. That's some dandruff you have there!" and she took a couple of steps closer to examine him further.

His still damp hair contained a mass of large white flakes, and there was what could best be described as a tide mark of red, angry-looking skin, which appeared to cover his entire scalp, ending in an almost straight line, just above his eyebrows.

"I just woke up like this, Annie. The more I wash it, the worse it gets!" he said at last. There was a look of panic in his eyes as his wife studied her husband's flaking, raw-looking scalp.

"Blimey! I dunno what it could be, Steve. Some kind of psoriasis, maybe?" she offered, and then shrugged.

"Psoriasis?" he almost whined. "Is that *serious*?" he added, eyes wide as he pulled the towel over his head once more.

Ann touched his shoulders before noticing that it had a fine layer of dead skin cells dusting them, and quickly removed her hand without thinking.

"Well, it's probably slightly more serious than Man Flu, longer lasting at least."

Steve let out a startled whimper, like a small child, and Ann continued, "But, I'm sure they have creams and stuff these days that'll soon clear it up. Take the morning off and go and see the doctor. That'd be my advice."

*

Two hours later, Steve was sitting in the doctor's waiting room, his head covered by his old beanie hat pulled tightly over his crusty scalp, a pair of large aviator sunglasses hiding his eyes and the collar of his jacket flapped up around his neck. He couldn't help but notice that the other patients were casting him sideways looks.

Although the waiting room was busy, the seats to either side of him were vacant, meaning that people would rather stand than sit beside him.

After what seemed like hours, his name was finally called, and as he stood up in a shower of flaky skin, there was almost an audible sigh of relief throughout the waiting room as he left.

"Sit down, Mr...er...Clarke. Now, what seems to be the problem?" asked the doctor, pen poised ready at his notepad.

Steve sat down nervously and removed his hat and sunglasses to yet another small blizzard of dead skin particles.

The doctor looked up from his notepad for the first time and his patient could see the look of undisguised horror on the medical man's face.

"Oh!" he said, simply, making no attempt to move from his position behind the desk. "And how long have you been like this, may I ask?"

Where the tidemark of red had stopped at his eyebrows only two hours earlier, it now continued down his face to just below his top lip, and what had been sore and angry skin before, had now become white, flaky and almost *scaly* in appearance.

"Well, Doctor, I woke up this morning with an itchy head, and now...it's like *this.*" And, as if to emphasise the problem, another storm of white skin cells drifted from his head as he spoke.

"I see," replied the doctor, though it was patently clear from the expression on his face that he really had no idea what he was dealing with.

His hand moved, spider-like, across to his computer and he continued speaking as he typed, without looking up at his patient again.

"We'll try you on this. Actually, it's a mixture of several things used for the treatment of Psoriasis, Eczema and other skin conditions, and we'll see how you go on that for now? If things don't improve within a week, I'll have to get you looked at by a skin specialist at the allergy clinic. Okay...Mr...er, Clarke?" and with that, he printed out the prescription and handed it to his patient, before busying himself with apparently very urgent paperwork.

Steve Clarke pulled his hat down over his scaly scalp, popped on his sunglasses and silently left the surgery. But not before hearing on his way out, "Nurse? Could you pop in here with the Hoover, please?" over the intercom.

*

By the time he'd had his prescription filled, at no small expense, and had returned home, the 'rash' or whatever it was had crept down to the base of his neck and was starting to reach downwards towards his chest.

When Ann got in from work, she found her husband lying in their bed, covered in some sort of greasy, oily substance, his hair plastered to his now totally white, scaly scalp with large clumps of hair lying on the pillow, where it had fallen out.

Incredibly, even though he was heavily coated in the unctuous ointment, his skin was still managing to shed flakes, and the floor on his side of the bed was several millimetres deep in dead cells, the duvet and pillows were a complete mess.

"Oh my God, Steve! What the hell did the doctor say?" She was attempting to exude calm, but the nightmare vision of her husband lying in bed, shedding hair and skin, did little to help her bedside manner.

Steve had been dozing, and awoke with a start.

"Oh...hi, darling...you okay?" he slurred, drowsily.

Ann wanted to sit on the bed beside him, she wanted to stroke his face and comfort him, but she couldn't bring herself to do either.

"Never mind about *my* day...what did the *doctor* say? You look *awful!*" she blurted, instantly regretting her words.

Steve tried to sit upright, but gave up after struggling for a few seconds.

"He didn't really seem to know, but thought it was probably something like Psoriasis, as you said. He prescribed me all these ointments and creams." He waved a scaly hand towards the plethora of bottles and tubes of medication littering his bedside table, adding, "It seems to have got a bit worse since then, so I phoned the surgery about an hour ago to make another appointment, but apparently the doctor's gone off sick now, and no one can see me until next week."

Ann looked appalled, and she stormed across to the phone on her side of the bed.

"I'm calling for an ambulance! This is bloody *ridiculous!*"

Steve made another huge effort to raise himself from the bed.

"*No!* I don't want an ambulance!" he wailed. "Just give this cream some time to start working, and I'll be fine," he added, pleadingly.

Against her better judgement, his wife stopped with her hand hovering above the receiver.

"If you're not showing any signs of improvement by the morning, it's the hospital for you...and no *arguing!*"

Steve tried to smile, but his lips were too cracked and scaly.

"Fair enough, Annie. Let's just see what happens, okay?"

*

As much as she would have liked to have snuggled up to her husband that night, Ann simply couldn't bring herself to share a bed with him, let alone *touch* him, and she therefore slept in the spare room.

She had looked in on him before going to bed herself, but he'd been fast asleep and she decided it was best to let him rest.

He was *still* flat out when she bustled in with a mug of coffee the next morning and asked softly, "Morning, darling, how are you feeling today?"

No reply.

Ann crossed the room and opened the heavy curtains, the bedroom flooding with morning sunlight, but still Steve hadn't stirred in the bed.

She could just see the top of his head poking out as she drew back the duvet, to be greeted by a completely fleshless, grinning skull which lay amongst several inches of dry, dead skin cells.

Without thinking, she continued to pull back the bed covers, and, as the scream formed in her throat, she realised that her husband's entire body was now nothing more than skeletal bones lying amongst a hideous dust, composed of dried skin and human organs.

As the terrified scream finally broke from her throat, she realised with dawning horror, that her *own* head had now started itching badly…

BLIND DATE

Norman Scrote wiped the palms of his sweaty hands down his corduroy trousers as he paced, impatiently, back and forth outside the Roxy Cinema, that fateful summer evening.

It was his first ever blind date and he was as nervous as hell. He had arrived a full forty minutes early, and had regretted having all that extra time to fret over whether his date would indeed turn out to be the girl of his dreams.

In fact, it was some time before he realised that the gangly, greasy haired, spotty faced creature who was standing beside a lamp post, pulling *the* most horrendous faces, was in fact his date. At which stage, he actually began to wish that he *was* blind!

There was no doubt that Norman would have legged it there and then, had it not been for the fact that Barry King, the instigator of the rendezvous, had assured Norman that the girl's family was absolutely *loaded*. She was one of the Thrashlightlys, the fish and chip shop millionaires (surely you've heard of *them*?) and Norman, being the sponging, money grabbing, gold digging little rat that he was, was quite prepared to date Quasimodo's *granny* if he thought it could lead him to getting his greedy little hands on a load of loot.

So, with this aim in mind, he steeled himself and stepped forward to greet the apparition before him. Grim and greasy-looking though she was, he was determined to sweep the young Miss Thrashlightly off her feet, and claim his prize.

"Hello, are you Hilda?" he asked, a nanosecond before stepping on a neat spire of dog shit, which caused him to skid forwards, and collapse in a heap at the girl's feet.

Hilda held out her hand, mechanically, and seemed not to have noticed that anything unusual had just occurred, as a very red-faced Norman scrambled to his feet, muttering something very unpleasant about dogs and their owners.

He pulled himself together as best he could, recalling the reason for being there in the first place, a vision of sack-loads of cash floating through his mind.

His 'date' simply stood there looking very blank-faced, with her hand outstretched and not so much as a trace of a smile on her thin lips to indicate that perhaps Norman hadn't made the most dashing of entrances.

Norman dusted himself down and peered closely at the strange girl. She continued to make the most peculiar, uncontrolled facial expressions that he'd ever witnessed, outside of a gurning contest. It was a blend of a leer, a snarl and a demented, manic grin and her mouth displayed two rows of uneven, green tinged teeth, with what seemed like every other tooth missing.

This, coupled with a disgusting cooing, bubbling sound that wheezed from somewhere in the back of her throat, gave Norman his only clue that Hilda Thrashlightly was attempting to *smile* at him. He fought back the urge to shudder, gritted his teeth and placed her right hand in his, before kissing it tenderly.

She had a faint *earthy* smell about her, and her hand felt odd, almost *slimy. Probably been helping her old man peel a few spuds?* thought Norman, resisting the urge to snigger aloud.

No sooner had his lips left her unsavoury-smelling hand, than she began making the most obnoxious *mewling* noise. She snatched her hand away and pressed it hard against her spotty, greasy cheek, stroking it as if it were a new pet kitten, while continuing to make a sound which was very reminiscent of two pigs copulating.

In fact, so loud was the racket she was creating, several passers-by gave her and Norman the oddest of looks. Norman merely shrugged his narrow shoulders and grinned, sheepishly.

He could see where they were coming from, though. They *did* look an odd couple, with the young, handsome, well-dressed man (Norman's thoughts, not mine) standing beside an escapee from a Hammer Horror film set, who was making an unseemly fuss over its own hand, while uttering the most stomach churning noises this side of an army latrine!

Yes, as Norman watched the small crowd assemble about them, he had to admit that they had good cause to be there. He was pretty thick-skinned, but now even *he* was embarrassed by the whole thing, and with his limited imagination, he could think of only two things to do.

The first, and *infinitely* preferable to Norman's mind, was to run away as though the Hounds of Hell were snapping at his heels, and to seek refuge in the nearest pub.

The *second* notion, was to stand his ground and take a deep bow to the assembled audience, and that, for reasons unknown to him, was what he did.

The crowd erupted into spontaneous applause, with some even throwing money at the odd-looking duo.

"Best street performers I've seen in a long time!" said one person.

"Must be an advert for a new movie?" queried another.

"Brilliant make-up on the girl. She was absolutely *horrendous!*" marvelled a third.

Then, as if from nowhere, appeared a light summer's breeze, wafting the smell of dog shit, which was liberally attached to Norman's trousers and shoe, and the crowd dispersed as quickly as it had formed.

Norman couldn't help but notice that there was *another* pretty unpleasant smell floating across from the persona of Hilda, as well. But he reasoned that anyone who came from a long line of fishmongers was *bound* to pong a bit.

Moments later, they were alone once more and Norman was pleased to see that she had stopped all that billing and cooing over her own hand nonsense. Then she made her first recognisably human gesture.

Hilda pointed at her incredibly flat chest and moved her mouth, emitting a sort of high-pitched, bubbly-wheezing noise which was something like 'Meeeee eeeengar' and then 'Eeeeeeengarr'.

It sounded as though she had the worst cold Norman had ever come across, either that or her vocal chords were bunged up with super glue, but as she finished making the weird noises, she stood there, obviously waiting for some kind of a response from Norman, while that dreadful parody of a smile played across her corpse-white face.

Norman, who had never been the sharpest knife in the drawer, scratched his head and looked at her for a while. Then the penny finally dropped and he realised that the grease-thing was introducing herself.

"Aaahh...right...gotcha!" he replied.

"*Your* name is HILDA!" he added, in a tone usually reserved for the mentally unwell or the hard of hearing. As he spoke, he couldn't bring himself to look her directly in the eye, not even for all the chips in her father's empire could he do that!

Hilda appeared either excited or upset, Norman simply couldn't tell which from the frightening expressions rippling across her face, but she 'spoke' once more,

"Neeeeeee! NeeeeeeeEEEEEE!" she squealed like a pregnant banshee with terminally painful haemorrhoids.

"Yes, Hilda...it's a *very* pretty name. For a *very* pretty girl!" replied Norman, ever the smooth talker as his date grimaced, shaking her head from side to side and making that strange mewling noise once more.

Norman considered whether it was actually a wise move to take her into the cinema. But at least, he figured, no one would be able to *see* her in there. A courting couple smooched by and they reminded Norman where his heart was; in his wallet. He decided to press on.

"My name is Norman...NORMAN," he repeated very slowly, looking for any sign that she had understood him.

Hilda was still mewling and thrashing her head wildly from side to side, her short, dark hair dripping with grease.

"NeeeeeEEEeeeeeoooooo!" she wailed, and, for the very first time, Norman accidentally gazed into her eyes.

It was like looking into a vacant plot in a lonely, windswept cemetery, on a moonless night in the dead of winter.

He shuddered involuntarily and quickly tore his eyes away from hers.

"Nooormaaaan," she managed to wheeze. "Yoooo Nooormaaaan... meee eeeengaaaarrrr!" she uttered in an almost intelligible voice.

The problem, thought Norman, was that now she'd *started*, the bloody loony wouldn't *shut up*!

And sure enough, Hilda repeated, "Nooormaaan...EEEeengaaar...Nooormmaaan...Eeeeeeengaaaaar," over and over, like a crazed minor bird on speed until Norman could stand it no longer.

"SHUT UP! SHUT UP! SHUT UP!" he screamed, and she did so immediately, almost as though he had slapped her for being hysterical. Her head dropped to her chest and she stood there, staring at her feet, which Norman noticed for the first time, were filthy dirty and clad in a pair of sandals so old that they may well have been left behind by one of the first Romans to set foot on this island!

If it were at all possible for the girl's normally uncontrolled facial muscles to, just for once, work in unison, Norman would have been able to detect that Hilda, was in fact sulking. As it was, Norman got the message when Hilda began to whimper like a starving puppy, only in *her* case, without a puppy's endearing ways.

"Now, now..." he tried to soothe the sulking girl, but carefully avoiding touching her until he relented, patting her on the arm and instantly regretting the action.

She clasped his hand in an amazingly strong grip, pressing it firmly to her face.

"Oy!" spluttered a shocked Norman. "Steady on, girl!" But Hilda was apparently in raptures and she bubbled, "AAaaaaaaaaarrrr...uuummmmmmm," while re-creating that realistic mating pigs sound.

Norman just managed to snatch his hand away as she began to lick and suck his fingers.

"GERROFF!" he screamed, in a rather high-pitched, shaky voice. He had never been a man who indulged in what he considered 'kinky stuff', and money or no money, even *he* had some scruples!

Hilda fell immediately into sulk-mode once more, and forcing himself to concentrate on the vast Thrashlightly fortune, Norman decided that he'd make one last effort at winning her over. *This* time without laying a hand anywhere *near* her.

"Come on, Hilda. Let's go and see the movie, shall we?"

The film playing that night was entitled *The Revenge of the Bone Crunchers*, an apparently scary little movie, which, had he been with anyone *other* than Hilda, would have guaranteed plenty of snogging in the back row of the cinema.

However, the very *thought* of doing anything like that with *her*, sent a shiver running down the length of Norman's puny spine.

While he went and bought the tickets, Hilda was engrossed in studying the still photos in the foyer, which showed graphic scenes from the film. As soon as Norman approached, she babbled, "Maaaaaaaaaaaaa," in that odd, wheezy voice, pointing at one of the stills in particular.

"Looooo!" she continued, dragging Norman closer by the sleeve of his faux leather jacket. He studied the still briefly. "Yes…man…*nasty* man," he said, managing to yank his sleeve free of her slimy grasp.

The main feature had already started, much to his relief, and he was more than grateful that they would soon be in the darkened cinema, before anyone he might know could spot them.

Hilda finally managed to drag herself away from the photos in the foyer and sauntered along behind Norman as he headed upstairs to the circle. She looked about her as though this was the first time she had been in a cinema, her strange, dead-looking eyes lapping up the atmosphere as she walked up the red carpeted stairway.

The cinema was not even half full and an enthralled Hilda dragged Norman towards a row of empty back seats, where she sat, spellbound. She was instantly attracted to the action on the screen, where some of the 'bone crunchers' were devouring their prey wholesale, and Hilda sat drooling and making revolting sucking sounds of her own as she looked on, clearly awestruck by the whole experience.

As she began mewling once more, Norman considered that rich people seemed to have no idea of teaching their offspring how to behave in a public place. *Surely* she must know that it's impolite to dribble like that? The seat in front of Hilda, mercifully, the whole row in front was empty, was now dripping with Hilda's saliva as she sat with her scrawny arms propped on its back, oozing drool like a starving man being taunted by a steak dinner.

No wonder her old man's never taken her to the movies before, if this is how she carries on! mused Norman.

The dreadful mangling on screen stopped for a while, due to an apparent shortage of 'good guys' to maim, and Hilda sat back in her seat, a more vacant expression than usual on her face.

"Would you like anything…some popcorn…a choc ice…anything?" he asked his date.

"Noooorrrmaaaan," she croaked, loud enough for a man four rows away to glare at them and say, "Shhhhhhhhhhhuuush!" before tutting loudly.

Norman held up his hand in apology. *This is a bloody nightmare!* he thought. *Just you wait till I get my hands on you, Barry-bloody-King! I'll swing for you, lumbering me with this…money or no bleedin' money!*

The slaying had started once more on the big screen and Hilda was transfixed and drooling again. Norman stood up and determined to get himself a lolly to suck on, when he recalled the unfortunate episode of Hilda sucking and licking his fingers, and he suddenly went right off the idea.

He resumed his seat, half watching the boring movie, half listening to Hilda dribbling, grunting and squelching, when the dog shit on his shoe and trousers, now warmed by the heat of the cinema, began to hum with a vengeance, adding to the general nightmare quality of his evening.

Suddenly, Hilda began tugging feverishly at his sleeve, pointing excitedly to the on-screen action.

"Looooo...Noooormaaaaan...meeeee...maaaaaar!" she oozed, jabbing a filthy finger screenwards.

This was a particularly stomach-churning scene, involving a young catholic priest being eaten alive by a couple of 'bone crunchers' as he continued to scream for them to confess their sins and return to Mother Church.

As the camera zoomed in to reveal one of the ghouls stripping the living flesh from the priest's right arm, Hilda became even more animated.

"It's alright...calm down! That nasty thing won't hurt you, Hilda," he tried to calm her as her grunting reached fever pitch. Norman cast a quick glance around the cinema to see whether anyone was looking, for it sounded for all the world as though Hilda was in the middle of a mighty orgasm! He was amazed to see that the handful of people in the upper circle were actually as engrossed in the movie as Hilda, and they were far too busy watching the film to look and see where all that orgasmic racket was coming from.

Hilda was now beside herself with excitement.

"NOOOOOOOOO!" she wailed. "MII MAAAMAA!" she pointed wildly towards the screen, clutching Norman's right leg with her filthy, claw-like fingernails.

He let out a girly squeal of pain, before slapping her hand away as though it were a Tarantula crawling up his leg.

"For Christ's sake...calm down, you fucking loony!" he wailed. "You hurt my leg with those bleedin' claws of yours!"

By now all thoughts of the Thrashlightly fortune, however vast, had evaporated from Norman's mind and he was unable to hide his revulsion of the girl for a moment longer.

"Just cos your old man's got a few quid, you seem to think you can carry on like some crazed *Aardvark*. Why, you can't even talk proper, you smelly, bloody crackpot!" And with that, Norman got to his feet.

"I'm off, and your old man can stuff his money where the sun don't shine!"

Hilda moved so fast that Norman had no chance to react, even if he had been *strong* enough.

Her hand darted out and clamped his throat in a grip of steel, dragging him back to his seat as though he were made of straw, and she held him there as he gasped for air.

Norman's eyes bulged from their sockets as Hilda struggled to summon up enough faculties to make one last attempt at communication. She pointed at the screen, and at one ghoul in particular, who was currently feasting on the remains of the priest's liver, and she said in an amazingly clear voice:

"Tharts...mi...mummeee...looook!" It was a command, not a request, and Hilda emphasised the order by twisting Norman's head around to face the screen.

As he watched the action through bulging eyes, on the verge of passing out through lack of air, he spotted the family resemblance between Hilda and the blood covered creature dining on the priest's internal organs.

All at once, and far too late, everything clicked into place.

The smell of earth and of things long dead which rose from the girl's clothing. Her deathly white pallor, the inability to speak due to her dried up vocal chords. It all came together, and as if to confirm matters, Hilda stretched his neck back and took a huge bite, severing his jugular vein.

As his life ebbed quickly away, his last thought was *Shit, I've been on a date with a film star's daughter!*

No one noticed the crunching, drooling sounds amidst the screaming and carnage on screen. Or the revolting slurping, gnawing noises coming from the back row of the cinema.

Nobody looked as the tall, greasy haired girl, covered in gore, left the cinema through a side entrance and slipped away into the gathering dusk.

And when, the next morning, a cleaner discovered the few remaining cleanly picked bones stacked beneath one of the back-row seats at The Roxy, a seat formerly occupied by one Norman Scrote, it was put down as a student prank, the bones disposed of in the recycling bin for composting.

Meanwhile, several hours earlier, a pretty blonde girl had stood outside the Roxy Cinema, looking at her expensive watch one last time, before she headed off to catch a cab back to her apartment.

That stupid bastard, Barry King! I'll give him a piece of my mind the next time I see him! thought Hilda Thrashlightly, as she headed away from what would have been her very first blind date.

HERBERT MANNING'S PSYCHIC CIRCUS

Herbert Manning stood in his shabby caravan, fastidiously ironing his white Ringmaster's jodhpurs, and daydreaming about the past.

It hadn't *always* been like this; time was when he would have had other people to do chores like ironing and washing for him. But in these hard times of political correctness, the growth of the animal rights lobby and the nightmare that had grown to become a zealous religion known as Health and Safety, the days of the circus, the *real* circus, were all but dead.

Modern times had dictated that circus midgets were now to be referred to as 'people of diminished stature', kids seemed to be terrified of clowns thanks to the likes of Steven King and his story *It*, the use of performing chimps was now frowned upon, and training of most other animals for entertainment in the ring brought about demonstrations from just about anyone who could carry a placard.

So now his once great circus consisted of a trio of tutu wearing dancing dogs (these had somehow managed to escape the interest of the animal rights people), a few assorted jugglers who doubled as slap-stick clowns...minus the 'scary' makeup, naturally, a strong man and a high wire/trapeze act which had been so hamstrung by health and safety issues that it was hardly worth watching. Who the hell wanted to watch a high wire act who was forced to wear a safety helmet and harness at all times?

Gone were the fire eaters, the lion tamers, the knife throwers, the dancing elephants and all the other acts which made circus as it used to be; family entertainment with just enough danger to spice things up for the crowds.

These days, Herbert mused, they would all be claiming unemployment benefit if not for the few ancient fairground rides which travelled alongside the circus, because the big top attendances were so meagre. It was now, alas, a world full of video games, endless so called 'talent shows' and cookery programmes on the television which captured people's imagination. The thrill of the circus had all but gone and today's youngsters no longer had any time or interest in it.

The steam hissed from his iron, splattering his white jodhpurs with little bits of rusty brown water, and Herbert screamed with frustration and threw the iron straight through his open caravan window.

"Even the fucking *iron's* against me!" he asserted to the empty van.

At that moment, an urgent knocking at his flimsy wood and aluminium door brought him back to earth. *Now* what?

The caravan door opened outwards and a well-dressed man clutching a small zip briefcase poked his head through the opening. Herbert took one look at the man and he knew that he was going to be trouble, in some form or another. He would almost certainly be either some moron from the local council wanting to check licences and permits, or a similar pain in the arse from some other official agency, looking to bring more grief upon him and his circus.

"Herby? Herby Manning?" asked the man, who by now had stepped, uninvited, into the caravan and was offering his hand to the occupant. The visitor's face cracked with a huge, beaming smile.

Herbert looked at the man suspiciously and pointedly refused to take his offered hand in greeting. Then he realised that he was standing there wearing nothing more than his tatty old boxer shorts and string vest, and he quickly pulled on his dressing gown to cover his embarrassment.

"It's *Herbert*. No one calls me *Herby*!" he finally replied, as he watched his uninvited guest carefully close the caravan door behind him and settle himself down in a vacant chair.

"Please, do feel free to sit down, won't you?" said the Ringmaster, sarcastically.

The stranger's smile hadn't left his face, despite the lack of any warmth on Herbert's part, and he handed him his business card before continuing with what he had to say. Herbert took the card in broody silence and glanced at the inscription.

"Stanley A Tan Enterprises," said the card, in bold, red, raised lettering.

"You can call me Stan, though, Herby...especially as we'll be working closely together, real soon."

Herbert was both perplexed and annoyed, though annoyed definitely had the upper hand of the two emotions.

"It's *Herbert! Herbert!*" he said angrily, adding, "And what the bloody hell do you mean by 'we'll be working closely together, *real soon*'? For crying out loud...who the hell *are* you?" Herbert was now steaming more than his late departed iron, and he looked at the business card once more to see whether that held any clues.

He fingered his neat moustache, swept a hand through his thinning, black-dyed hair and stared hard at the man, waiting for some kind of an explanation.

"Okay, Herby...*Herbert*...whatever. I'll come to the point," said the other man, the smile still splitting his well-tanned face. Herbert shook his head and took a seat opposite his unwelcome guest.

"Go on then. What are you selling?" he asked, in resignation.

Stanley Tan nodded contentedly.

"Okay, Herb...ert," he began. "It's like this. We both know that business is, to say the least, bad, and I'm here to help you turn things around!"

Herbert frowned. "How much?" he asked, simply.

Stanley laughed a loud, booming laugh and shook his head.

"Hey, hold your hosses, Herby! I haven't told you what I have in mind yet, and *I* don't want anything from *you*. Not until things get a whole lot better around here, at least."

Herbert was nobody's fool, and the fact that this man apparently didn't want any money up front warmed him to the idea of at least hearing the man out. After all, what did he have to lose?

"Go on," he said.

Stanley Tan's smile grew even wider and he laughed that booming laugh once more.

"Good man, Herb...ert! Good man!" and with that, he leant across and slapped Herbert heartily on the shoulder. Herbert looked a little shocked, but managed to force a weak, trembling smile to his thin lips.

"Right then, my man...it's like this," continued Stanley Tan. "I have an idea that'll turn this whole circus of yours right around, and make you a very rich man, *when*...not *if* it works! What do you think of that, Bertie?"

Herbert Manning's nose wrinkled at being called Bertie; nobody had called him that since he was a child, and he'd always hated it, even then. It was an enormous struggle, but he remained calm.

"I don't really know *what* to think, Mr. Tan," he began.

"*Stan*, please call me Stan," interrupted the other man.

Herbert continued. "Stan, then. I mean to say, you haven't actually told me anything of your idea yet, have you?"

Stanley guffawed suddenly, startling Herbert.

"Quite right, Bertie baby...I'm coming to that part...you just be patient for a while longer!" Herbert did as he was told and sat patiently waiting for the man opposite to finish laughing and continue with his spiel, though he glanced nervously at his watch, as the next show in the big top was in two hours, and he was nowhere near ready for it.

"Don't worry about the next show, Bertie boy," said Stanley, almost as though he had read the Ringmaster's mind. "We both know that there'll only be a handful of customers, and the others can handle things without you for a while, surely?"

"But..." began Herbert, and the other man raised a silencing hand and ploughed on with his sales pitch.

"I have a couple of friends, well more *clients* I guess, that have some very special 'powers'. I look after them and they...*we*, need an outlet...a venue so to speak, for their amazing gifts to be shown to the world. Now *that*, Bertie my boy, is where *you* come into the picture!"

It was Herbert's turn to interrupt now.

"*Gifts*?" he asked, incredulously. "What sort of *gifts* are you talking about?"

Stanley smiled, but spared Herbert the deafening laugh this time.

"Why...*Psychic* gifts, Herby. Very special and *genuine* Psychic gifts! The kind of gifts that people will come from near and far to witness and, more importantly, pay a whole lot of money for the privilege, too!" Stanley sat back in his seat and waited for Herbert to react. It wasn't quite what he had been hoping for.

The Ringmaster smiled, twitched for a bit and then burst into uncontrolled laughter, the tears rolling down his chubby face and soaking into his neat little moustache, the rouge he'd applied to his cheeks earlier running in small red rivulets, and all the while, Stanley Tan looked on, a puzzled frown on his face.

When at last Herbert had finished laughing, he said, *"Psychics? Are you bleeding mad, man? Who the hell would come to a circus to see a couple of bogus bloody ghost botherers, for Christ's sake?"*

"Bogus?" snapped Stanley Tan. "Who said anything about them being *bogus*? I can assure you, Bert-O, that I wouldn't waste a single second of my time on *bogus* psychics...no, these are the real McCoy...*both of them!"*

The smile left Herbert's face.

"Go on...get out! You're wasting my time, friend!" he snapped, angrily.

Stanley smiled and shook his head sadly. Then, without another word, he unzipped the leather case he'd been holding and emptied its contents onto the small Formica-covered table in front of him.

Herbert Manning greedily took in the pile of money spread out before him, his piggy eyes trying to estimate how much was there, before Stanley spoke.

"There's fifty grand there, to save you counting. Fifty big ones...more money than you've ever seen at one time in your entire life, I'm guessing, Herby?"

Herbert was speechless for possibly the first time ever. He licked his thin lips and stroked nervously at his immaculately groomed moustache.

Stanley Tan pulled one more thing from the briefcase, and he placed it carefully on top of the pile of money, blocking the cash from Herbert's view, so that it had his full attention.

It was a small poster.

HERBERT MANNING'S ALL-NEW PSYCHIC CIRCUS

it said in bold, in-your-face lettering.

"So, what do you think, Herb-O?" asked Stanley Tan.

"Er...yeah, I like it. When do we start?" replied the Ringmaster.

"I knew you'd see things my way, Bertie boy! Right then, this is what we're gonna do." And for the first time, Herbert Manning leant forward and listened with genuine interest to what this strange man had to say.

*

A little over a month later everything was in place. The first venue had been selected, a completely revamped big top had risen from the metaphorical ashes of the old Manning's Family Circus, all new advertising hoardings had been erected and the staff, at least those who hadn't thought the entire thing a complete farce and who had walked out to find circus rings anew, had been kitted out in brand new uniforms and trained by Stanley Tan himself, to act as ushers for the new style customers coming to see the act.

Herbert had allowed himself to be swept along on the tsunami of progress, and had been a willing, though slightly baffled participant when Stanley instructed him on how things were going to be in the future.

Gone were the white jodhpurs, the bright red Ringmaster's coat and the tatty old black top hat. In came an outfit more befitting a far eastern mystic, comprising of a long, embroidered Chinese silk gown, a pair of neat black Chinese style slippers, topped off with a black silk skull cap. Herbert had felt ridiculous at first in his new get up, but had soon warmed to it after a couple of the old staff told him how good he looked in it.

Stanley, for his part, had been busy drumming up custom by organising local press coverage, and, as Herbert peered nervously through the curtains covering the new stage area, he was amazed to see that the house was already half full of punters. The first time he had seen so many customers in many a long year.

"Nervous, Herby?" Herbert almost jumped out of his costume, as he hadn't heard Stanley Tan creep up behind him.

"A little...it's all new to me, and rehearsals are one thing, but this is the real thing," he replied, turning to find that Stanley was wearing the same suit he'd worn the first time they'd met.

"Ah, you'll be fine, Herbert! You've done all this stuff before. This is just a different kind of act."

"I know," said Herbert. "But it would have been a big help if I had actually met these psychics of yours before the big night."

Stanley Tan smiled and clapped Herbert on the shoulder.

"Trust me, Herby...this really ain't the kind of act you can rehearse in advance! Things will happen, and they *will*, you'll see. But what happens will be different on every occasion. Now...if you're ready?" and with that, a pre-recording of suitably mystical music played from the PA system out front, as the curtains drifted slowly apart to reveal the spot-lit stage with nothing more than Hebert Manning and two empty leather wingback chairs upon it.

"Good evening, Ladies and Gentlemen," began a nervous Herbert to a silent audience. "What you are about to witness here tonight is entirely real. There is no trickery, there are no special effects, no 'plants' in the audience, and I have as little idea of what will happen here as you do."

There was a murmur from the crowd as he spoke, and someone shouted, "Yeah, sure! We believe you, mate!"

Herbert, a long-time expert in ignoring hecklers, continued with his introduction.

"I will now ask our psychics to come and join us." And he turned to see for the very first time two beautiful young Chinese women seemingly *glide* across the stage and take their seats either side of where he stood. The only illumination in the whole big top was the pair of spotlights carefully and cleverly targeted, so that the two women were half lit and half in shadow, making them appear somehow ethereal and other-worldly.

Having never been introduced to either of the women, Herbert only knew them by name. "And now, Madam Ling and Madam Yow will begin..."

"'Bout bloody time too, mate!" shouted the same heckler.

"Are you *frightened* of the spirits, Robert? Yes...I see you are, but you are also interested in them?" said the psychic seated to the left of the stage.

The heckler was suddenly lit up by an overhead spotlight, and he squirmed uncomfortably in his seat, shielding his eyes from the bright light.

"Hey...what's going on here? How do you know my name?" he shouted, as much in embarrassment as in anger.

"Your father told me your name, Robert...your father Terry, who passed over two years ago. He says that he is well and happy on the other side and that you must no longer grieve at his passing."

The heckler now went on the offensive.

"Oh yeah? *Anyone* could have found that stuff out, missus! You people are all the same...same old crap every time...with absolutely no proof!"

Suddenly, the psychic, Madam Ling, rose from her seat and walked slowly to the centre of the stage, carefully followed by the overhead spotlight. She stood still, her arms held wide, when a mist, small at first, grew slowly from the bare stage until it formed into a perfect column, directly in front of her.

The mist vanished suddenly, and a man was standing there as clear as day and in perfect detail. It was obviously not some sort of faked photo or projected image, as everyone could plainly see that the man was actually *breathing*, his eyes *blinking* with the glare from the bright spotlights.

"Dad? Is that *you?*" asked the heckler, incredulously.

The man on the stage spotted the heckler in the audience and smiled.

"Robbie! yes, it's me, son!" The man was both elated to see his son, and confused as to how he came to be there.

Robbie stood up from his seat and started to move towards the stage.

"Stop!" warned Madam Ling. "Your father is a spirit, and though you may *see* him, you may not come near him…for your own safety!"

"But, he's my *dad*…I *have* to talk to him…I *have* to see him!" cried the young man.

"Robbie…stay there, son. Listen to the lady, please."

The young man stopped in his tracks, uncertain whether or not to ignore the advice and jump up onto the stage anyway.

"But Dad…there's so much I want to say to you. So many things I wanted to ask you…"

The spirit smiled. "I know, Son…but I don't have much time. Just know that I love you and I always will do, and be happy in your life. Know that I'm really sorry for what I did…" and with that the image began to fade and waver, the mist returning and then shrinking like a genie going back into its bottle.

The young man leapt onto the stage.

"Dad!" he screamed, but there was nothing there other than the passive figure of Madam Ling and Madam Yow seated in the other chair.

The boy looked stunned and angry.

"It's a *trick*! It *has* to be a trick!" he said, in a bewildered voice, though it was clear from the look on his face that he knew it hadn't been a trick. Madam Ling smiled at him.

"It *was* your father…you know in your heart that it was him," she said, soothingly, adding, "But the spirit's time on earth is very limited…the connection very weak, and we can only communicate with the other side for a brief while."

She touched the grieving young man's arm gently, and he became calm.

"Thank you. Thank you so much," he said, quietly, and allowed himself to be guided back to his seat by one of the ushers, where he remained for the rest of the evening in stunned silence.

There were many other 'connections' that night via the two mysterious psychics, and each one, as the first, with a seemingly real and easily identified presence appearing on the stage. By the end of the show there were a lot of new believers leaving the big top, all talking in hushed, excited voices about what they had witnessed.

Herbert found Stanley Tan counting the evening's takings back in Herbert's new luxury mobile home.

"That was *incredible*, Stan! How the hell do they *do* that?" he asked in genuine amazement. Stanley finished counting, jotted the figure on a notepad, and handed the cash over to Herbert.

"There's over five hundred there, Bertie-me-boy. Not a bad start for the first night, with plenty more to come. Trust me!" he said.

Herbert took the money and placed it without any real interest, on a chair beside him.

"Stan, please tell me how they do it?" he asked again.

Stanley smiled. "They just *do* it, Herby. It's no trick, what you see is all *real*. Real spirits...*ghosts* if you prefer, but they can only stay here for a few minutes at a time. It is *not* a trick!"

"Bloody hell!" was all Herbert could manage to say at that precise moment.

*

From that evening onwards, Manning's All New Psychic Circus was a sell-out wherever it went.

Word of mouth soon got around, as did press and television coverage and instead of the usual two, or at most, three nights spent in each town, they were performing to packed houses for anything up to a month at a time. They were also playing larger cities rather than their usual small town, backwater audiences.

People of all types, rich and poor, black and white, the famous and the unknown were these days *begging* to attend the shows, every one of which was a complete sell out. And there was no sign of any let up on the horizon.

"I think that it's time to go the *next* stage now, Herby," said Stanley after another packed-house show had ended.

Herbert looked puzzled. "The 'next' stage, Stan...what did you have in mind?"

Stanley put an arm around Herbert's shoulder and smiled.

"This Big Top can only hold so many people, as you well know. I'm talking about *much* bigger venues, theatres...arenas...the *big* places where we can *really* pack 'em in! *Thousands* of punters, instead of just a few hundred at a time!"

Herbert fell silent.

They were *already* making money far beyond his wildest dreams, and Stanley had been more than honest, always giving Herbert the night's takings to look after. But then, Stanley had been the one to come up with this incredible show in the first place, so what could he, in reality, say against going bigger?

But he *would* miss his Big Top...it had been his life, though, not always a *good* life, it had to be said.

Stanley looked at his business partner and frowned.

"I *know* what you're thinking, Herb. You'll miss the old Big Top...all those memories. But, if I were to tell you that I've already booked us into the biggest Big Top in the country for our first new-style show, what would you say?"

It was Herbert's turn to frown.

"The *biggest* Big Top?"

Stanley grinned so wide, that Herbert feared his face would split.

"I've booked us the O2 Arena, in London! The Millennium Dome, man! And...it's already a complete sell out! Over twenty *thousand* punters!" he added, triumphantly.

"Wow!" was all that Herbert could say in reply, as he began to feel decidedly light headed at the very idea of such a huge crowd.

*

The stage was literally set for the big show that night.

It was even to be filmed for release on DVD at a later date, an event which would surely secure many more packed houses all across the planet.

Herbert was as nervous as hell about performing to so many people packed into one venue. He was even *more* nervous, after what Stanley Tan had told him, only one hour before lights up.

"Thought I ought to mention, Herby my boy, that tonight will be ever so slightly different from our usual show."

Herbert, who was already quaking in his silk slippers, almost passed out with the news.

"*Different*? How so, *different*?" he whined.

Stanley grinned that huge smile of his and fixed Herbert with a piercing stare.

"It's nothing for *you* to worry about, Herby. You just do your normal thing, and all will be fine. There could be a few more spirits appearing than usual, that's all. After all, this is the *big* time, and we want the paying public to get their money's worth, don't we? Especially as we'll be filming the whole show."

Herbert realised that this sudden revelation shouldn't make much difference to his part in the night's events. After all, all he really did was to get the thing off the ground. Nevertheless, he couldn't help feeling a little uneasy about any changes to what he considered to be a winning formula. And Stanley hadn't let them down so far, had he?

Herbert had earlier stood on the stage when the house had been empty, and he had felt completely *overwhelmed* with the size of the building even then. But when he walked out into the completely *packed* house, through a haze of theatrical stage mist, he almost wet himself with terror as he saw the sea of expectant faces all around him.

He caught sight of himself in one of the gigantic overhead monitor screens and almost decided to run off there and then, before he spotted Stanley Tan standing at the side of the stage, watching him intently, and he rose to complete the job in hand.

"Good evening, O2!" he said excitedly into the tiny microphone taped to his face, only to realise that he hadn't switched on the sending unit attached to his belt.

"Good evening, O2!" he tried again, this time he was greeted by a massive, almost deafening cheer from the twenty thousand plus capacity audience.

Herbert forced himself to remain calm and he tried to imagine himself in his more familiar Big Top environment. Slowly, he warmed to his task and he found that his nerves had all but disappeared by the time the two psychics arrived on stage.

You could have heard the proverbial pin drop, even in such a vast arena, as he introduced the two women.

"And now…Madam Ling and Madam Yow, will begin!" he said, before executing a deep theatrical bow and walking slowly off stage, where he could watch the proceedings from the shadows.

The whole place was still in total silence, as first one and then another of the now familiar misty columns began to appear on either side of the stage.

A murmur buzzed around the huge building as a third and then a fourth, quickly followed by yet *more* and *more* of the columns emerged from the ether until the whole stage was full of them.

The columns of mist began to firm up into more solid shapes and there were sudden screams of terror erupting from all over the venue as yet *more* columns appeared, this time in amongst the audience, on the main floor area, way up high in the stalls, in every exit and on every stairway.

Herbert looked on in undisguised horror at the what was emerging throughout the entire vast complex. The smoky, ethereal forms were firming up alright, but these were not the usual deceased relatives that he'd witnessed so many times before.

These were…he didn't know *what* they were!

Some kind of hideously deformed, demonic *creatures*, with huge slavering mouths full of razor sharp teeth, long, curved talons and small, leathery bat-like wings on their backs!

And the *smell*! God, it smelt like the biggest stink bomb in the world had been let off! He could see people in the audience both screaming and retching at the same time.

He looked over at the two psychics and saw that they were in a deep, trance-like state. Their eyes had clouded completely white and although they were wide open, they apparently saw nothing of the horrors which they had conjured up.

By now, every one of the misty columns had evolved into similarly terrifying creatures as on the stage, and, en masse, the crowd of more than twenty thousand people were on their feet and running in blind terror towards the exits, while the things from hell attacked as one, ripping the audience apart, tearing off heads and limbs, disembowelling people and feasting on their flesh before they moved onto their next victim.

There were by now thousands of the creatures as they covered every area of the huge arena, and they butchered the audience in a well organised fashion, as though following a preconceived plan.

Incredibly, within minutes, the carnage was over and not a single living soul remained. Twenty thousand odd men, women and children had been slaughtered in the most appalling way. There were no cries of anguish or of pain. The place was totally and utterly silent, save for the thump of Herbert Manning's heart, beating erratically within his chest.

The demons or whatever they were, once more reverted to funnels of mist before disappearing back to whichever nightmare place they had been summoned from, and the two psychics stood and then walked silently from the stage, as though they were completely unaware of what had just happened.

Herbert stood there, wide eyed and almost insane with the horror of it all. His feet felt soaking wet and he realised that he had soiled himself, when a gentle touch on his shoulder snapped him out of his nightmare.

"Always a bit of a messy business I'm afraid, Herbert, old son. But not a bad night's haul though, I'm thinking? Twenty thousand souls captured in one go, is nothing to be sniffed at, eh? I usually have to wait for a *war* to get that many in one go!" smiled Stanley Tan, placing a scaly hand on Herbert's shaking shoulder.

"And I *certainly* couldn't have done it without *your* help...you're a *great* showman...almost as great as *me!*"

Herbert stared at Stanley with unabashed horror in his eyes, as his former mentor started to dissolve like one of the manifestations brought about by the two psychics

Just before he vanished completely, he said:

"I'll leave *you* to clean up the mess, Herby, old son. Oh...and enjoy all that money...while you can!" All that was left was that familiar booming laughter ringing in Herbert's ears, reverberating through the vast arena.

Herbert Manning bent down and picked up the small visiting card which was all that now remained on the spot where Stanley Tan had been standing seconds ago.

He flipped it over.

Stanley A Tan Enterprises.

It was now *Herbert's* insane chuckle which echoed around the huge complex, and he was still cackling like a madman when heavily armed police found him sitting on the edge of the stage, staring at the card.

As they led him gently away, he was chanting over and over:

"S.A.Tan...S.A.Tan...S.A.Tan...!"

THE BOY

No sooner had he walked through the front door after another long, hard day at work, than his wife was on at him.

"*He's* been a little swine again!" she screamed, pointing at their eleven-year-old son who was busy cowering in a corner of the living room. All afternoon, he'd been listening to his mother say those dreaded words, "Wait till your father gets home! *He'll* give you what-for, my lad!"

And the sad thing was, the boy *knew* that he would get 'what-for', as he seemed to get it at least three or four times a week, but he couldn't help himself. He was simply a normal, naughty, pain-in-the-arse boy, no better or worse than any other boy of his age.

Okay, maybe *slightly* worse; certainly, no angel by any stretch of the imagination, but then, no demon either.

His father had barely had time to take off his coat, as his wife continued her verbal assault on him, bombarding him with every tiny misdemeanour, every minor infraction of the rules carried out by his son during the day.

"*And* he called me an old cow, too! I told him you'd give him what-for when you got home...I *warned* him!"

The boy's father was in his early fifties, and truth be told, he was not a well man. These days, he would have been diagnosed as still suffering from the effects of post-traumatic stress disorder, following the nightmarish scenes he had witnessed during his time serving in the army in the Second World War. Sights which he had never spoken about, not to *anyone*. Sights that had left him a nervous wreck of a man, only able to function on any level because of the cocktail of drugs supplied by an understanding GP.

The father's nervous tic grew more pronounced the more his wife continued to berate him about their son's behaviour, and when at last his short fuse ignited, he dragged the boy roughly from his hiding place, somehow managing to remove his thick leather from his trousers at the same time, and thrashed the squirming child while his mother looked on, a smug, self-satisfied smile on her hard face.

When it was over, for today at least, the boy ran sobbing to the bedroom he shared with his younger brother, and flung himself on his bed. Although his father administered the beatings on a regular basis, the boy somehow knew that he didn't *want* to carry them out; that he didn't *enjoy* doing what he did. It was just his way of shutting his wife up, of stopping her constant nagging, of getting a bit of peace and quiet after a hard day.

The boy also remembered that it hadn't *always* been this way.

He recalled the day it had all started, the day he had been taken to a neighbour's house and left there for what had seemed like months, but in reality it was probably no longer than a few weeks.

One minute, the then three-year-old had been happily playing with his Dinky cars on the lino in the kitchen, the next, he had his coat thrust onto his back and he was marched six houses up the street and deposited with some strange woman and her daughter. People he didn't recall having ever seen before.

Then his father was gone, saying he'd be back when he could. The young boy cried himself into a bewildered sleep on the stranger's settee.

He knew it had been around Christmas time; he remembered that, because the strange woman had taken him to visit Santa's Grotto at the big department store, and he had sat on a fat man's lap who had given him a small plastic toy boat filled with toffees.

During those days, weeks...months(?) he only saw his father three times, and then only when he called round to the neighbour with some money, presumably payment for looking after the boy. His father would promise to be back to see him soon, but the days seemed to drag on endlessly and each time the boy saw his father during those fleeting visits, it only served to stir up more feelings of abandonment and highlighted the fact that he was no longer wanted, no longer loved by his daddy.

There had been no sign of his mother, his one-time *loving*, caring mother. She seemed to have vanished from the face of the earth?

Then, finally, it was over.

His father came to collect him, wearing his big old tweedy overcoat. He held the boy's hand and they walked the six houses back to their home. The small boy looked up at his daddy, his face full of joy, elated that they were back together again, *thrilled* to be holding his father's hand.

They entered the living room, and there, silhouetted in the bay window, backlit by watery January sunlight, sat his mother on a hard-backed kitchen chair. She was holding something carefully in her arms; something wrapped in a small blue blanket and she was smiling, not at the son she hadn't seen for such a long time, but at the bundle which she held so gently.

"This is your new brother!" she announced, proudly, without preamble. The father held the three-year-old firmly by the shoulder, perhaps in an attempt to comfort the boy from the shocking news.

The small boy was led slowly across to where his mother and new brother sat, almost as though he was in the presence of royalty and he had been granted a special audience.

Mother pulled the blue blanket away from the baby's face so that the boy could get a better look at his new sibling.

"There," she cooed. *"Here's* your brother. What shall we call him, eh?"

she asked in a sugary-sweet voice, her eyes still fixed adoringly on the infant.

The boy was in shock.

He was too young to know anything about babies or understand where they came from. All he *did* know was that he had been dumped with strangers for weeks on end, without setting eyes on his mother, and with only the briefest glimpses of his father. And now *this*? This *stranger*, who had come from nowhere and was apparently his *brother*? This brother sitting on *his* mother's lap, in *his* place? And *she* was smiling at *him!*

"Rover!" said the boy, suddenly.

"What?" asked his mother, still too engrossed with the new-born to listen to her elder son.

"Rover...call him *Rover!"* repeated the boy.

His mother laughed, giving subliminal permission for his father to do the same.

"We can't call him *Rover*...he's not a dog...he's your *brother!"*

The boy thought for a moment while his parents laughed at him.

"Chum then...let's call him Chum?" suggested the boy, in honour of a pet which had died back when he was still crawling.

His parents laughed again, his mother with a strange look in her eyes. She was smiling, but there was something *behind* the smile, something the boy had never seen before. It was something *nasty*, as though she didn't like him anymore.

"No. We've already decided to call him Clive. Clive is a *nice* name...not a *dog's* name."

"Clive's a *stupid* name!" said the boy, and he felt his father's grip tighten on his shoulder.

So Clive, aka Rover, came into the boy's life and stayed there.

As it turned out, Clive was a very sickly child. If anything was going around, any sort of childhood malady, he was certain to pick it up, and he'd be screaming the place down day and night, which made their father, whose nerves were already shattered at the best of times, even *more* uptight than usual.

Then, after a while, another strange thing happened,

The boy's father just vanished one day.

He'd come home from the local infant school, and Dad was gone! It was even *more* peculiar, because Dad always picked the boy up from school in his little van, but on this occasion, there was no one there waiting for him and, after hanging about long after all the other kids had gone home, he decided that his dad wasn't coming and had walked home on his own.

"Where's Daddy?" asked the boy of his mother, who was busy trying to comfort the eternally sick Clive.

"He's gone away for a while," she snapped, without elaboration.

The boy was confused and scared. It reminded him of that *other* time.

"Has he gone to get another baby?" the boy asked, earnestly.

His mother shook her head and snorted with derisive laughter.

"No...he...hasn't!" she spat. "Now get that uniform off and wash your hands ready for tea."

"But, *where's* my daddy?" whined the boy.

A firm slap to the left side of his face silenced his whining.

"I said, he's gone away for a while! Now get changed, you little sod!" This, together with the frightening glare that his mother gave him, made it clear that the subject was now closed.

He didn't see his father for many weeks after that, and, despite asking after him on a regular basis and receiving yet another slap for 'being defiant', he was never given an answer.

All he *did* know was that he was forbidden to go into the back bedroom and that their doctor would pay regular weekly visits to the house, where he would whisper with his mother. At these times, the boy would be locked in the front room and he would hear the doctor climbing the stairs and the back-bedroom door open and close.

Then the visits stopped.

His mother became ever more hostile towards the boy, while Clive became ever more wonderful in his mother's eyes.

After what seemed like an eternity, his mother together with Clive in the pushchair (although he was easily now big enough and old enough to walk unaided) and the boy, went for a walk together. A rare event indeed, so the boy asked where they were going.

"We're going to meet your father from the station," she replied, somewhat nervously, adding, "And you had better bloody well behave yourself!"

His father had lost a lot of weight. His old tweed coat was now hanging from his once broad shoulders, almost as though it belonged to someone else, and stranger still, he no longer had any teeth. Just a gaping mouth full of red raw gums! But the boy was thrilled to see him again, teeth or not, and he threw his arms around his father's waist and burst into tears.

The walk back home from the station was very quiet, neither of his parents spoke to one another, as Clive grizzled in his pushchair, demanding the attention of his doting mother.

Over the coming weeks, the boy heard the words 'convalescent home' and 'nervous breakdown' a lot, as his mother chatted to the neighbours over the garden gate. None of it made any sense to him, of course, but his dad was back and that was all that mattered.

He was a lot twitchier than the boy remembered, the tic in his eye had now been joined by a non-stop flexing of the fingers in his right hand, which grew worse in direct proportion to how much his wife nagged him.

Suddenly, the boy could do nothing right. Every action or gesture was pounced upon by his mother as a sign of 'defiance', every word deemed to be 'argumentative' or 'rude', so much so that it was almost impossible to do or say anything without her uttering those fateful words:

"Just you wait until your father gets home!"

And, when he wasn't receiving a belting from his harangued father, he would feel whatever object came into his mother's hands around the back of his legs or, worse, the back of his head. On one occasion, she had actually hit him alongside the head with a frying pan snatched from the hotplate. And he then got another beating from his father because the frying pan had been full of fat and his mother had had to clean the kitchen as it had splattered everywhere!

There was no escape.

He had been promised his own bedroom at one point, but his mother and father now had a room each to themselves for some reason, so he was forced to continue sharing with Clive.

His father, never big on DIY, had created a set of narrow bunk beds made from two ex-army cots bolted together with angle iron.

To make matters worse, Clive had been given the top bunk and he delighted in wetting the bed at night, which showered down onto his brother beneath.

His mother and Clive found this *most* amusing, even though it was *she* who had to clean up the mess and change Clive's bedding each morning. Though she didn't change his, no matter *how* damp and smelly it became. *His* would have to last a fortnight.

The more that she doted on Clive, the more he would go out of his way to torment and antagonise his older brother, which in turn, seemed to make his mother happier.

The boy was now eleven and his brother eight. This was when the boy decided that enough was enough; he would kill Clive and things would go back to the way they *used* to be. Just him, his dad and his mother. All happy again with no more beatings and no more *Clive* around to ruin everything.

But just *how* do you kill someone? It was easy on the television; you simply shot or stabbed someone and they fell down dead...easy-peasy. That was on TV however. How would *he* get rid of his brother, yet not get into trouble again? After all, despite his apparent 'defiance' and 'rudeness', the boy was no fool and he realised he would be in *serious* bother if anyone found out he had done it.

He prayed every night that one of Clive's endless illnesses would kill him, and there was a brief moment of real hope when his brother was taken into hospital suffering from some mystery virus. But he returned after a couple of weeks to continue his tormenting ways.

Time passed, and the boy kept the notion of dispensing with his brother on the back burner, as the six-week school holidays had arrived.

His last such break before 'the big school'.

Freedom!

He was out every day with his friends, building camps in the park, playing football, climbing trees and having fun from dawn until dusk in the bright summer sunshine. He'd more often than not return home late for tea, covered in dirt and mud and receive a beating for both his tardiness and for being mucky, but it was worth it just to be out of that depressing house, and more importantly, away from *Clive* and his snivelling ways.

Then his mother found a part-time job in a baker's shop, and the boy was instructed that *he* would have to look after his younger brother until she returned from work.

Not only did he have to suffer the ignominy of having his friends taking the piss because he had his baby brother tagging along everywhere he went, but Clive would tell their mother everything his elder brother got up to, which inevitably led to yet *more* punishment.

Fortunately, their mother didn't entertain the notion of grounding the boys, as she knew that the house would be wrecked in her absence, so they were allowed to continue roaming free, so long as the boy agreed to look out for his brother and keep him safe.

Great news for Clive, dire news for his brother.

With every day that passed, the boy hated Clive a little more and the feeling seemed to be entirely mutual, as Clive would relish any and every opportunity to cause grief for his brother when they returned home each evening.

The worse occasion being when the gang of boys had seen a drunken flasher in the park one day, and, after failing to persuade Clive to go and touch the man's cock, they had stripped ferns, uprooted the stems and then used them to chase the drunk and whip his genitals until he had screamed for mercy and run off. Comically, he had tried to pull up his pants and trousers while still running and he fell heavily on the uneven ground. The boys had seized their chance, thrashing the pervert mercilessly until he crawled off, bleeding and sobbing into the bracken.

The boy received the worst beating of his life for that little episode.

Not because he and his friends had punished a paedophile, but because he had endangered the precious Clive with his antics. Clive and his mother sat side by side on the settee, each wearing an identical smug smile on their faces as the boy came back into the room after his thrashing, and tried to sit while his buttocks were ablaze with pain.

"That'll teach him to look after me properly, won't it mummy?" whined Clive.

"Yes, it *will*, my darling!" confirmed their mother.

*

104

The old sewage works had always been a great place to play and hang out. Despite, or rather *because* of all the DANGER-KEEP OUT! signs, the gang always felt compelled to go there and rummage about in the various tunnels and shafts, as well as the long abandoned pump house, which still stank of shit even after all the years of disuse.

Rats scurried in dark corners, bats lived in what remaining roof hadn't been vandalised, stolen or simply collapsed from old age and lack of repair.

It was a *magical* place to the boys, full of mystery and adventure, a veritable treasure trove of excitement to anyone with half an imagination.

Clive, however, had *no* imagination.

He would whine constantly that the place stank, that it was too dirty, too scary and too far away from home, though in reality it was less than a mile away.

The boy used his newly learnt words on his brother,

"Fuck off, Clive...you little shit!" and the other boys laughed long and hard. There wasn't a single one of them that didn't feel the same way about Clive.

Clive stuck out his bottom lip and began to whimper.

"I'm telling my mummy you said that!" he whined and would have run off back home right then, except for the fact that he didn't know the way. And he was also far too frightened to move about the old sewage works on his own.

"Let's play hide and seek!" called one of the boys, to unanimous agreement from the others. All bar one that was; Clive, naturally.

"NO! I DON'T WANNA PLAY THAT!" he screamed, his shrill words echoing eerily around the high walls of the pump house.

The boy walked over to his brother, his fists clenching and unclenching, resisting the almost overwhelming urge to punch Clive straight in the mouth.

"Okay, you sissy-boy! *We'll* hide, and *you* can find us, if you're too chicken too hide!"

"NO!" screamed Clive.

"*TOUGH!*" retorted his brother. "You can play, or you can fuck off back home on your own. And I don't care *what* dad does to me!"

Clive's fleshy lips puckered and tears rolled down his grubby cheeks, while the rest of the gang looked on, smirking at this unexpected standoff. It had been a long time coming and they were enjoying every second of it.

"It's up to you, Clive. We can leave you here with all the rats and the bats, or you can try and find us and then we can all go home."

Clive, slowly realising that he was in a no-win situation for once, wiped his snotty nose on the sleeve of his jumper and nodded, accepting defeat.

"Wahoo! Let's go! Close your eyes and count to twenty!"

And with that, the rest of the boys scattered around the huge old pump house, fighting amongst themselves for the best hiding place.

The boy had already decided in advance where his hiding place would be, and he headed across to the far wall, scrambling over a large pile of rubble towards his goal.

He had been to the pump house many times before being lumbered with having to take Clive everywhere, and he knew that there was an old covered cistern with a heavy, cast iron lid on the inspection hatch. He also knew that, although the pump house had been long redundant, the access hatch and all the machinery in that section of the plant was still maintained, as there was a sluice gate separating the cistern from the canal which ran outside the works. This cistern was, on rare occasions, used when the canal threatened to flood following very heavy rainfall.

It was easy for him, therefore, to lift the well-oiled inspection lid and to clamber down the vertical ladder which led down into the old Victorian, brick-lined cistern. It hadn't rained in an age, so he knew he would be safe from the risk of flooding.

The lid was heavy, but he hefted it a few times to make sure he'd be able to open it again from the inside, then he closed it silently behind him and descended the metal ladder once more.

It was pitch black now that he had closed the lid, but that didn't worry the boy one bit, as he knew that no one would find him down there. And Clive *certainly* wouldn't have the balls to look in such a place. Even if he did manage to overcome his terror of dark places, scramble down the vertical ladder and discover his hiding place, the boy would make certain that he would never leave alive. He suppressed a snigger, and sat down to wait on the dry, rubble-strewn floor of the cistern.

"Nineteen, twenty...coming, ready or not!" announced Clive, with no enthusiasm, and he proceeded to make a great pretence of looking for the hidden gang of boys.

In reality, he hadn't kept his eyes closed while counting to twenty. In fact, he had made a point of watching *exactly* where his brother had been heading towards, and he made a beeline in that direction.

As soon as he spotted the heavy lid covering the access chamber, he knew immediately that this was where his brother would be hiding and he grinned broadly to himself. That was just *too* easy!

Then he spotted the wheel which operated the sluice.

Liberally coated in grease, it would be as smooth to operate as the day it was installed, way back in Victorian times.

Clive released the safety break and began turning the wheel, as fast as he could. He could hear the sluice gate opening in the cistern beneath his feet, and the barely audible muffled cries from his brother, as the cold, dirty grey canal water poured into the old tank with a faint roaring sound.

The shock of the cold water battering into his body made the boy go rigid with terror.

The force of the deluge knocked him off his feet and swept him into the far corner of the inky black darkness of the cistern. He tried to stand, groping blindly for the safety of the vertical ladder, but every time he attempted to clamber to his feet, the sheer force of the water knocked him over again.

He screamed for help at the top of his lungs, but was rewarded with a mouthful of foul-tasting water which forced its way down his throat, up his nose and into his lungs, making him choke and retch.

Turgid canal water mixed with one-hundred-and-twenty-year-old Victorian shit that had washed from the crevices in the brickwork and from cracks in the cistern floor, filling his lungs with the foul mixture, almost drowning him.

He tried one final time to flounder his way to the hatch in the ceiling of the cistern as the water steadily rose, but he had swallowed too much water, and when his flailing hands touched the vertical ladder, a brief glimmer of hope flashed through his mind, before he sank slowly to the bottom of the tank. Dead.

It was all a dreadful accident, of course.

None of the boys should have been in the old sewage works in the first place, and surely no one would ever have been crazy enough to enter the cistern when it had been full of water?

The coroner entered a verdict of Accidental Death.

As nobody amongst the gang had actually witnessed what had really happened, what else could the verdict be? The coroner issued a strong rebuke against the owners of the site for their complete lack of any form of security, but that was that. Case closed.

Clive and his mother stood beside the open grave as the priest jabbered on with the funeral service. Father hadn't been able to make it; he'd suffered a bad relapse and was 'away' at a convalescent home for the foreseeable future.

As the service ended and Clive and his mother walked away from the graveside, they held hands, turned, and smiled at one another.

"It's just us now, mummy," said Clive.

"Yes, darling, just us," replied his mother, happily.

TEN WEEKS

Five minutes! Three hundred seconds...a mere three hundred heartbeats or so.

If only he had arrived just those three hundred seconds earlier, how different things could have been. *Would* have been!

His work was nearing completion.

No, not *work*, for it had been anything but a chore to him. No, *vocation* was a more appropriate word, his calling from God. Yes, a God-given vocation to carry out His will, for the greater benefit of all mankind!

But then everything had gone so badly and so *quickly* wrong. All because of those five minutes! He would now never be able to complete his mission. His *Holy* mission. Yet he had been so very close to doing so. As close as *any* man could have.

He had been so careful up until then.

Never making a move without the most intense research beforehand. No matter what those penny-dreadful newspapers might have said about the 'random victims' and of him 'having the luck of the devil' in the way he managed to avoid capture by the mighty Metropolitan Police.

It was far from luck! Although he would have to admit that perhaps he had been a little *fortunate* on occasion? Especially by the way the stupid police had followed so many false leads. But he was more than happy that these dead-ends distracted their eyes away from him and his mission.

No, it was all to do with his very careful observations of his victims, their haunts and their habits. This, together with his scrupulous planning, had enabled him to continue.

But, if luck had ever been a part of what he had been doing, then it was surely very *bad* luck which had ended his assignment so abruptly and led him here to this terrible place? Bad luck and his own stupidity.

He had always, up until that fateful day at least, been so meticulous with every detail. So careful with his preparation for the next undertaking. Yet, for something as brainless and dim-witted as not checking that his pocket watch had been fully wound? To be thwarted because of a stopped *watch*? It was almost unbelievable!

To make matters worse, his *previous* mission had been so successful, that his skill, his *art* was now shared by appearing not only on the London newspapers, but he had heard he was now renowned across the entire *world*! He was perhaps the most famous person on the globe, yet *no one*, not one single soul knew of his identity.

That something so banal as a stopped pocket watch should have led to such an ignominious end to his work, was almost beyond his comprehension.

Worst still, no one ever *would* now know anything of him. The whole world knew of his work, and people would undoubtedly speak of it a hundred years from now. But of the man *behind* that work? Or the very *reason* that he'd carried out these sacred acts, would all be a mystery, sadly. No one would know his name, or his reasons.

He had spent many hours, both night and day, watching the comings and goings at that seedy room in Miller's Court. He knew enough about her habits, erratic as they often were, to form a plan.

She had, in fact, seen him on numerous occasions, even propositioned him more than once as he lingered in the vicinity of her room. Not close enough to arouse suspicion, of course, just close enough to keep a careful eye on the woman.

She had never been suspicious of him. More often than not she was the worse for wear with gin anyway.

So, she had not been at all perturbed when at last this man had finally agreed to her offer and had accompanied her back to her seedy den that fateful November night. She had been even *more* excited with his company as he'd produced a bottle of gin from his small leather Gladstone bag.

That woman had been his greatest success to date, but he had planned an even *more* elaborate exhibition of his skills for the following night. Saturday the 10th of November 1888. Another whore, who lived only three streets away from the Kelly girl's hovel.

A girl which he had been tracking for the last two months.

She would be his *pièce de résistance!*

At least, she *would* have been, but for his own stupid negligence and those five minutes!

The streets were abuzz with vigilante groups and more police than he had ever seen. Whores now worked in gangs rather than individually, and their pimps stood watch on every corner.

He had easily managed to evade them all in the past, and tonight would be no different than any of his previous excursions. The danger of it all always gave him a wonderful frisson of excitement anyway. That was almost as thrilling as the work itself. Almost.

Emily Jones was an angel-faced, dark haired nineteen-year-old girl who had fled from her native Wales to escape her abusive father. Sadly, the life she had chosen for herself, or rather fallen into, was surely far harsher than anything before?

However, she was stubborn as well as beautiful, and she had decided to continue working as a whore until she could save enough to leave the dreadful streets of London's East End and find somewhere sweet smelling to live, perhaps in the countryside.

To this end, Emily had no pimp controlling her clients and no man to steal her hard-earned money each night. She would only go with 'gentlemen', and she amassed a regular clientele of well-heeled men to call upon, so she had no need for street walking or the pimps who offered their dubious 'protection'.

He had become one of her regular clients over the last couple of months, unlike his previous victims, who were merely common, diseased street whores to his mind. He was therefore trusted by Emily, who was always happy to receive him or, rather, the not insubstantial sum of money which she was able to command for her services.

The tenth of November was his next appointment for a night of pleasure and he was expected at 9:30 sharp. Punctuality was her only demand, aside from payment, naturally. Anyone arriving late would be refused access for the next month.

"Time is money, sir," was her catchphrase. And he had paid for the whole night in advance, as usual.

Almost all the streets in the East End were now subject of regular patrols by both the police and the Whitechapel Vigilance Committee, but his was a regular face in the area, and as such he never attracted attention or the suspicions of either group.

The penny-dreadfuls had whipped up suspicion of all foreigners, and the two factions seemed to be concentrating on any swarthy-looking types, with accents or a pointy-toothed demon butcher wearing a leather apron and a mad wild-eyed look on his face.

They were certain; it was *definitely* some foreigner. No *Englishman* could carry out such horrific atrocities!

Whereas *he* was a respectable-looking middle aged man, with light blue eyes, pale skin and a gentle air about him. A man who blended easily into the background. A man who would arouse no more suspicion than would a priest, which, incidentally, was his former occupation before that unfortunate incident with the young girl arranging flowers at his old church.

The incident which ruined not only his career but his whole life. If only the stupid bitch hadn't made so much *fuss* over such a trifling matter? If only her parents had not been so stubborn by insisting that the *Bishop* be informed about the incident?

He knew by heart the times of the regular patrols in the dingy street of Whitechapel. He glanced at his pocket watch in the light of the flickering gas mantle above his fireplace to confirm when the next one was due.

He would arrive at Emily Jones' rooms at precisely 9:30 and commence with his work immediately.

He looked at the pocket watch once more, a slight frown creasing his brow. He placed the gold half-hunter next to his ear and listened carefully. It had stopped!

Christ in Heaven, he would be late, perhaps *so* late that the whore would be finding another client in his stead?

The man panicked as he had never done since commencing his

undertaking.

He quickly donned his dark grey hat and threw a velvet cape about his shoulders, before bolting out of the door and into the misty November night.

He maintained a steady pace, though not so hasty that he would draw attention to himself, and he strolled confidently through the narrow streets and twisting alleyways towards his goal.

But what *time* was it? Just how late *was* he?

Then, through the chill mist, he heard a distant clock strike the half hour. 9:30 already! And he was *still* a good five minutes from the girl's room.

He quickened his steps to almost a trot, brushing through the crowds of drunken whores and their pimps, through the sight-seers and the newspaper sellers, as angry oaths were uttered behind him, but he never stopped nor looked behind him.

He was now less than a minute from Emily Jones' rooms, when he realised with sickening horror that he had forgotten to pick up his bag; the bag with all his equipment inside. The bag without which he would be unable to implement all of his intricate planning!

What to do?

If he returned home now to fetch it, he would be far too late for the whore. If he carried on without it, then his mission would be a failure as he could never hope to exceed his previous night's work without his equipment.

He stopped dead in his tracks, leaning up against a rough, damp wall, gulping in the misty night air as he tried to think. He found himself panting, and he loosened the stud in his starched white collar to make breathing easier.

"Are you alright there, sir? You look ill, if I might say so?"

The young constable shone the light from the Bull's Eye lantern into the man's face and watched him with genuine concern.

The man started with shock. He had not heard the constable emerge from an alleyway behind him. Quickly, he attempted to gather some semblance of normality to his usually well-ordered self. He nodded politely at the young policeman.

"I am quite well, thank you, constable. I just seem to have got myself lost in this fog and I became a little anxious. That's all."

The constable looked somewhat dubious at this reply.

"You look more *ill* than lost, if you don't mind me saying so, sir? Let me take you back to the station where you can compose yourself and rest for a bit?"

"*NO!*" screamed the man, with sudden rage; rage at himself for his lack of precision. Rage at leaving his watch unwound. Rage at leaving his vital bag of instruments behind in his rooms.

The constable stepped back, alarmed by the man's sudden outburst, and he automatically drew his truncheon from his belt and held it before him.

"Now then, sir...I'm only trying to be helpful. There is no need for that attitude. I think perhaps you'd better come along with me and we'll see what's up with you."

The man snatched the truncheon so quickly that the young constable had no chance to react or defend himself.

He rained down blow after blow onto the young man's face and skull, until his head was little more than a bloody pulp of torn skin, shattered bone, and oozing grey mush.

The man stood there, eyes wide and breathing heavily, gore dripping from the head of the truncheon, the coppery stench of fresh blood filling the chill night air. Suddenly, he looked about him to get his bearings and he fled down the nearest alleyway.

All of his careful plans were now forgotten as he ran in blind panic through the narrow, twisting alleyways. The shrill sound of a police whistle pierced the night, heralding the discovery of his foul deed in the darkness behind him.

As he rounded a tight corner, he ran slap into a group of drunken vigilantes who blocked his path, with staves, hammers and knives.

"Where you goin', matey?" asked one man.

"'Ere, there's blood all down your clothes, you murderin' bastard!" cried another.

He was beaten so badly by the outraged mob, that it was thought the man would never live to see his trial, let alone recover enough for his execution.

But, against all the odds, he *did* survive to be tried for the murder of constable George Pike, an eighteen-year-old policeman who had been on his first night's solo patrol out of Whitechapel Police Station.

Although the man was unable to speak in his defence at his trial, or write a single word in mitigation, as he had received multiple fractures to his jaw and both hands, he was subsequently found guilty of murder in the first degree. An outcome which was hardly surprising as he still clutched the blood-soaked, brain-spattered murder weapon in his gore covered hands, when at last the other officers were able to drag him from the baying East End crowd and exacted their own form of justice upon him.

He was sentenced to be hanged by the neck until he was dead.

So here he was.

Legs strapped together at the ankles as he stood on the wooden trapdoor, a noose fitted around his neck, the large knot pressing tightly against the left side of his head, just below the ear,

A muslin sack covered his face, his breath coming hard and fast as he heard the muffled words of a priest droning somewhere behind him.

Five minutes...three hundred seconds...three hundred heartbeats.

Nobody would know of his great mission now.

He was to be put to death for the murder of a mere policeman!

He would be no missionary, no visionary. They would never realise that it was *he* who had ended the lives of those whores.

Mary Ann Nichols. Annie Chapman. Elizabeth Stride. Catherine Eddowes, And his final, greatest triumph, Mary Jane Kelly.

He wanted to call out to the assembled witnesses, to tell them *who* he was and *what* he had done...and *why*!

But his shattered jaw was held in place with a linen bandage, and would not allow that to happen.

The trapdoor dropped open.

He fell suddenly, *violently* into the void.

His neck snapped with a sound like breaking wood.

His tethered legs kicked briefly as he voided both his bladder and his bowels.

And then...nothing.

The ten weeks of horror which had begun on Friday the 31st of August, and ended on Friday the 9th of November 1888, terrifying the residents of Whitechapel in the East End of London and gripping a nation with each new and ever more ghastly revelation, was at an end.

DIN-DINS FOR BINKY

Mary White was a sad sight.

She was only 33 but looked at least 20 years older, and that was on a good day. Aside from having the dress sense of a vagrant and the personality of a freeze-dried slug, she was several stones overweight and her incredibly plain features were topped off with a shock of bright red, unkempt hair. Her skin had the unfortunate tendency to wrinkle for no apparent reason. She had never worn make up and had studiously avoided the sun due to the combination of her red hair and very pale skin, therefore quite why she had become so wrinkly at such a young age was something of a mystery.

When she had first met Victor, her future husband, she had been at teacher training college and Victor had been a lathe operator in a small engineering firm.

Alas, Mary turned out not to be the great success that both her and her parents had hoped for, failing many of her vital teaching exams, though she did however manage to scrape through and gain just enough qualifications to allow her to teach in an infant school.

When she had been dressed in her peculiar assortment of clothes in those days, Victor had thought that she had looked cute and he understood that someone living on a student loan simply couldn't afford decent attire with such a meagre allowance.

Months later, after Victor had proposed to her and she had accepted (in hindsight, rather too quickly) he felt positive that as his wife, she might make more of an effort with her appearance. He had been swept to the altar in a tsunami of activity hastily organised by Mary and her mother and it didn't take long for Victor to realise that his new bride was in reality going from bad to worse. It seemed that now she had bagged herself a man, there was simply no need for any sort of effort on her part.

She never did take on any kind of work, paid or otherwise after their marriage, and now, six years on, Mary couldn't even be bothered to rustle up her hardworking husband's sandwiches as she once had, preferring instead to remain in her bed the whole time, watching endless daytime television, reading horror stories, eating chocolates and breaking wind with incredible gusto.

The couple had shared a double bed for less than a week at the start of their life together before Victor discovered that his new wife apparently had a terrible phobia of anything to do with sex, and he had been transferred to the spare room, much to his frustration and to Mary's obvious delight.

However, the final blow to this disastrous union came when Victor was made redundant from his beloved job. His only solace in a world otherwise filled with misery. Victor, who was well used to being handed life's Booby Prize, was now completely distraught at the prospect of not only being unemployed, but being forced to spend more time at home with Mary.

He haunted the Job Centre on a daily basis, signed up with employment agencies and scoured the local papers avidly. He even called in person at every likely source of employment in the area, alas, all to no avail.

The bills were mounting. They were now in arrears with the mortgage and his car had been repossessed by the finance company. The wolves were at his door and they weren't being too quiet about announcing their presence.

Meanwhile, Mary was being a fat help as usual. About 26 stone of fat to be more accurate. She wailed incessantly about the shortage of food, more specifically chocolate, and she announced that Victor's lack of income was causing her to die from both starvation and neglect. With this in mind, she added an extra blanket to her bed as a means of comfort and lay there sobbing pitifully whenever she knew that Victor was within earshot.

He rarely caught sight of the apparition that was his wife outside of her bed, apart from the times she tottered from her bedroom to the toilet, as always clad in a heavily stained, bright yellow candlewick dressing gown and green fluffy slippers. On reflection, he was now *very* pleased that he had been banished to the spare room and he had in fact secretly installed a lock and heavy chain on the inside of his bedroom door, lest Mary should ever overcome her terror of the delights of the flesh.

He spent every moment that he could away from the house. He would rather walk the streets in the rain than listen to Mary's endless complaining and demands for his attention. When he wasn't out pounding the pavements searching for work, *any* work, he would sit in the library or visit the little cafe around the corner from his home.

It was in that cafe that he had first clapped eyes on, and then fallen hopelessly in love with Iris Jenkins, a waitress who worked alternate weekdays. Iris, of course, was totally unaware of Victor's secret yearning for her. She merely thought of him as a nice, polite and pleasant customer. Victor had nursed his repressed passion for the lovely Iris for some five months and he was barely able to contain himself when on one occasion their hands had briefly touched as she took away his tea cup.

Finally, after what had felt like an eternity, Victor found himself a job at the local pet food factory, where he was employed as a machine operative. He found the work hot, smelly and very unpleasant, but at least it paid the bills and kept him away from Mary and her endless carping.

He had been assigned the task of operating the Pulveriser, a fearsome looking contraption that mangled and crushed the bones and carcasses of the horses, sheep and cattle used in the manufacture of pet food. As he carried out his grisly daily task at the Pulveriser, Victor would do his utmost to put Iris from his thoughts. He tried to convince himself that it was nothing more than a teenage-like infatuation with her body. But *what a body though!*

The weeks plodded slowly by. Three long months later, as Victor was strolling home from his shift at the factory, he spotted something in a pet shop window which he hoped might encourage Mary to be a little more civil towards him. It might even encourage her to heave her lazy, fat arse from her bed.

It was the saddest looking, cutest little puppy that he had ever clapped eyes on. He felt an instant empathy with the poor pathetic creature in the window. A melding of two lonely souls sailing on the choppy sea of despair. And of course, there were very few perks to his job, other than a weekly allowance of pet food, so feeding the beast would be very cheap.

So, without further consideration, he entered the pet shop and purchased the tiny Yorkshire terrier and the pup licked his new owner's face all the way home, expressing its eternal gratitude at being rescued from its miserable position in the flyblown store window.

Victor hadn't seen Mary look as happy since that fateful day he'd proposed to her. She'd made such a fuss over the tiny pooch that he feared her chunky great arms would crush the poor animal. She immediately named the unfortunate pup 'Binky', and from that day onwards things for poor Victor went from bad to diabolically awful!

He was banned from making any kind of noise in the house, lest he upset poor Binky. He had to suffer the indignity of taking the creature walkies and clearing up its mess before and after work each day, a chore which he ultimately refused to carry out after an unfortunate encounter between Binky and an extremely amorous Jack Russell in the local park.

His refusal to go walkies with the creature eventually forced Mary to shift her mighty bulk from her much abused, sagging mattress and take the dog out herself. So perhaps his strike action had done *some* good at least? Over time, Mary actually appeared to lose a little weight and her usual deathly white pallor began to turn into an almost healthy looking colour.

But of course, it didn't last.

Things really turned ugly, however, when Victor returned home from a particularly gruelling day at the Pulveriser to find their small kitchen resembling a vet's surgery. A hastily cut-down cardboard box placed on the floor contained an assortment of Yorkshire Terrier/Jack Russell miniature clones, every one of which seemed to be mewling noisily and demanding attention.

"*Wonderful* news, Victor!" babbled an overexcited Mary. "Our Binky is a *girl* doggy and she's given us this beautiful little family, all of our own!"

Mary was stroking the proud mother so hard that Victor feared its fur would fall out, as he cast his mind back to the incident in the park. The Jack Russell climbing all over Binky's back and the penny dropped with an unpleasant clatter of realisation.

It was shortly after this that he took to roaming the streets of an evening. *Anything* to escape his wife's endless billing and cooing over her precious babies, as she referred to the puppies. During one of these lonely evening treks, Victor's mind once more returned to the lovely Iris Jenkins.

As he entered the cafe for the first time in months, he was surprised to see Iris flash him a beautiful and genuinely warm smile of recognition.

"Long time, no see?" she said as he sat at his usual table in the corner of the small cafe. "I thought maybe you'd moved away...?"

Victor could hardly believe his luck. Iris, the woman of his dreams, was actually talking to him as though she had missed his presence.

"I started a new job, so I haven't had much time to pop in as often as I would have liked," he replied, and he flashed her what he hoped was his winning smile.

When she brought him his regular order of tea and an Eccles cake, she smiled again. "Well, it's lovely to see you again...you've been missed," she added. Victor's hand was trembling as he sipped his tea and watched Iris buzzing around the cafe, serving and tidying up as she went.

The days passed and the two became a little more friendly with his every visit. Eventually, Victor found the courage to invite Iris out for an evening and he was flabbergasted when she accepted.

One thing led to another, as they often do, and within weeks they became lovers. He had confessed from the very beginning that he was a married man and he'd described his dire home life with Mary and her eight dogs in vivid detail.

Iris hadn't entirely believed his tale of woe until she decided to loiter near his house one day, and witnessed first-hand the grossly overweight woman wiping the backside of a yapping Yorkie after it had left a neat pile of shit in the middle of the pavement outside her front door.

That very evening when Iris and Victor met, she came straight out and suggested that he ask his wife for a divorce. "It's not right that a lovely man like you should have put up with a dreadful woman like her! It's not right at all!" she insisted. And, as if to emphasise the benefits of him getting divorced, Iris introduced a grateful Victor to two more positions taken from the pages of the Kama Sutra that night, and he had to concede that she put up a damned fine argument.

When he finally arrived home several hours later, a knackered Victor had indeed put the suggestion to Mary. Unfortunately, she had gone berserk, telling him that she would never divorce him as she was a devout Catholic and that it would be totally against her deep-rooted religious beliefs, all of which was news to a bemused Victor. When he dared to question why she hadn't mentioned her faith before, having never seen her so much as attended a midnight mass at Christmas, she told him that the subject was closed before she forcibly ejected him from her room.

Dark thoughts began to fester within Victor's brain the next day as he fed clean picked carcasses into the mighty Pulveriser. *Why* couldn't she see things from *his* point of view just for once? Why did she have to be so *selfish* about everything?

That evening, as he drove home in his recently acquired and somewhat battered old Ford Focus, he had decided to make Mary an offer he felt she could not refuse.

The discussion, such as it was, was very brief.

Victor, a normally calm and placid character, had seen a red mist descend before his eyes and he had throttled Mary with Binky's dog lead. "Must've been a choke chain!" he cackled insanely, as the great bulk that had been Mary slithered dead onto her bedroom carpet.

He stared at the vast heap of flesh at his feet and watched in distracted fascination as a damp patch spread through the front of her pyjama trousers and a foul odour pervaded the room as she had evacuated her mighty bowels at the instant of death. Her nondescript, piggy eyes bulged hideously from her puffy cheeks and a thin trickle of blood oozed from beneath her mighty torso.

"Blood?" said a puzzled Victor. "What the...?" he mused. But the mystery was soon solved when, with great effort, he managed to roll her over only to discover a flattened and very much dead Binky lying beneath its mummy's corpse.

"Oh well...one down, seven to go!" said Victor, cheerfully as he struggled with his late, though not yet departed wife's body.

It had been a nightmare task, hauling her mighty carcass down the stairs from her bedroom and then dragging her outside before forcing her body into the back of his Ford without being spotted by anyone. Fortunately, they lived at the end of a very quiet lane and Victor was pretty fit after operating the Pulveriser day after day, so he eventually managed the task. There was a brief moment of panic when he couldn't get the rear door closed, but it turned out to be nothing more serious than one of Mary's puffy feet wedged in the hinge, and the problem was soon rectified.

The journey to the factory had been very nerve wracking, especially as he managed to hit every red light on the drive there, but he arrived safely and opened the large double doors to let himself into the loading bay with the spare key which he'd purloined from the foreman's office earlier that day.

Firstly, he attached her beefy legs to a hoist, and, after winching her from the back seats of his car, he dragged her body across the floor of the factory. He was able to raise her up and then lower her into the huge vat normally used for rendering animal carcasses, where he simmered her on a medium heat for one hour and twenty minutes. When he figured that she was 'done' (he ascertained this by prodding her vast buttocks with a pole) he hauled her from the vat, and pulled her via the overhead track and hoist system to the next phase of the procedure.

The now brilliantly red, boiled corpse dribbled great globules of fat and grease as he dragged her across to one of the many butchery tables which lined one side of the factory, and he gently lowered her down onto its stainless-steel surface.

Victor had been watching the men who worked in this section very carefully from his position, high up on the Pulveriser and he soon had pieces of Mary dissected and spread about the metal bench. After her boiling (could've done with another ten minutes, he considered) her flabby flesh came away from the bone with relative ease, and, in little under an hour, he had a sizeable heap of Mary meat on one side and a slightly smaller pile of her bones on the other side.

He was quite amazed to discover just how much flesh there had been on his late wife's carcass, and especially as he had never actually seen her naked. She would surely have fed Battersea Dogs Home for an entire month?

The next stage of the process was pretty straightforward, but again he had made a point of covertly observing the women who operated the rows of mincing machines. Although he had always prided himself on his lack of squeamishness in the past, Victor did find himself gagging somewhat as he fed handful after handful of par-boiled Mary flesh, intestines, organs and gristle into the whirring steel blades of the mincing machine, and he dearly wished that he'd had the foresight to don one of the Perspex visors which the regular operators wore, as his face was splattered with visceral matter flicked up by the rapidly rotating blades.

The smell of minced Mary churning up from the bottom of the machine combined with a revolting, squelching, plopping sound as the chopped meat dropped into a large plastic collection bin below, finally convinced Victor's stomach that it urgently needed to eject all contents held within, and he vomited violently into the gaping intake hole of the mincer.

He stood there retching for several minutes and the foul stench of minced Mary combined with his own vomit made him feel quite light headed and he was mightily relieved as he fed the last joint and handful of intestines into the machine.

Mary was now all but gone and Victor (and his stomach) could begin to relax as the worst was now over.

He wheeled the steaming, stinking plastic bin of minced Mary, together with what he now thought of as his own secret added ingredient, through to the final part of the process, the cannery. Alas, this section was in another part of the building and he had no idea as to how any of the equipment worked, so he was unable to package his dear departed wife into Wuffles Dog Food tins. He therefore tipped the large container of Mary bits into the cannery hopper which would be packaged up the next morning, and he left to set about the final stage of his plan.

He fed her fleshless bones into the Pulveriser and ground them into dust which he knew would later be sold on as fertilizer, the ultimate form of recycling, thought a proud Victor. Just as he was about to switch off the machine, he noticed with horror that Mary's head was still sitting on the butchery table, her hideous, bulging, boiled egg-like eyes glaring at him accusingly, and her fat, sulky mouth pouting as it had always pouted since the day after their wedding.

His already delicate stomach began to churn alarmingly once more, as he quickly scooped up her surprisingly heavy head and dropped it unceremoniously into the Pulveriser, being very careful not to look into her face again as he did so. He heard a hideous cracking/popping noise as the powerful machine made light work of crushing the mush-filled skull into oblivion.

After a thorough tidy up, there was not a single trace of Mary to be found and an exhausted, but very happy Victor drove home and collapsed into his bed for a well-earned sleep.

Victor couldn't resist the urge to buy a few extra cans of Wuffles that week and he was convinced that the whining dogs could somehow sense that their beloved mummy was still feeding them, which in a way, she was.

Not long afterwards, Iris moved in with him, and, as it turned out, she *too* turned out to be a great dog lover. As if that wasn't coincidence enough, Victor also discovered that Iris also suffered from the most appalling ill health and she had to spend much of her time closeted in her bed while he waited on her hand and foot.

But then again, Iris was a rather more clever and imaginative woman than her predecessor had been, and she had left a letter with her solicitor which was to be opened in the event of her sudden death or disappearance.

A REFLECTION OF THE TIMES

It's a strange thing, but have you ever noticed how certain mirrors seem to make you appear slightly different than others? 'Different' perhaps is the wrong word...maybe 'better' is more accurate?

It could possibly be to do with the light refractive properties of the glass, or even the silvering of the actual mirror, but I have spoken to many people on this subject and they have all agreed. They each have their favourite mirror. The one they always use before going out for an evening. The one they know will be the most flattering.

The odd thing is, this may not be the same mirror for different people.

Sophie Parry believed that she would never find her perfect mirror. She certainly had enough of the things in her small Dorking flat. Mirrors ranging from Swedish superstore purchases to older ones bought from charity shops and from small make-up mirrors to full length. Dozens of them, but she was never happy with the way she looked in any of them.

She was always too fat, too thin or just plain ugly!

But the reality was that Sophie, at just 23, was what most people would consider to be beautiful. She was tall and slim, had huge brown eyes, a fashionably full mouth, a figure to die for and long tapering legs. Alas, her reflection would never confirm any of this to her.

Men would flock to her, and her friends, her *true* friends at least, would always say how gorgeous she looked, but Sophie always believed that they were just being kind to a plain, dumpy girl.

So, it was with some amazement that she walked past a dusty old antique shop in a small village near Guildford one day and caught sight of her reflection in a fine old mirror displayed in the window.

She did *indeed* look beautiful!

She nervously entered the shop to take a closer look. It was very expensive. Far more than she would ever want to pay for a mirror...but *what* a mirror! As she stared at her reflection, it seemed as though time stood still and nothing else mattered. The sounds of the traffic outside faded as she continued to admire herself. She had honestly never realised how attractive she was. Sophie could at last see what other people could see.

The shop owner had spoken to her several times before she finally heard him and she reddened with embarrassment when she turned to see the old man standing behind her.

"I see that you like this piece, Miss...?" he asked, slightly awkwardly, nodding his head towards the mirror.

Sophie had to force herself to stop admiring her reflection. "Yes...it's very beautiful. But I guess it's far too expensive for me, I'm afraid," she replied, her voice full of regret.

The old man smiled. "Well...it *is* a beautiful piece...but then, I've had it in stock for quite some time now and it's been a bit quiet, sales-wise, recently. I'm sure we can come to a suitable figure that satisfies both of us?"

When it was delivered to her Dorking flat a few days later, Sophie found herself physically shaking with anticipation as the delivery men gently placed the mirror against the wall in an area she had cleared especially. She was still shaking as she carefully peeled off the wrapping paper and multiple layers of bubble wrap before once more resting her precious find against the lounge wall and stepping back to admire it.

For some reason, she hadn't bothered to look closely at the mirror's frame while it had been in the Antique shop. For the first time, she noticed the finely carved giltwood and marvelled at the delicate way it had been worked. The four sides of the frame had the most beautifully crafted flower buds, flower stems and intricately modelled leaf pattern surrounding the mirror. It was an amazing work of art in its own right.

The mirror itself was in incredible condition given its age, which the antique dealer had put at around the early 1700's It had none of the usual signs of tarnishing or silvering peeling off from the back of the glass, the things normally associated with mirrors of the period. The glass itself was in perfect condition as well. In fact, if she hadn't known better, she would have sworn that it was brand spanking new.

As Sophie stood admiring her reflection, everything else around her, the music playing on her radio, the sound of traffic from the busy Surrey street outside her flat seemed to fade into stillness.

She looked beautiful, she looked slim and she looked healthy. The first time in her adult life that she had felt any of those sensations while looking at her own reflection.

The next day, a couple of workmen arrived to hang the heavy mirror for her, as she didn't trust herself to do it without causing damage if she tried. She watched the men uneasily and didn't leave the room until it was hanging safely on the wall.

It wasn't until a week or so later that Sophie's friends began to notice a change in her behaviour. A party to be held at her flat, which she had been organising for weeks, was suddenly cancelled as she feared her mirror might get damaged. And although she was still totally enamoured with her reflection (all other mirrors in her flat had now been consigned to local charity shops and the dump) she noticed that she had gained a few pounds since buying it and decided to diet and get back into shape.

Her friends invited her out for the evening but she would refuse, telling them that she had things to do. And, anyway, if she went out drinking she would only pile on even more weight. They invited her to the gym to help shape up, but she told them she couldn't afford it and it was a waste of money anyway.

As a designer, it meant that she worked from home and it wasn't at all unusual for her to be closeted in her flat for days, sometimes a week or so at a time when she needed to complete a project, but it had been more than a month since she'd made contact with any of her friends. Her mobile had been switched off, she didn't reply to any emails and the landline went straight to answerphone.

The last person to have seen her was her closest and oldest friend, Marie, who'd been informed by Sophie that she was in the middle of a very big project which she had to complete in six weeks for her demanding, wealthy client. Marie had thought that her friend had looked very pale and thin and when she had asked Sophie if she was okay, she had been curtly told, "I'm fine, thank you. Don't worry about me...I'm just very busy at the moment." And with that Sophie closed the door in her friend's face and Marie heard it being locked and bolted on the other side.

Sophie *had* lost weight. She didn't know how much, as she never weighed herself and didn't even own a set of scales, but she knew she looked so much better for it as she admired herself in her wonderful, precious mirror. Mirrors, she knew, could lie. But this one certainly didn't. As she gazed once more at her reflected image, something which she seemed to spend most of her time doing of late, she knew that she was trim and lovely. She had never looked this good before...not *ever*.

Her hair was long, thick and beautiful, her complexion hadn't been this perfect since childhood and she looked and felt like a woman reborn!

Marie had called round at her friend's flat on the odd occasion over the following weeks hoping to see Sophie, but now she wasn't even answering the door, and she noticed that the doorbell had apparently been disconnected. Two months after her last visit, and after hammering at Sophie's door for some ten minutes with no reply, she decided to call the police.

She was still banging on the door when two officers, an older sergeant and younger constable, appeared on the stairs behind her, accompanied by a local locksmith.

The stench as he unlocked and opened the door was sickening and the locksmith actually threw up on the landing outside, adding to the already horrendous miasma.

"Best you wait here, Miss," advised the sergeant, but Marie looked far too horrified and pale to venture far from her spot on the landing outside her friend's flat.

The older policeman nodded at his white-faced colleague and the two men carefully entered the flat.

"Miss Parry...Sophie Parry...hello...?" the constable called nervously. Neither man knew exactly what to expect, but the sweet, sickening stench of corruption was a familiar clue to them both.

And then they found her...*it*.

Curled up in the foetal position beneath a large, ornate mirror were the putrefying, almost skeletal remains of what had presumably once been Sophie Parry. Her hair was sparse and thin; her once beautiful eyes had turned to a slimy mush which oozed a watery substance from their sockets and ran down the taut, rotting flesh of her face. Dozens of large, black fat flies swarmed about her corpse, buzzing greedily around her ruined eyes and flying in and out of her gaping, shrivel-tongued mouth.

The ashen faced younger officer watched in stunned amazement as he noticed the horrific corpse's stomach moving gently in and out.

"Jesus, Sarge, she's *breathing*! She's *alive*!" he spluttered, incredulously.

As the younger man knelt at her side, the skin of her abdomen heaved upwards and then split open with a disgusting liquid sound, as tens of thousands of well fed, bloated maggots erupted from within Sophie's body, spilling out across the floor and onto the legs of the kneeling policeman.

Many months later, in an old Antique shop in a small village near Guildford, a large, delicately carved gilt mirror was on display in the dusty window.

The craftsmanship was exceptionally fine. In particular, the beautifully carved frame with its four sides wreathed in full and life-like flowers, so fresh looking that they could have been carved very recently.

AND THE DEAD SHALL SPEAK

"Is there anybody there....?"

Craig sniggered and Tina kicked his shin beneath the table to silence him, a warning look flashing in her dark eyes. Craig looked suitably admonished and struggled to keep a straight face, looking down at Tina's small hand held on the one side and the stranger's hand on the other; a Mrs. Battersby, apparently? The medium cast Craig a withering glare and went back to work.

"Is there anybody there? Come forwards...come into the light..." she continued, her voice gentle, almost pleading.

Craig squeezed Tina's hand and, at the same time, the candle in the centre of the round mahogany table guttered slightly. Tina shot Craig a sideways glance as if to say 'I told you so!', but her boyfriend simply closed his eyes and shook his head. He knew about this stuff. A shifty puff from the mediums mouth was all it would have taken to move the candle flame. How could anyone buy into this shit? Christ, the next thing would be table-rapping or bloody ectoplasm, all things which had been debunked a century or so ago.

"I can feel your presence...is there somebody here you wish to contact?"

The candle flame guttered once more, and this time Craig was paying particular attention to Madame Orloff's mouth. No sign of any subtly exhaled air. She was good, this one. But then, he had no idea who the other people around the table were; they could just as easily be working in league with the medium.

Suddenly, Madame Orloff broke the chain by removing her hands from those either side of her, and started scribbling on the large sheet of paper spread before her, her eyes wide and staring straight ahead, transfixed on some distant point...or person. She wrote frantically, mostly complete gibberish, but the odd word forming here and there, as Craig and the others looked on in fascinated silence. His fascination was no doubt completely different to the others present, as they were believers and he decidedly was not.

"With whom do you wish to speak?" continued the medium, pausing briefly from her scribbling as she pretended to listen to the spirit apparently present in the darkened room. She began the frantic writing once again, and this time the words were more legible until there were actually more words than gibberish forming on the paper. Her assistant, seated to her left, removed the now full sheet of paper and replaced it with a fresh one, which Madame Orloff began to fill with yet more scribbled writing.

Then, as suddenly as she had started, she stopped and slumped forward in her chair, supposedly spent after her communications with the other side. The candle guttered once, twice and then went out completely, leaving the parlour in darkness until the assistant switched on a standard lamp at his side, and they could see the pale face of the medium seated quietly with her eyes closed as though asleep in her chair.

Craig tried to get up but Tina gripped his hand and made him stay where he was. She was trying to read some of the words the medium had scribbled across the paper, but it was not easy as the paper was upside down and halfway across the table from where she sat. Slowly, and very theatrically, the medium made a great display of coming to, shaking her head from side to side and fluttering her eyelids against the brighter light of the lamp. She took a sip of what could have been water, but to Craig's mind was more likely gin, and cleared her throat.

"Did anyone come through…did we make contact?" she asked as though she had no idea that she'd been writing on the paper for a good five minutes, even though the evidence was right under her nose. Mrs. Battersby, who Craig suspected was a long-time victim…sorry, *customer* of the medium, was the first to reply.

"Ooh, *yes*, Madame Orloff…indeed you did! You were writing like someone possessed…if you'll pardon the expression, dear?" She sat back in her chair, embarrassed that she had mentioned possession, something that Madame Orloff was allegedly terrified of ever happening to her; possession by an evil entity during one of her trances.

Tina was still trying to read the scribbled words on the paper, craning her neck now to get a better look, as the medium did her best to move the two sheets out of sight before anyone realised that what was written was indeed gibberish and random words. However, as she slyly shifted the papers to her side of the table, she couldn't help noticing that there were words on them that she definitely had *not* written, words which she didn't understood and certainly wouldn't have been able to spell, even on a good day. She stopped trying to hide her handiwork and moved the papers into the centre of the table so all present could see.

"Now what have we here…?" she asked, as though this sort of thing happened every time she held a séance. Tina stood up and walked around the table to get a better view and Craig and Mrs. Battersby joined her so that there were now five pairs of eyes scanning the sheets for some sort of a pattern.

The first sheet was more or less complete rubbish; words and short phrases deliberately written by the medium to impress her audience. LOVE. MISSING YOU. AT REST. I AM HERE. Generalisations which could have meant anything to anyone, depending on how gullible they were feeling at the time. A *placebo* of words, suitable for any grieving person hoping to hear from their dead loved ones.

But the words on the other sheet were very different. Even the style of writing was clearly not the same. Whereas on the first sheet the writing was in a flowing, flowery script, the words on the second sheet were in block capitals and looked spiky and somehow demanded to be read. Mrs. Orloff threw the first sheet to one side, quickly looking at her paying customers to see whether they had noticed, before drawing their attention to the second sheet of paper. Her eyes widened in genuine shock as she read some of the words written upon it.

MURDERING BASTARD. KILLER! UNDER WHORESON! BOARDS.

Both the medium and Mrs. Battersby reddened, the latter saying a prim "Oh...good lord!" before hastily reading more.

YOU KNOW WHO I AM! ILL GET YOU! REMEMBER ST.RICHARDSON. 62. FLOOR. ANLEY. HE DID IT

These were the words which appeared to link together and make any kind of sense. The rest seemed to be little more than random swear words interspersed with yet more gibberish. The five people, the medium, her assistant and the three paying customers all crowded around one end of the table trying to make some sort of sense from the writings. Madame Orloff appeared to be genuinely stunned by what she was reading and even Craig thought that she was either an academy award winning actress or something very odd had occurred in that small room this evening.

Tina was highly impressed and asked the medium if she could perhaps take the second sheet home with her to try and make sense of it, but was quickly refused, Madame Orloff folding the paper and placing it in a drawer secreted in the end of the table nearest to where she sat. Craig, ever the sceptic, thought that was a very handy little secret drawer and he motioned to Tina that the time had come to leave.

"What a load of old bollocks!" he erupted as soon as they had left and were no more than a few yards from the medium's house. "Did you see that secret drawer...and the way she was so keen that we shouldn't take her precious scribbles away with us? I wouldn't be surprised if all *three* of 'em were in it together!" Craig idly kicked at an empty beer can sitting in the middle of the pavement, missing it completely, before he crushed it underfoot instead, feeling faint satisfaction and a vague sense of triumph.

Tina stopped, turned and looked him in the eye. "I know you don't give any credence to this stuff...I *know* you think it's all a load of rubbish, and normally I'd agree with you. But there was definitely *something* strange happening there tonight. She may well be a bloody great fraud, but even *she* was surprised by the things written on that second paper."

She let Craig think about that for a second before marching off along the street towards the bus stop. Craig stood mouth hanging open for a while, before following her. As they waited in silence for the bus to arrive, Craig's brow furrowed as an idea came into his head.

"Okay," he said. "So why don't we go back there, break into her house and get that piece of paper. If it'll put this crap out of your mind, it'd be well worth the risk!" Tina turned and smiled smugly, just as their bus turned the corner. "No need for that. I managed to snap it on my phone before she whipped the thing away!"

The next evening, Craig returned home from work to find the living room carpet covered in sheets of A4 paper, each with a single word written on it. Tina was kneeling in front of them, moving each sheet around trying to make sense of the words. "What the hell are you doing? Hasn't this party trick of hers gone far enough, Tina?" he asked before slumping down on the settee, searching for the tv remote.

Tina looked up in surprise as though she hadn't heard Craig come in.

"There's a pattern here, I'm sure of it," she stated, matter-of-factly, and continued staring at the sheets spread about the carpet. Craig shook his head. "There's a pattern alright; do any of those words make the sentence: gullible fucking idiot?" Tina stood up and then sat on the settee beside him.

"*You* can think whatever you like, but I'm convinced that *someone…something* was trying to pass a message on. Didn't you see the expression on her face when she read this?" Craig pulled a face and, having found the remote control, he began flicking through the television channels looking for something interesting to watch.

Tina sighed. "Okay, granted the first sheet was undoubtedly her doing; a load of randomly selected words to hook people in. But *this*…this is entirely different and she had no idea what she'd written on this sheet!"

Craig pressed the off button and stared at his girlfriend. "Tina…so what? So what if she didn't know what she'd written; what does it prove and why do you give a shit anyway?"

Tina glared at him with undisguised anger on her face. She pointed at the first few sheets on the floor. "*Someone* is trying to tell us something, you moron! Look…" She bent down and picked up the first four pages, holding them in front of him like cue cards, and then placed them carefully on the carpet in front of his chair. KILLER. UNDER. FLOOR. BOARDS. "Read!" she said, and Craig begrudgingly glanced at the words.

"So? There's a killer under the floorboards? It doesn't make any sense…you're scratching for an answer to a non-existent question here!"

He stood suddenly and stared at the other words scattered across the floor.

"Okay...so who the bleedin hell is St Richardson and where does 62 come into your plan?" he snapped, feeling unreasonably angry. Tina bent over and shuffled the sheets about for a second. They now read: KILLER UNDER FLOOR BOARDS 62 RICHARDSON ST. Craig's brow furrowed as he studied the words, then he shook his head. "This is crazy! You're playing with words like this is some kind of game of Scrabble! You could make a dozen...a *hundred* different sentences from those words if you tried for long enough!"

Tina was surprised by his anger. She knew he had a temper, but losing it over something so...so *minor*? But she knew when it was time to back off and leave well alone. "Okay...it was just something to do until you got back...forget it." And she began to pick up the sheets of paper, placing them into a pile before leaving them on the coffee table. Craig stepped forward and hugged her.

"I'm sorry, babe! I just don't want you to get sucked into something that's so obviously a put-up job, that's all." He held her close and gently stroked her back, and slowly she melted into him and returned the hug. "Okay," she said finally. "I'll leave it alone...let me go and make supper and we'll have an early night." Craig smiled at the insinuation in her voice and released her.

But as Tina prepared their supper, she determined to find out more about number 62, Richardson Street, whether Craig liked the idea or not.

*

Madame Orloff, it seemed, kept very strange hours. Tina had been ringing her doorbell and knocking for a good five minutes before the medium appeared, somewhat dishevelled, as she eased open her door a couple of inches and peered out, somehow managing to resemble a hamster disturbed from a lengthy hibernation.

"Whaa...oh, it's you. What do you want at this hour of the day, may I ask?" Tina glanced at her watch; 1:30, the day almost half over for many of the population. Tina smiled her best smile, and stepped forward as the medium remained staring at her through the three-inch gap between door and jamb. "I need to talk to you...about last night."

Madame Orloff's eyes narrowed warily. "What about last night? What do you want?" she repeated, making no effort to open the door any further. Tina smiled again. "You *know* what I'm talking about," she replied. "The second sheet of writing...something odd about it."

The medium looked more wary than ever. She was well used to prying snoopers trying to de-bunk her and her kind in these so-called enlightened times. Suddenly, she opened the door wider, stepped out onto the porch and peered over Tina's shoulder, scanning the street either side of her. "What's wrong?" asked Tina, somewhat nervously.

Madame Orloff peered at the younger woman for several seconds, before stepping back into her hallway, leaving the door ajar for her visitor. Tina cautiously walked into the house as the medium closed the door quickly behind her, clicking the lock and fixing the door chain in place. "You can't be too careful these days, young lady. I know there are always reporters, television people and the like who enjoy nothing more than trying to expose so called bogus mediums! It's happened to a couple of my colleagues and I have to be careful..." she petered off, before heading down the hallway towards the parlour where she had held the séance the previous evening.

Tina followed her in silence and looked the medium up and down as she did so. She guessed that Madame was in her late fifties – maybe even mid-sixties. She was wearing a silken dressing gown over an old-fashioned lace nightdress. Her greying hair was awry and the carefully applied make up she'd been wearing the night before was now smeared, her eye liner now smudged which made her resemble a raccoon. Tina thought that Madame Orloff looked very much like Bette Davis in *What Ever Happened to Baby Jane*.

She was led into the séance room and Madame motioned for her to sit. The medium sat in the same place she had occupied the previous evening and Tina automatically sat in her original position. Madame Orloff, to Tina's amazement, lit a long, thin cigar, took a long pull and then coughed heartily for several minutes, before stubbing the thing out and fixing her visitor with a steady gaze.

"Right...get to the point! What are you talking about?"

For the first time since deciding to call on the medium, Tina suddenly felt nervous. It was one thing to bring up the subject of the second sheet, but something completely different to insinuate that the first one had been totally bogus. And especially when sitting face to face with the very person she was accusing!

"Okay," she began. 'I'll get straight to the point. There was something very different about the second piece of paper compared to the first one you'd written." The medium's eyes narrowed once more, but she said nothing. "I had the distinct impression that *you* were as surprised by what it said as *we* were. Am I right?" Tina sat forward and folded her hands on the table. Madame Orloff did almost the complete opposite; she sat right back in her chair, wringing her hands nervously, her eyes darting from side to side as though searching for a reply somewhere in the darkly furnished room.

After several minutes, she said, "Are you working for one of those hateful rags? Because if you are..." She left whatever threat she had in mind unspoken, and Tina almost smiled as she thought of Madame Orloff summoning up some hideous demon to carry out an awful revenge upon her. "Absolutely not! I came to your séance for genuine reasons…though I'll admit that I had to drag my boyfriend here against his will, and he *is* the biggest sceptic in the world. But I've been to several séances in the past…and as we both know, not everything is as real as perhaps it could be?"

The medium shot her visitor a withering glance, but Tina help up her hand and ploughed on. "However, after last night, I'm convinced that you actually *do* have the gift…even though maybe you weren't aware that you had it." Tina raised a querying eyebrow and watched her host's face carefully. Madame Orloff stared at her for a while, before lowering her gaze to her hands, which were clenched tightly together as though her very life depended on it.

"This is a very hard life these days. Time was, there were dozens…possibly hundreds of us mediums throughout the country. But then the likes of Houdini and many more of his ilk gradually destroyed the business with their witch hunts…and now there are very few of us left…" She re-lit her cigar, took a long drag and exhaled a huge pall of grey-blue smoke, before extinguishing it once more. Tina smiled encouragingly for her to continue.

"I admit it…I have never been blessed with the true gift…though I've had my moments, mostly many years ago. So, when I saw that second sheet of writing, I confess it proper scared me! I like to think what I do here gives a lot of lonely people some sort of hope for the future…hope that there is an afterlife…that they will be re-united with their loved ones. And what harm does it do, anyhow?" Tina could have said many things at that point, but she wasn't here for a debate about the rights and wrongs of dodgy mediums; she was here for information, so she bit her tongue and smiled.

"So what happened last night then? What was different about that from all the other séances you've held here?" Tina prompted. The medium's eyes grew wide and she shook her head. "I don't know…I have no idea!" Tina sat back in her chair and considered the medium's reply. There must have been *something* unusual, something different, surely?

"Think, Madame Orloff…try and *think* what was unusual about last night's séance. What did you do that was different from any other night?" The older woman leant forwards and held her head in her hands, eyes closed, mulling over the events of the séance.

"I can think of nothing out of the ordinary…other than the fact that you and your friend were new clients. Mrs. Battersby has been coming to me for several years…she used to bring her husband, but he hasn't attended for a few months now, and my assistant, Mr. Cardew, has been with me for over two years. So, in answer to your question; no, nothing different apart from you two arriving."

Madame Orloff sat upright in her séance chair and absently mindedly brushed back a wayward lock of her long, greying hair. "But," she added,

"I will confess, though I'd deny it vigorously if questioned, that I did *feel* …what's the word? *Different…odd…strange* as the séance progressed. I actually *did* go into a trance-like state for a time, and the words written on that second piece of paper were as much of a surprise to me as they were to everyone else around the table."

Tina nodded and smiled thinly at the old woman's confession.

"Can we look at that second paper again…please?" she asked.

The medium thought for a moment, then nodded her head. It seemed almost as though she was scared to read the words on the paper, but realised that they would never get to the bottom of the mystery until they did. Tina noticed immediately that her camera phone hadn't picked up all the words on the sheet. In fact, she must have only snapped around half of them. But then, she had taken the photo pretty rapidly out of necessity.

Madame Orloff remained seated as Tina looked over her shoulder and they studied the writing together. "Apart from all the swear words, most of it looks like gibberish to me," said the medium, her brow creased, trying to make head or tail of the jumbled mass of words.

"That looks like it could be an address, possibly?" Tina pointed out the 62 and the Richardson St. The medium nodded slowly in agreement, still trying to form the random words into anything other than just that; random words. Then suddenly, she had an epiphany and slammed both hands on the mahogany table, causing Tina to jump.

"Look!" she said, pointing with a slightly gnarled index finger. "There! KILLED UNDER FLOOR BOARDS…it's there, clear as the nose on your face!" There was a look of triumph on the old lady's face as she swivelled round to face Tina. Tina, of course, had already spotted the UNDER FLOOR BOARDS part, but could hardly share that fact without raising the medium's suspicions. But she thought it had said KILLER, whereas it definitely read KILLED.

They studied the words for the next ten minutes or so, but no other sentences immediately leapt out at them. It was very difficult without any sort of punctuation to help. Finally, Tina made a suggestion.

"Would you mind if I were to make a copy…take a photo of this and then study it when I get home? I could come back to see you tomorrow and we could compare notes…if you're happy with that?"

The older woman looked very dubious about the whole idea, and sat quietly for a few moments to consider her options. But then, she was as intrigued about what all this meant as her visitor was. "Alright, but only on condition that I keep the original here with me…and that no one else knows anything about this, or anything else we've discussed here today. Agreed?"

"Agreed!" And they shook hands like the fellow conspirators they were.

*

Fortunately for Tina, that night was Craig's boys' night out, and she knew that he would either stagger home in the wee small hours and crash out on the settee or, as he often did, sleep on the floor at one of his mates for the night. Either way, she was free to study in peace and quiet, for tonight at least. The longer Tina studied the words now once again spread all across the lounge floor, the more confused she became. She had already compared the photo she had taken on the night of the séance with the photo taken earlier that day, and there definitely seemed to be more of them?

"Im-bloody-possible!" she said aloud. "How can that be?" but the more she looked at them, the more new words she discovered in the jumble of lettering. It was only when she started printing them off, that she realised just how many extra words there actually were.

There was now a ME, PIN, HEAD, BATTERED, MURDERED on the printed-out sheets, as well as a lot of other words which made no sense whatsoever, such as ANGEL, ASLEEP, CHAIR and, bizarrely, SLIPPERS.

Tina thought that she would make a point of asking Madame Orloff whether Richardson Street meant anything to her tomorrow, before realising that the medium had already seen that address and it had, apparently, not registered with her. She was feeling pretty tired after all her detective work, a headache was starting to throb behind her right eye. Enough! She headed off to bed and would start again in the morning.

Tina was rudely awoken at 6:30 by Craig throwing open the curtains and flooding their bedroom with sunlight. "I thought you were leaving all this crap! You promised me you'd forget all this nonsense, but could you leave it alone? Oh, no…not you! Miss bleedin Marple!" He was holding a handful of screwed up papers, the papers he had snatched off the lounge floor when he returned home moments earlier.

Tina knuckled sleep from her eyes and propped herself up on a couple of pillows, pulling the duvet up to cover her nakedness. She felt oddly uncomfortable with the situation for some reason, almost as though Craig were a stranger who'd burst into her room, and she didn't like the look in his eyes or the fact that he'd woken her up so abruptly. She brushed back her matted hair and looked at him coldly.

"Don't come back here still half pissed, and then tell me what I can and cannot do! I find this stuff interesting, and if I decide to look into it…then I bloody well will!" Craig's face was a picture of rage. He coloured a bright red and screwed up the papers in his hands, before ripping them, awkwardly, into small pieces before her eyes. "Fine! Then you can look into it without me around to watch you make a fool of yourself!" and with that, he tossed the rest of the torn paper into the air and stormed out of the bedroom. Moments later, Tina heard the flat door slam, shortly followed by his car door, and he was gone.

"Fine!" she said to the empty room, shaken by his crazed outburst.

*

By the time she arrived at Madame Orloff's house later that morning, she had managed to calm down. For the life of her, she couldn't imagine why Craig had been so enraged by her interest in the events of the séance. She had seen a totally different side to him these last couple of days, and was, on reflection, quite happy that he had left. As she rang the doorbell, a fresh set of printed sheets carefully placed in a folder beneath her arm, she was musing whether she would have to wait five minutes for the medium to answer, when the door suddenly opened and Madame Orloff, fully dressed and made-up this time, ushered her quickly inside.

"Follow me," said the medium without preamble, as she swept, majestically, down the dingy hall towards the séance room. She motioned for Tina to sit, this time beside her, as she took the original sheet from the secret drawer and spread it out on the table top.

"There's something *very* odd going on here...er...?"

"Tina." The medium nodded. "There's something very odd going on here, Tina. Look!" Tina rubbed her eyes as she stared at the paper. Where yesterday, there had been random words spread haphazardly across the sheet, there were now lines of writing...part *sentences* even, and there were a lot more of them!

"This is *crazy!*" said a stunned Tina. She was shaking her head and for the first in her life, she genuinely could not believe her eyes. Madame Orloff nodded brusquely then placed a motherly hand on the younger woman's shoulder. "Crazy, yes...but we can both see it, so it must be real? I was beginning to think that I was going mad...so I'm very pleased that *you* can see it too!"

The two women fell silent as they sat beside one another, staring at the words written on the ordinary looking piece of paper spread before them.

The part-sentences were tantalisingly incomplete, but at least they were more helpful than the random words had been. "I saw this yesterday." Tina pointed excitedly at one group of words in particular.

BATTERED WITH ROLLING PIN KILLED ME

The two women looked at one another, and then back to the words. "So..." began Tina, "it seems that someone was murdered...beaten to death with a rolling pin, of all things, and then hidden under some floorboards...possibly at 62, Richardson Street...wherever *that* is."

The medium nodded in agreement, adding, "And my guess would be that they were asleep in a chair at the time...maybe wearing slippers."

It was Tina's turn to agree. "Yes, that makes sense!" she replied, excitedly, "but the big questions are who and where."

Madame Orloff shook her head. "Who, where and *when* more like. Don't forget, this is a message from the grave...it could be someone who died last week or a hundred years ago, for all we know."

"I don't suppose you have a computer, do you?" asked Tina, doubtfully.

The older woman laughed and shook her head. "Now why would I need one of those contraptions?"

Tina shrugged. "Not to worry, I can do it when I get home." And she suddenly thought of Craig and that strange, almost insane look on his face earlier that morning. She shuddered as though someone had walked over her grave.

"How about an A-Z then...?" she asked.

"Now you're talking my kind of language, young lady! Books, I do have!"

There were three Richardson's in the book, one Richardson Avenue, and two Richardson Roads, but not a Richardson Street to be found. They also tried St. Richardson on the off chance, but no joy there either.

"There's nothing to say that it's even in this area, is there? It could be miles away," suggested the medium as she snapped the A-Z shut and shoved it across the table.

"Hmmmm, you're right...it could be anywhere. I'll Google it when I get back."

Madame Orloff had not the faintest idea what Googling involved, but nodded as though she understood.

Tina looked thoughtful. "There are a couple of other *huge* questions that need answering of course; why is this person contacting you, and, more bizarrely, how on earth does the writing on the paper keep changing from day to day."

*

She was pleased to note that the lights were out at the flat as she arrived outside. The day had simply flown by and she was amazed to see that it was 8:30 when she looked at her watch, bidding a hasty farewell to Madame Orloff before rushing off to catch the bus home. She hadn't eaten all day, as they had been too engrossed with their work to think of food, but now she was ravenous. As she entered the flat, she could see that Craig had been back at some stage to collect some of his things. There was a terse note blue-tacked to the lounge door: *I'm not staying around to see you make an even bigger dick of yourself! I'll be back when I've found somewhere to get the rest of my gear.*

And that was that. End of relationship and over *what*, exactly?

A wave of sorrow swept through Tina and she hugged herself as there was no one else around to do it. She poured herself a large glass of Rioja and stood in the empty kitchen, wondering why Craig had acted so weirdly. "Nothing different apart from *you* two arriving..." The words of Madame Orloff drifted into her mind for no apparent reason, and she sat down heavily on a kitchen chair and sipped thoughtfully at her wine.

"*You* two arriving..."

Tina suddenly had the overwhelming urge to lock the front door and attach the security chain. She found herself shaking and as she picked up her wine once more, it splashed over the side of the glass, a blood red stain forming on the white kitchen worktop. "Jesus...NO!" Surely all this wasn't somehow connected to Craig?

"*You* two arriving..."

But why *had* he acted so strangely both before and after the séance? And why did he lose it when he found that she'd been working on the random words again? She actually knew very little about him, now she came to think of it. They had met at a friend of a friend's party some five months ago, and, what with one thing leading to another, he had moved in with Tina two months later and they had been very happy for all of that time.

Okay, so he'd always had his regular nights out with the boys, she'd been fine with that, but she had never actually *met* any of them and he'd always been loath to discuss his past or his friends, other than the mutual acquaintance who had held the party. The more she thought about Craig, the more she realised that she actually knew *nothing* about him. Tina shivered, though it was warm in the flat.

The phrase *you* two arriving had now morphed into *him* arriving.

Tina didn't sleep much at all that night. She had even dragged the settee across the room and wedged it against the door as an added security measure. As soon as nine o'clock finally arrived, she was on the phone to a local locksmith arranging to have a new, upgraded lock fitted as soon as possible, and only when that had been done, did she leave her flat and go to see Madame Orloff.

This time, the door opened before she even rang the bell, and a white faced Madame Orloff ushered her into the séance room without a word passing between them. Still without speaking, she opened the secret drawer and handed the sheet of paper to Tina, jabbing a finger at one particular phrase which had appeared overnight.

HES DID IT. HES MURDERED ME. HES DID IT. SIX MONTHS. KILLED ME

The medium was ashen faced and trembling slightly as she finally broke the silence. "I don't know how to say this, Tina...but I think that maybe your young man has something to do with all this. *He's did it*...so the murderer was clearly a man...and the only man present, aside from Mr. Cardew, who is sixty-seven, was your friend." She rested her hand lightly, reassuringly, on the younger woman's arm, waiting for her response.

Tina was as pale as the medium and trembling every bit as much.

"I came to the same conclusion last night...before I'd even read this ...and to think, I didn't even know him six months ago."

Madame Orloff looked genuinely shocked. "But how will we *prove it*? We don't even know who it is he's killed, let alone where or why."

The pair sat in silence for several minutes, contemplating their next course of action. Suddenly, Tina sat bolt upright and slapped her forehead with the palm of her hand. "We hold another séance! That's the answer!"

Madame Orloff looked doubtful about the idea, but Tina continued, undaunted. "This jumble of words is all very well...we're slowly learning things day by day, but it's all too slow! He could be out there murdering someone else in the meantime, and without a body, there's no proof...we have nothing at all. But whoever was murdered clearly has some sort of affinity with you and we might get the answers we need before something else happens. Please...?"

*

It was arranged for the following evening. The same people would be present, with the obvious exception of Craig. Madame Orloff looked understandably nervous as Mr. Cardew lit the candle before switching off the lights, and Mrs. Battersby, Tina, Madame Orloff and Mr. Cardew linked hands around the small mahogany table. The room fell unnaturally silent as the medium asked the question:

"Is there anybody there...?"

It was so quiet in the parlour, that Tina was convinced everyone around the table could hear her heart hammering inside her chest. "Is there anybody there...come forward...come into the light...?"

The candle gave the smallest of flickers, then burnt straight and upright once more. Madame Orloff gave Tina a quick sideways look, their eyes meeting briefly, before she concentrated harder than she had ever done, willing the unhappy spirit to make contact as it had earlier.

Abruptly, the medium began to twitch, her hands clawing at the table, and her assistant quickly placed a pencil in her hand and slid a clean sheet of paper in front of her. Immediately, she started to write, not in her own delicate, flowing script, but using the now familiar jagged lines she and Tina had been studying over the last few days.

HES KILLED ME! HES DID IT!

There were more unintelligible words and then some familiar ones, coming faster and faster. The pencil snapped clean in two and Mr. Cardew replaced it with a new one.

STRICHARDSON62KILLEDUNDERFLOORAN LEYBOARDSHESDIDITROLLINGPINSLIPPER SWHORESONSIXMONTHS

The letters came out in a continuous string now, almost impossible to read or decipher, and as one sheet was filled or a pencil broke or wore down, it was instantly replaced by Mr. Cardew, who looked in a state of shock, as he had never witnessed anything like this in his time with Madame Orloff.

Suddenly, the writing stopped.

Madame Orloff, or rather the person or thing inhabiting her body, brushed the written sheets of paper to one side and snatched a fresh one from an astonished Mr. Cardew.

HES DID IT   HES HERE NOW!

Tina's mouth fell open and her heart was now racing so fast that she thought she may well pass out. She looked across to Mr. Cardew who shook his head and stared dumbfounded at the medium. Then Tina glanced over at Mrs. Battersby, who, although wide-eyed and ashen coloured, had a slightly bemused expression of her face.

ITS HER! HES DID IT! HES KILLED ME! WHORESON! BITCH!

Madame Orloff collapsed face down on the table. At first, as Mr. Cardew fussed over her, Tina thought the séance had been too much for her and she had died of exhaustion; she was no spring chicken, after all. But then she let out a low, agonised groan, coughed as though her lungs would burst and suddenly sat up, very pale looking and visibly shaking as she looked across to Tina.

Mr. Cardew switched on the standard lamp behind the medium's chair before fetching her a glass of water, which she knocked back in one.

"Right..." she said, her voice wavering slightly, "tell me what happened. *Did* we make contact?"

Mr. Cardew patted her shoulder gently. "Please, Mabel...you must rest...please." But Mabel was not for turning.

"Tina...?" she implored. Tina looked her steadily in the eye, a weak smile on her face. "Yes...you made contact. But the result may not be exactly what you had in mind..." The medium looked both exhausted and utterly bewildered. The three other people present were all staring at her as she struggled to comprehend what had taken place while she was in her trance state.

"Read the last sheet," suggested Tina.

Madame Orloff noticed the scattered papers on the floor beside the table and then drew the final piece of paper towards her and focused on what was written there.

ITS HER! HES DID IT! HES KILLED ME! WHORESON! BITCH!

The medium looked more confused than ever now, her brow furrowing as she tried to digest the words upon the paper. They didn't make any sense...

"He never could spell, the dumb bastard! Partially dyslexic, you see...could never manage the simple words...like SHE. Always wrote it as HES...the prick!"

The tension was palpable as all eyes turned towards Mrs Battersby, who was leaning back in her chair, smiling as though she didn't have a care in the world, just chatting about an old friend. It was Tina's turn to be dumfounded now.

"You *know* this person...this *spirit*?" she asked.

Mrs Battersby howled with laughter until the tears ran down her cheeks, she slapped her chubby hands on her meaty thighs and rocked from side to side until Tina thought the chair might break under the strain. Slowly, she stopped and wiped her tear-streaked face with her hands, even now, the odd giggle erupting from deep within.

"Oh Lord...sorry about that, dears. But you have to laugh, don't you?" she asked, matter-of-factly. When no one replied, she elaborated. "Of *course* I know this person. I ought to; I lived with the nasty old shit for thirty-four years before I smashed his head in with a rolling pin!"

The room was silent after this revelation, three pairs of eyes stared at the face of Mrs Battersby. Mrs Battersby, the lovely old school dinner lady, who was liked by all and wouldn't hurt a fly.

"But..." began Mabel Orloff, "but the names on the paper? Richardson Street...number 62...?"

Mrs Battersby laughed again, grunted loudly as she bent to pick up the discarded sheets from the floor, snatched up a pencil, and set to work.

"Look!" she said, and started underlining what appeared to be more random words. "I knew it was Stanley the moment you wrote HES the other night. And there was me thinking you were another bleedin fake like all the others. Ha!"

When she had finished, the gibberish started to make sense.

STANLEY RICHARDSON, 62. KILLED SIX MONTHS AGO. UNDER FLOORBOARDS. ANGEL

"You probably figured most of this out already," she continued. "What you didn't know, of course, was that Stanley and I were never actually married. I'm Angela Battersby from my first marriage...and he, of course, was Stanley Richardson. He was sixty-two when I did for him...and all over a row about me fetching his bleedin slippers for him! The lazy whoreson!"

The room fell silent again as the others digested what they had just been told.

"I'm glad it's all over, truth be told; he's been stinking up my living room for the last six months, lying there, rotting under the floorboards. He always was a smelly old bastard!"

Tina shook her head in disbelief.

"And to think," she began, "that no one would ever have known until Madame Orloff here made contact with him," she said, her voice full of awe.

Angela Battersby started laughing once more. "That silly daft mare? She couldn't make contact with someone sitting next to her on a bleedin' *bus*! It's *you*! *You're* the one with the gift...didn't you know...?"

Before Tina could reply, the bulb in the standard lamp flickered abruptly and went out, plunging the room into darkness. There was an ear splitting, terrified strangled scream followed by a hideous thud and a soft, wet squelching sound. When at last Mr. Cardew found the presence of mind to grope around and locate the main light switch, Tina looked in horror at the body of Angela Battersby slumped in her chair.

Her eyes had been plucked out and they dangled down her puffy cheeks, her tongue lolled from her mouth like a fat, pink slug, and the heavy candlestick, which had once sat in the centre of the séance table, was now imbedded deep within her brain, grey matter and blood running freely from the hideous wound, trickling down her nose and dripping from its tip onto her ample chest.

Stanley had had the last word, it seemed, and all this over a row about a pair of slippers?

The three survivors sat looking at one another in shocked silence. They were clearly thinking the same thing: *This* was going to take some explaining!

Tina turned to Madame...Mabel Orloff.

"Do you know where Mrs Battersby lived?" she asked.

The medium thought for a moment. "Yes...I have her address in my file. Why?"

Tina didn't reply, instead turning to Mr. Cardew.

"Do you have your car here, Mr. C?"

Mr. Cardew looked perplexed. "Yes, it's parked outside. Why?"

Tina smiled.

"Then I think it's time we re-united these two love birds...under the floorboards, back at home...where they belong."

Mabel Orloff and Mr. Cardew considered the suggestion for a moment, and then smiled at Tina.

"Good idea!" they said in perfect unison.

BOYS WILL BE BOYS

The whole experience had been nothing like he imagined it would be.

Watching too many Hollywood romantic movies had lulled him into a false sense of wellbeing which had left him ill prepared for the grim realities of it all. He felt cheated. Cheated and sick, and not necessarily in that order, the truth be told. No, *sick* definitely had the upper hand of the two emotions.

It should have been a wonderful time, according to all those movies, as well as many of his friends. Something that would stay within his memory for the rest of his life, a truly *unforgettable* experience which he would treasure forever. And, in truth, it *would* linger inside his head for the rest of his days, but for all the wrong reasons.

He had pleaded with his wife to be excused, *begged* her to tell the midwife and doctor that she didn't want him present at the birth of their first child. Even though the poor woman had been suffering the agonies of labour for over six hours and had now been given an epidural to help numb the pain, he could only think of himself; of his phobia with blood and his terror of hospitals and all things medical.

Then, the unborn infant had shown signs of stress and the doctor roughly brushed the father aside, telling him in no uncertain terms that he must remain in the room to comfort his wife as they carried out an emergency forceps delivery to save the baby's life.

While his wife endured the agonies of the cold metal forceps being pushed inside her, her husband could only squeeze her hand in a half-hearted attempt at easing her suffering and trying to show his empathy with her plight. In reality, he was battling with a rising nausea and the overwhelming urge to pass out, right there on the delivery room floor.

Then, it was over. A nurse whipped the freshly born child over to some kind of device which sucked the mucus and blood from the baby's nose and it took its first gasping breath of air after living in fluid for nine months.

So, no slap on the backside from a hefty, rosy-cheeked midwife, then? Another Hollywood myth blown out of the water.

The child was wrapped in a clean white towel and handed unceremoniously to its mother. "It's a *boy!*" said the midwife, unenthusiastically, while the doctor worked feverishly with needle and suture to repair the damage to the mother's torn vagina, caused by the emergency use of forceps.

Unremarkably, the mother began to throw up, and the midwife pushed the tiny child into the arms of its father, before fetching a bowl for his wife.

In the movies, the new born babe is a lovely clean, pink hue with fluffy hair and rosy cheeks. Whereas *this* baby was covered in a thick white creamy substance, mingled with traces of his mother's blood.

"It looks like snot...or *spunk*?" the father couldn't help thinking as he gazed down at his new son, as though it were a creature from another world.

Then he looked at the misshapen head and involuntarily held the child at arm's length. Not only did the head resemble the shape of a coconut, but it was also *yellow*! In fact, the boy's entire body was yellow, and, worse yet, the baby was covered in a thick, coarse dark *fur*! The tiny arms, back and legs were as hairy as any chimp, hair growing like sideburns forming a tiny beard on the infant's trembling chin.

"Look, Mum, Daddy's already bonding with his new son!" cooed the midwife. Mistakenly, as it happened. Nothing could be further from the truth in fact, as all 'Daddy' wanted to do was to hand the monkey-boy back to the midwife and then get the hell out of there to have a stiff drink or ten.

But his wife was in a bad way; she had lost a lot of blood during the birth and she was in a state of collapse after the strenuous hours of labour. A worried-looking doctor spoke in hushed tones to the midwife, and, much to the father's relief, he was ushered out of the delivery room and instructed to remain in the waiting room until he was called for.

Okay, so it wasn't the stiff drink he really needed, but anything, *anything*, was better than being in that room with the kidney bowls full of bloody instruments and what could only be described as '*bits*' of his wife. Those and the umbilical cord and placenta, together with the blood ...lots of thick red blood.

*

She died that night without regaining consciousness.

The doctor had missed the artery, severed during the forceps procedure, until it had been far too late to do anything about it, and though they worked on his wife for a very long time, she was now a cold, dead body down in the mortuary.

And even *now*, all he could think about was himself!

Never mind that she had suffered all that pain giving birth to their child. Never mind that she was cold and lifeless and lying alone on a stainless-steel trolley deep in the bowels of the hospital.

What would *he* do now? After all, *he* was alone, too. Just him and, oh God, him and the Monkey Boy, of course. The thought crossed his mind, more accurately, it didn't just *cross*, it remained resolutely within his brain, that he should flee the hospital. Run away and leave Monkey Boy in the nursery and never return, never see that misshapen skull, or the yellow skin covered in thick, coarse hair again.

But then, a very rare spasm of guilt entered his head. Even *he* couldn't leave the dead body of his wife in the hospital morgue.

His mind conjured up the scenario of the police getting involved if he didn't return to sort out 'the arrangements' for her burial. He could imagine the press getting hold of the story and them dragging it out for weeks, possibly months. His business would be ruined, his friends would desert him, his life would also be over, just as surely as his wife's was.

The newspaper headlines flashed before his self-pitying, tear-filled eyes:

"HUSBAND FLEES HOSPITAL AFTER WIFE DIES GIVING BIRTH TO MONKEY BOY!" and " COWARDLY 'FATHER' LEAVES BRAVE, DEAD WIFE AND HORRIBLY DEFORMED BABY TO ROT IN HOSPITAL!"

Those and a dozen other banner headlines ran through his mind, and he knew, for no other reason than self-preservation, that he could not simply leave here and slip out, unnoticed, into the night.

He also realised. with dawning horror, that he couldn't leave his...the word almost refused to form in his head...his 'son', the Monkey Boy, either.

*

As it turned out, the yellow tinge to the boy's skin was caused by a touch of jaundice, which was soon remedied. Also, the misshapen skull had apparently been caused by the forceps delivery and it quickly returned to a more skull-shaped skull after a few days.

Even the 'thick fur' somehow rubbed off after a week or so. "Perfectly natural. Many babies have exactly the same thing at birth," he was assured by a nurse, and she had been right. The boy was now a healthy pink colour and had no more hair than any other baby of a similar age. "So what are you going to call the little chap, then?" asked the nurse, whose specialist subject appeared to be baby fur.

"I, erm...I haven't thought about that just yet. A lot on my mind; you know how it is?" he replied. The truth be told, he had only ever thought of the child as Monkey Boy since its birth, but at least he had the good sense not to mention this to anyone else.

Even *he* realised that a child couldn't go through life with a name like Monkey Boy. Suppose he ended up going to Eton or Cambridge? What then?

"Well, best to think of a name, and as soon as...just in case?" added the nurse, mysteriously. He had no idea what "just in case" meant, but agreed to put some thought to the matter, more to shut her up than anything else.

He considered 'Kong' and 'Cheetah' briefly, but they were simply ludicrous notions. 'Damien; was also in the running (after all, hadn't *he* killed *his* mother?) but thought maybe that was a tad obvious. Then, the idea to Google the word 'death' came to him and that led him to *mors, mortis*, the Latin for death or 'of death' and he decided to corrupt these words into Morris, which was what the child was finally called.

There would be no christening; his father figured that anyone who came into this world by causing the death of his own mother did not deserve the protection allegedly offered by such a sacred ritual. The boy would just have to fend for himself in that respect.

Morris was a strange boy from day one.

He never cried, not *ever*; even when he was wet or hungry, he would just lie patiently in his cot until the rapidly hired nanny attended to his needs.

"He's such a *wonderful* baby!" she would enthuse about her charge. "Just a little *angel*, he is!"

His father thought that 'angel' was just about the complete antithesis of what the child *really* was.

He would lay there, his big dark eyes staring up at his father with no trace of emotion, no hint of a baby mind behind the steady, cold stare. Just a chilling sensation that the adult was being studied by the baby, like a specimen in a laboratory. His father was convinced that his son had been brain damaged during the birth, but the hospital strenuously denied that anything of the sort had occurred.

No, he was just a very *quiet* baby, perhaps a little unusually so, but by no means brain damaged.

Morris could speak fluently by the age of three. This in itself was not that strange, but there had been none of the usual baby language. No 'da da daas', no 'goo goo goos'. No blowing bubbles while learning to use his mouth for anything other than eating.

No, he simply couldn't speak, and then he could; it was as straightforward as that, and not one of the so-called 'experts' could explain why it should be so. For once in Morris's short life, they couldn't use the well-worn phrase 'perfectly normal'.

The child read as well. Not baby books, *real* books, proper *novels*, newspapers, scientific journals, in fact anything that he could lay his tiny, yet unusually strong hands upon, and *no one* had ever given the boy so much as a single second's worth of tuition in the fine art of learning to read.

He could also write. Not childish nonsense, not fairy tales or silly rhymes, but proper adult prose, together with a lot of technical stuff which even his father could barely understand.

Morris was thrown out of playgroup on the excuse that he wasn't 'engaging' either with the staff or the other children, but his father knew that his son had intimidated the adults working there by constantly studying them and speaking to them as though *he* was the adult and *they* the children. He had also refused point blank to join in with any of the childish games or to sing the infantile songs.

While the other children napped during 'quiet time', Morris could be found either engrossed in some mighty tome or he would be sitting crossed legged in the corner, quietly observing the staff as they chatted amongst themselves, casting the occasional nervous sideways glance in his direction.

Infant school was a similar experience of course: the headmistress confiding to Morris's father that there was simply *nothing* they could possibly teach the boy. In fact, she admitted, the lad could undoubtedly teach some of her *staff* a thing or two!

So, what to do with a five-year-old boy genius?

Obviously, he was far too young for secondary school. Not mentally, of course, but the boy would be tormented from day one by the larger children. And, even though the father had no feelings towards the boy whatsoever, he didn't want to see his son suffering needlessly.

Fortunately, aside from the fact that his father earned a very good living as the proprietor of a chain of successful estate agencies, there had also been an insurance pay-out on the death of his wife as well as a hefty out of court settlement from the hospital in an attempt to keep their obvious negligence quiet. In short, they were a little *more* than comfortably off when it came to finances.

It was possible, therefore, to hire a private tutor for the boy, someone suitably qualified to teach such a young, but incredibly intelligent child as Morris. It was *possible*, but very difficult as it turned out.

*

The first tutor, an elderly woman by the name of Doris Hoskins, lasted only three days before she fled the house, never to return. She had babbled something about Morris being 'too strange' to work with as she beat her hasty retreat, sending a friend round to collect her belongings a couple of days later.

The second tutor faired only slightly better by making it through the first week. He was a retired public school master who suddenly discovered the urgent need to visit a sick relative in Australia.

The third and fourth didn't see a whole day out between them and the fifth simply refused to be interviewed for the job by a five-year-old child.

The *sixth,* however, seemed to make everyone happy, and Morris especially so.

She was a woman in her late twenties by the name of Jayne Mitchell and she had come very highly recommended by the agency employed to find the right person for the job.

The boy's father was also smitten with the woman and they got along like the proverbial house on fire from the moment he opened the door and saw the very attractive, blue-eyed Jayne beaming a broad smile at him, before offering him her delicately manicured hand to shake.

Even *Morris,* who had never in all his five years on earth been known to smile, had a fixed grin on his small face as he stared in open admiration at his new tutor.

At *last,* someone who both father and son liked and could get along with.

*

Within six weeks, the father and the new tutor were getting along very well indeed, and had begun a passionate affair, with her creeping into his bedroom when Morris had gone to sleep, and staying there all night, every night.

Morris was very quick to notice the change in Jayne and his father. He spotted the way that they looked at each other, how they would brush against one another when passing in the hall or in the kitchen. He spied his father playfully pinch her perfectly shaped bottom and saw the way she giggled when he did so.

He observed all these things and, for the very first time in his life, Morris was feeling confused. Confused, and another emotion which, after researching through his extensive library of books, he discovered was called *jealousy.*

Being an emotionless child throughout his life, Morris wasn't sure that *jealousy* was the correct diagnosis for this new felt sensation, but *something* was definitely wrong with him. And if this was indeed jealousy, of what or of *whom* was he jealous, exactly? This was something he couldn't understand, something which, although he could look it up in a reference book and understand the *words* he read within, he could not apply the learned facts to himself. He couldn't figure out the root *cause* of this feeling, and it bothered Morris. It bothered him a lot!

*

Six months had now passed and the boy, though still deeply puzzled by these strange and persistent sensations, was happy in his own way with life, and his tutor in particular.

He had never known any real love or affection, but he felt sure that

Jayne loved him. She was always very kind towards him, at least, and used to playfully ruffle his hair when he managed to solve a particularly difficult problem, which he, of course, invariably did. He found the hair ruffling very annoying at first, until he realised that this was her way of showing him affection. Or, perhaps, *love*?

So, it was with some amazement that his father called him into his study one evening to find Jayne and him holding hands and seated on the settee, both wearing a broad grin on their faces.

"Ah, Morris," his father began, nervously, "Jayne and I...well...we've decided to...ummm...get married! Jayne will become your mother." And, as if to confirm this fact, Jayne held up her left hand to show Morris the large diamond engagement ring which glinted brilliantly on her finger, flashing the boy an equally wide smile of happiness.

Morris's reaction took the happy couple completely by surprise.

Initially, he stood with a slightly puzzled frown creasing his young brow, but moments later he rushed across the room and flung his arms around Jayne's neck, hugging her close.

"Oh *Mummy*, I *love* you!" and there were, incredibly, tears in the five year old's eyes. Morris, who had never been known to shed so much as a single tear in his entire life. This was a complete revelation to his father. The boy clung to Jayne's neck for an uncomfortably long time, and she was forced to gently ease him away from her so that she could breathe.

"Don't you think that you should congratulate Daddy as well, Morris?" she asked, quietly.

Morris stepped back and wiped the tears from his eyes with the back of his hand. He took a long look at Jayne and his father. Then, he stepped forward and shook his father's hand as you would shake a stranger's.

"Congratulations, Father," was all the boy said, almost, but not *quite*, grudgingly. There had never been any kind of affection between the two, and it seemed to be quite an ordeal for them both.

"Thank you, Morris. I'm pleased that you're happy with the news."

Morris turned his attention back to Jayne and smiled.

"I'm *very* happy, thank you. And now, if you'll please excuse me...?" And with that, he left the study, closing the door quietly behind him.

"Strange boy, that one," said his father upon hearing his son running upstairs to his bedroom. "*Very* strange."

Jayne leant across and kissed her husband-to-be full on the lips.

"He's just a kid. A very *intelligent* kid, but a kid all the same. And *now* he's a *happy* kid too. We have no idea what it must be like to lose your mother at your birth. It's enough to make *anyone* a little odd, knowing that they had died, bringing you into the world."

Her fiancé pulled her close and kissed her forehead.

"I guess you're right. Jayne. I've never really thought of it like that," he said. But he was also thinking, *but why the hell was he so weird even as a baby? He had no idea about his mother dying in childbirth back then.* He kept the thought to himself, however.

*

Morris lay on his bed, arms crossed behind his head, legs crossed at the ankles, eyes wide and staring up at the ceiling. He was experiencing another unfamiliar emotion, or was it the same one he'd felt previously, perhaps in a different form?

He was perplexed about the whole thing and he had no idea what to think. He decided that further information was required to enable him to make a balanced judgement on the matter.

He had by now read and outgrown every reference book in the house and Jayne had talked his father into buying the boy a laptop, which would open up the whole world of knowledge to the child.

Morris sat up on his bed, flipped open the laptop and switched it on.

He typed the word EMOTIONS into the search engine and waited for the results.

Morris was busy reading very late into the night, way past his usual 9:30 bedtime, and he was perturbed by some of the articles which he read, and perhaps more so by the strange noises coming from the direction of his father's bedroom. Noises which could be construed as either pleasure or pain, he could not decide which. Noises which culminated in Jayne screaming, "Yes!Yes!Yes!" before the sounds ended and the house fell silent once again.

Silent, that is, apart from the gentle tapping of Morris's small fingers on the laptop keypad as he now decided that further investigation was needed on the matter of these strange sounds coming from his father's room.

*

The boy was late getting up the next morning, which in itself was very unusual, as Morris was never late in rising.

Jayne took one look at his pale, tired face and asked, "Are you okay, Morris? You look very white this morning," and she placed a cool hand against his forehead to see if the boy had developed a temperature in the night.

Jayne's hand against his brow felt somehow very pleasant, and an involuntary shudder made its way through the boy's body.

"Morris! You're *shaking*! You are definitely not well, young man, so it's back to bed for you, I think!" she said, and took him by his clammy little hand before leading him over to the staircase.

"I'm alright, thank you. Just a little tired this morning. I didn't sleep very well last night," replied the boy, gripping tightly onto Jayne's hand as he spoke.

The thought crossed her mind that maybe he had heard their enthusiastic lovemaking the previous evening, and Jayne blushed automatically. She smiled nervously at the boy and said, "I hope nothing disturbed you, Morris?"

Morris looked her square in the eye and held her gaze. "No, nothing disturbed me. Why would it?"

Jayne tried to disguise the relief in her expression, but it was almost impossible with Morris's dark eyes boring into hers. Attack was her only defence.

"Well, whatever it was that kept you awake, young man, it's back to bed for you for a few hours to catch up on some sleep!" and she playfully slapped his scrawny rump and pointed a well-manicured finger towards his room.

The boy did as he was told, as he always did in fact, and returned to his room. He climbed beneath the covers but couldn't sleep. The only thing in his young mind were the images he had seen on various websites last night. Images of men and women coupled together in various positions, with the women calling out as Jayne had called out to his father.

"YES!YES!YES!" they screamed, together with other things like "FUCK ME!FUCK ME!" and although they appeared sometimes to be in pain during those acts, it also seemed that they were enjoying themselves as well.

Once again, Morris was feeling very confused by the whole gamut of emotions affecting, or perhaps *infecting* his young mind.

But one thing seemed very clear to him; these were definitely the same sounds he had heard the night before. Sounds made by his father and Jayne as they must have been doing the same things he had witnessed on the internet.

Things which he realised could only lead to one ultimate conclusion, if they were to continue. And *that* thought brought yet another new emotion crashing into his five-year-old mind.

*

The wedding arrangements appeared to be all that Jayne and his father could talk about these days, it seemed to Morris. It had originally been planned to take place in mid-August, but for reasons unknown to the boy, the wedding had been hurriedly brought forwards and would now occur only two days after Morris's sixth birthday.

"We can have a double celebration, Morris!" enthused Jayne, ruffling the boy's hair in her usual manner. Morris smiled dutifully, but mused that none of his *previous* birthdays had ever been a cause for celebration, so why should this one be any different?

*

Then the bombshell was dropped. The very scenario that Morris had both envisaged and dreaded beyond anything else in life, came to pass.

Jayne and his father were seated on the settee in the study as before. They linked hands as though their very lives depended on their close contact, as Father asked Morris to take a seat.

"Er...Morris," began his father, "I have some wonderful news to tell you." His father looked particularly nervous, while Jayne just sat there beaming a smile at her future husband, squeezing his hand as though to urge him on with relating their 'wonderful news'.

His father cleared his throat and continued.

"We...Jayne and I...are...we're..." His voice petered out. He knew the words, had rehearsed them several times before calling the boy into the study, but simply couldn't speak them.

Jayne smiled, squeezed his hand one last time and continued on his behalf.

"What your father is *trying* to tell you, is that you are going to have a baby brother or sister, Morris! Great news, isn't it?" And as Jayne and his father stared in goggle-eyed admiration and love for one another, they failed to notice the look of utter horror on Morris's young face.

The boy turned on his heels and left the room, closing the door quietly behind him.

"MORRIS!" his father bellowed, angry that their moment, their *special* moment hadn't met with at least *some sign* of enthusiasm, even a token 'congratulations'; anything but silence and departure.

He made to stand up to follow the boy, but Jayne pulled him back.

"Leave him, darling. He's in shock at the news, that's all. It's only been the two of you for so long, and now, suddenly, there'll be four people sharing this house. It's a lot to take in, and after all, he *is* only five years old. No matter *how* smart he may be, he's just a very young kid at heart." Jayne leant across and kissed the father of her unborn child.

"He'll come round, you'll see," she added.

*

Morris was lying on his bed, arms folded behind his head in his usual thinking mode. But, unusually, there were tears in his eyes; tears of anger, of self-pity and of bewilderment. All of the confused and unwelcome emotions he had been experiencing since Jayne had arrived at the house had finally bubbled over into one huge cascade of jumbled feeling, which in turn erupted into stinging tears and choking sobs.

Morris had begun to believe that things were improving in his life. He had someone, Jayne, who actually seemed to *care* about him. Even his father had started to show him an almost considerate side, which he'd never witnessed before Jayne's arrival, and the whole house had seemed to be a better place in which to live.

His life had definitely changed for the better.

But now this!

It had been inevitable, he realised that much. But so *soon*?

Just when, for the first time in his life, he was getting some attention, it was now to be shared with another. And Morris was wise enough to know that *his* share of the love would be considerably outweighed by the portion of loved which would be heaped upon the new baby. *Their* baby. A shared part of themselves, created when they made those noises every night, just along the landing.

Morris sat upright on his bed and wiped the tears from his eyes with the cuff of his jumper. He rubbed a hand across his face as though wiping sleep from his eyes. No more tears, he told himself. There would be no more crying and no more emotions from him! He had let things get to him, and this was the result.

The boy left the bed and crossed to his desk where he flipped on his laptop and waited for it to come to life. It was almost dawn before he finally switched it off again and climbed into his bed, falling asleep within moments.

*

It was Morris's sixth birthday, and Jayne and his father had managed to somehow find the time between wedding planning and visits to the hospital, to arrange a small party for him.

'Small' being the operative word, as Morris had no friends and no opportunity to make any. Anyway, he would have had as much in common with the average six-year-old as he would have had with a Neanderthal. And he would surely have found the Neanderthal much more interesting.

So, the party consisted of his father and Jayne, his former nanny, and, as his father had no living parents or siblings, he had invited a distant aunt and her equally distant daughter.

Morris was both embarrassed at being the centre of attention and annoyed at the way his former nanny and this great aunt who he had never even heard of before today, made such a fuss over him.

He was a *'wonderful lickle baby!'* crowed the nanny. 'A proper *angel'*, he was. "Never cried, did you, Poppet?" and she pinched his cheek affectionately, as Morris squirmed and tried to escape back to the safety of his room, only then to be cornered by the great aunt and her dopey-looking daughter.

"You look so much like your mother, Morris. The dead spit of her, you are!" she said, before turning to her daughter. "You remember Aunty Jill, don't you, Celia? Doesn't Morris look like her, eh?" Celia, however, looked as though she may well struggle to recall her *own* image, even if she had a mirror in front of her to help.

No one had ever mentioned the fact that he looked like his late mother before then. He considered that perhaps this was the reason that his father had despised him so much over the years? But then, until Jayne arrived, his father seemed to have despised just about everyone, so maybe that had nothing to do with it after all?

Finally, after what seemed like a lifetime to Morris, the party was over and the guests, such as they were, had left. There were a few childish toys and games given to Morris as presents, left unopened and unplayed with on the floor beside the settee. Jayne and his father were clearing away the plates and glasses, feeding them into the dishwasher and busily chatting about the wedding in two days' time, when Morris interrupted them.

"Thank you for my party. It was nice," he offered, half-heartedly.

"That's okay, Morris. Glad you enjoyed yourself," replied Jayne.

"Now it's off to bed for you, birthday boy. You've had a busy day!"

Morris could hear them talking about the wedding once more as he climbed the stairs to his room, his birthday already forgotten as they engrossed themselves in their plans for the future, and the future of the new baby.

*

The gentle, muffled tapping sound awoke Jayne first. The curtains were closed, but she could see daylight creeping around the edges and she glanced at the bedside clock. 8:25 am.

There was another light knock at the door. Jayne pulled the duvet cover up to hide her nakedness and called out, "Yes? Come in," as Morris's father stirred beside her.

The door opened slowly, and in came Morris carrying a tray heaped with breakfast things, making his way carefully across the gloomily lit room and setting the tray down gently on Jayne's bedside table.

"There!" he said "You made a birthday party for me last week, and I've made breakfast in bed for you!" he grinned broadly, before opening the curtains and flooding the bedroom with early morning light.

His father struggled to sit up, his eyes squinting in the sudden brightness, and said, "Whatsup? What's going on?"

"Nothing is up, darling. Morris has kindly brought us breakfast as a reward for giving him a birthday party," replied Jayne.

"Ah...right...thank you, Morris. Very kind, I'm sure."

Morris smiled tightly and said, "I'll leave you to it then. There's tea, coffee, orange juice, toast and marmalade. Enjoy!" He left the room, closing the bedroom door, before he put his ear to it, listening as his father expressed incredulity while Jayne laughed quietly as he spluttered his amazement.

*

Morris left them for one and a half hours before he returned to their bedroom.

He had calculated that would be more than enough time for the drugs mixed in the tea, coffee and orange juice to take effect. He had already experimented on a neighbour's cat and had simply extrapolated his results to account for the increased body mass of adult humans.

Thank God for the internet, he thought. You can buy almost *anything* on there, these days. His father's credit card had also helped, of course. He had tried, however, to purchase Rohypnol, but discovered that it was banned in many countries, and anyway, his research had led him to believe that it wasn't powerful enough for his needs.

So, he had looked further and had discovered that Ketamine mixed with a small amount of chloral hydrate should be ideal, and his new experiments with the cat confirmed this. Alas, his first trials on a couple of grey squirrels in the large back garden had gone badly wrong, leaving one stone dead and the other permanently paralysed down one half of its body.

*

He opened the bedroom door cautiously and peered inside.

They were both completely motionless. Jayne was out for the count and lying on her side, but his father was lying propped up on his pillows with his eyes wide open, and staring straight ahead.

Morris checked on Jayne first. He felt her pulse. It was slow but steady.

Then he checked his father. He was quite shocked to see that his father's eyes were trying to follow him as Morris made his way around the king-sized bed towards him. However, Morris realised that his ability to see what was going on, to witness what was about to happen, would make the whole thing more enjoyable and worthwhile.

The boy left the room and soon returned with yet another breakfast tray, only this one was covered with a tea towel.

Morris set the tray down carefully on his father's bedside table and whipped the tea towel away before tilting his father's paralysed head so that he could see the array of knives and other implements arranged carefully upon it.

A look of horror came into the man's eyes and Morris noted with delight that his father was trying to call out, to move, to run away. But he remained motionless. The combination of drugs was working well and would continue to do so for some time yet. Time enough for Morris to complete his work at least.

Morris stripped off the duvet and threw it into a corner of the room.

He noticed that both of the adults were naked, which was good as it saved him the trouble of struggling to remove any night clothes.

He then flipped Jayne over onto her back and arranged her, ready to carry out the operation he had watched several times on the internet. He had paid very careful attention and had made copious notes to assist him, should he need them.

Morris selected a couple of very sharp kitchen knives from the tray beside his father, and, as an afterthought, he picked up a pair of garden secateurs as well, and popped them into his back pocket. He had decided just last night, that he would operate on Jayne first, so that his helpless father would have the pleasure of watching the whole thing, knowing that *he* was to blame for the situation.

With this in mind, Morris adjusted his father's head so that he could better see what was about to happen.

Morris opened Jayne's legs and spread them wide. Most six year olds had never seen a vagina before, but Morris had been doing his homework and had seen plenty, one way or another, on the internet and he was completely unfazed by the experience.

He took a small knife and jabbed it into her genitalia, just to ensure that Jayne was still out for the count. When there was no reaction, he plunged the knife deep into her lower abdomen and started to cut across just above the pelvic bone, as he had seen surgeons do while they performed caesarean section deliveries.

The knife was sharp, but it was no scalpel and it took Morris quite some time to hack his way across so the pouch was large enough for him to see what he was doing for the next phase of the procedure.

The sheets and mattress were now covered in blood and Morris had to keep wiping his small hands on a towel taken from their ensuite bathroom, as the knife became too slippery to use.

After several minutes of delving about inside Jayne, Morris was certain that he had found what he was looking for and removed it with a few deft cuts of the kitchen knife.

Satisfied, he withdrew the uterus and dropped it unceremoniously onto the bed between Jayne and his father. He briefly considered sewing up the gaping slash in Jayne's abdomen, but quickly discounted the idea as a waste of time. And what would be the point...she was going nowhere.

Morris turned his attention to the uterus, and he easily located the sack containing the tiny foetus; his would-have-been brother or sister. The foetus was just as he had seen in books and on the internet. It looked more alien than human at this stage of its existence, with the head disproportionately larger than its body.

Making sure that his father could see, he removed his sibling's head with the secateurs, and threw the severed parts back onto the bed.

Morris allowed himself another rare smile. It was a job well done. A successful operation.

Now it was his father's turn, and a much simpler procedure.

He once again adjusted the paralyzed man's head so that he could clearly see what was about to happen, this time to him. Only the man's eyes gave any hint that he was aware of the horror of it all, but he was completely unable to prevent it from happening. He couldn't even close his eyelids to block it from his vision.

Morris held his father's penis in his left hand and stretched it so that the testicles were dangling like two fat plums. Then he picked up the bloody secateurs and snipped through his father's manhood at the very base, holding his trophy triumphantly before the adult's eyes, blood dripping from the severed scrotum, forming a gory puddle on his chest.

"There!" said the boy, "that'll stop *you* two having any more children, I think!" Morris left the room, his father still forced to remain staring at the place where his genitalia had once been, the blood welling up from between his thighs in thick, red gouts.

*

Morris struggled back into the room with the heavy cans of petrol and placed them just inside the bedroom door. He then gathered up all his equipment and took it downstairs to the kitchen before returning to collect the drugged breakfast things.

He carefully cleaned every item in boiling water laced with bleach, making sure that there was no trace of blood or remaining signs of the drugs he had used. He had already dumped the bottles they had arrived in at a bottle bank, several miles from his home.

Satisfied that every trace had been removed, he closed the kitchen door and headed up to his *parents'* bedroom.

His father was now trying to move. Morris could see the fingers of his left hand twitching and there was a faint movement in his left foot. Good, the boy thought.

He would not only *know* what was happening, but he would *feel* everything as well.

Morris unscrewed the tops from the petrol cans and began pouring it around the room, paying particular attention to the two people on the bed, ensuring that they were thoroughly doused in the highly flammable liquid.

He removed the cans from the bedroom, took a new box of Swan Vestas from his pocket, showing them to his terrified father, before stepping back into the doorway, lighting a couple of matches and flicking them onto the bed.

Despite all his research, Morris was shocked at the powerful way the fire ignited and took hold of the room. Within seconds, it was ablaze and he only just had time to shut the door before the flames were almost upon him.

He hurried downstairs and returned the cans to the large, triple garage where he had found them. The garage was directly beneath his father's bedroom, and when, Morris had calculated, enough time had elapsed to completely destroy all evidence of what he had done to the two adults now being cremated above, he would set *another* fire, which he was confident would disguise the one he had lit in the bedroom.

When the floor gave way, and the upstairs bedroom crashed into the garage below, not even the best fire investigation officer in the world would be able to tell where it had initially started.

And, after all, Morris was just a six-year-old kid. Kids played with matches, didn't they? He'd be very sorry, he'd clearly been very *naughty*, but then, boys will be boys. Won't they?

A NIGHT TO REMEMBER

I can't recall exactly how old I was when the first conscious thoughts entered my head, but I know that I was still in the womb.

Obviously, I had then no real concept of time; the hours, weeks, *months* that I was trapped within the suffocating confines of my mother's stomach, seemed endless to me and I almost went insane in there. In the dark, with strange noises vaguely discernible, coming from outside. From the great big, open world.

Then there was the ignominious and wholly messy birth to be endured. The *horror* of being ejected via my mother's vagina before being man-handled by nurses who sucked the mucus from my nose and wiped my small body with a rough towel, then attached a plastic tag to my ankle prior to shoving me into an incubator, as I was, apparently, a rather underweight infant.

Maybe my body *was* sickly and underweight, but my mind *thrived*!

Finally, I was released from the maternity unit and I still vividly recall the journey to what was to become my home, accompanied by my mother seated safely in the back seat of the car, holding onto me tightly, while a man, who I later discovered was my grandfather, drove us. I had no father, it seemed. At least not one who gave enough of a shit to have hung around to watch the fruit of their loins emerge into the world.

I suffered all the dreadful billing and cooing from one and all.

Strangers talking *at* me rather than *to* me, bouncing me on their knee as I gurgled inanities and made all the expected idiotic baby noises. My only pleasure being the instances when I was able to either throw up a stomach-full of milky vomit down these strangers backs as they hugged me to their shoulder, or better still, urinate or defecate as they had me on their lap. Even *more* rewarding if I happened to be nappy-less at the time.

But these small moments of pleasure in no way made up for the rest of my interminably boring existence. You cannot imagine the terrible frustration I endured by not being able to communicate via my voice. The *horror* of being unable to walk with those rubbery, weedy infant legs, while waiting for a more substantial musculature to develop.

I *loathed* the way that my head, as yet only supported by feeble neck muscles, wobbled almost uncontrollably, the difficulty I had in focussing my young eyes and all those enforced afternoon 'naps'.

My only way of exacting revenge being the frequent middle-of-the-night screaming sessions, which were poor recompense for the indignities I'd had to undergo.

My mother, although at the point of exhaustion with the effort of raising me on her own and with minimal outside assistance, clearly doted on me and she devoted her life to looking after me and pandering to all my infant whims.

Things started to improve, marginally, as I first learnt to crawl and then, after much practice and many painful knocks and falls, to toddle and finally walk. Those pathetic little baby legs gradually filled out with muscle, I no longer had the indignity of wearing a nappy as I could use a potty, my eyes could focus properly and my head no longer wobbled uncontrollably. I was *almost* a human being, finally!

Then, just as I thought that my life was at last starting to be worth living, *he* arrived.

I have no recollection of how or where my mother met the man.

He must have somehow contacted her and I gathered that he was my father. The same man who had not been there for my birth. The very person who had let my mother struggle to raise me on her own, with only scant assistance from my grandfather. However, he was not a well man himself.

But there he was and it seemed as though he was here to stay.

My cot was removed from my mother's bedroom and re-sited in the box room on the very evening that he moved himself into our small flat. Although I was to all intents and purposes still a very young child of three years of age, I could sense the hatred this man had for me. The way that he looked at me with loathing on his face when he thought no one else was watching.

I endured the sly slaps and the crafty pinches he would give me without crying, and, when my mother asked him where a random bruise had come from, he would simply tell her that I had fallen and knocked myself.

"He's a clumsy little sod sometimes," he would say to her, speaking as though I was not even in the room.

Over time, the slaps developed into punches and when on one occasion Social Services became involved, after severe bruising was discovered on my back during a routine check-up, the man...my *father*, managed to convince the authorities that it was *my* clumsiness that was the cause and they took the man at his word.

At first, I felt certain that my mother was totally unaware of his cruelty towards me, but over time I realised with horror that she knew exactly what was going on, and, although she would never condone such brutality to her only child, she was content to turn a blind eye, so long as things didn't go *too* far.

I noticed that she too had apparently become very accident prone, as she would often appear with bruises on her arms and once she had a black eye which was allegedly caused by walking into a door.

"A boy needs a firm hand, or he'll turn out wrong!" was the man's maxim, and for some reason my mother was evidently completely blind to the fact that her *lover*, my *father*, had turned out more wrong than she was ever willing to admit to herself.

There was a brief respite from the misery, almost a year later.

My 'father' was arrested for dealing drugs and burglary and as he had many previous convictions, he was sentenced to five years in prison. Although my mother was clearly upset about his sudden incarceration, I could not have been happier that he was no longer there to rule the roost and make my life unbearable.

It was just before my seventh birthday when the two worst things in my young life occurred, simultaneously.

My grandfather, a man I had sadly seen too little of, died after a long illness. And the other, was my father's early release from prison 'for good behaviour'. This bullying pig of a man had clearly been a coward in prison, where men of his own type would stand up to him and there were no small children or women to beat up and humiliate.

There was no birthday celebration for me that year. My grandfather's funeral upset my mother a great deal, as he was her only remaining relative apart from me. There had only been the two of us at the graveside, together with a couple of his neighbours, so it had been a very brief and upsetting affair.

And then *he* was back again, demanding her attention almost before my grandfather was cold in his grave, shouting at my mother in that coarse way he had, clipping me around the ear for no reason at every opportunity.

"Maybe the old bastard has left you some money?" he asked my mother, only two days after returning into our lives.

Mother shook her head. "He lived in that old council house his whole life and he hadn't been able to work for years because of his bad back. No...there's nothing there that *I'd* want," she replied, wistfully.

"Well, we can flog it all then...make a few quid out of his old tat," insisted my father.

Mother shook her head and smiled tightly. "I've told the Cancer Research people to come and get the lot and sell it in their shop. It was cancer that killed him, so it only seems right."

My father stood up, bristling with rage and crossed to my mother, his face only inches from hers.

"You've done fucking *what*, you stupid cow? We could've done with that money, never mind fucking *charity*! *Charity* begins at home, you moron!" and he shoved her heavily to the floor, before he stormed out of the flat, leaving the front door wide open behind him.

I rushed across to help her up as she lay hunched up and weeping on the rug beside the sofa, clutching her side when she'd hit the edge of the coffee table as she fell. As I eased her over to her chair and she sat down, I asked:

"Why do you let *him* live here?"

She held my hand and grimaced at the pain in her side.

"Because he's your *father*...and...because I'm too scared *not* to let him stay with us. Scared of what he might do…" And I knew for certain that the actual reason was the latter. I could see the terror in her eyes, the terror which I had mistakenly thought of as a look of love.

My mother suffered two fractured ribs after that attack and she was in pain for several weeks. Of course, she told the hospital that she had fallen; tripped over the rug and landed heavily against the table, which I suppose was at least *partly* true.

So, while *she* was out of action assault-wise for a while, he turned all his violence against me, and there were several visits to A&E over the following weeks for attention to my various 'football' injuries. Though a cigarette burn to the back of my neck, which had turned septic, was a little more difficult to explain away.

Unfortunately, along with his propensity for harming people smaller and weaker than himself, he seemed to have an amazing ability to invent the most incredibly convincing and elaborate lies. The burn on my neck was blamed on a passing gang of juveniles who had targeted me for no apparent reason.

So all of these incidents passed by unchallenged and with no suspicion falling on that jailbird son of a bitch bully.

It's odd, but when you endure such bullying month after month, year after year, it almost becomes the norm rather than the exception.

That is, of course, unless something happens to break the cycle of abuse. Something which snaps you out of the almost ritualistic behaviour and acceptance of the treatment you are receiving.

*

My mother was now a mere shadow of her former self.

There was no longer any glimmer of hope in her eyes and she seemed to almost sleepwalk through our daily lives. She had changed very much for the worse.

He meanwhile was becoming more and more heavily involved with ever harder drugs, and mercifully spent a great deal of his time staring off into some horror-filled world of his own creation. This at least gave me some peace, but there were times when both he *and* my mother were stoned out of their skulls, and I was left to fend for myself for days at a time.

I have to admit that I looked forward to these occasions. It was the only time that there was any *real* peace in my life. Time to sit and think without fear of another beating from *him*, or receiving a tirade of abuse from my mother, who, due to his influence and her new and habitual drug usage, was almost becoming as bad as him.

Then, one day as I was sitting watching television and tucking into the beans on toast I'd just made myself, *he* came staggering into the living room, wild-eyed and insane looking.

The first thing he did was to rip the television plug out of the wall, before he crossed the room and began cuffing me about the head and then dragged me out of the living room into the hallway, where he bundled me into the understair cupboard and slammed the door. I could hear him outside, apoplectic with rage and swearing insanely as he barricaded me into the small, dark cupboard which smelt heavily of dry rot and gas.

"You fuckin' little bastard! eating my fuckin' food like you own the place! Stealing my money, you fucker!"

Shortly, I heard the front door slam and sometime later, he returned, no doubt with a fresh supply of whatever dope he could beg, borrow or, more likely, steal and I heard him clambering up the stairs above my head followed by a bedroom door closing noisily.

Apart from a very narrow chink of light seeping through from the bottom of the door, it was pitch black in there. The smell was making me nauseous and there were faint scratching, scrabbling noises in the darkness which made me feel uneasy and afraid.

I have no idea how long I sat there in the cramped darkness, but I somehow managed to stretch out a little and I slowly fell into an uncomfortable sleep. It must have been night time by now as the faint sliver of light from under the door had now disappeared and, as I dozed fitfully, I imagined that I was once more inside my mother's womb, safe, but bored and eager to emerge into the world outside.

Faint noises filtered through the thin wooden door into my makeshift cell and I felt almost comforted to know that there was life outside. Even the sounds made by *him* and my mother as they stumbled about in their drug-addled way were strangely comforting.

I guess it was a couple of days later that the door to my prison was opened, the light blinding me after so long spent in almost total darkness. A plate containing two slices of stale bread and a plastic beaker of water were thrust into my face as my vision still struggled to clear after the sudden brightness.

"Fucking hell, boy! You've stunk that cupboard out!" said my father. I tried to clamber out into the light, but my legs were both numb after sitting on the hard floor for so many hours and I found that I couldn't move.

"Oh no you don't! You've made your stink so you can lie in it and think about what you've done." And before I could utter a single word, the door was once more slammed shut and I could hear him dragging something heavy against it to prevent my escape.

We may not have inherited anything monetarily when grandfather died, but my mother had somehow managed to persuade the council that she should have first option on his now empty house. And so, we had moved in some six weeks after his funeral and it was much nicer than the dreadful, damp flat we'd been living in on that horrendous housing estate.

At least this place was in a semi-rural location and had a reasonably sized garden. And it did, very briefly, stop my father from buying drugs so easily from his regular supplier. Until he made a new contact, that was.

Hours and then days passed in the cramped understair cupboard. I had tried to eat the bread and drink the water sparingly, but hunger was becoming a constant gnawing pain in my stomach and my throat was parched from the dry, musty-smelling air and my meagre rations had been devoured far quicker than I had intended. I was now starving hungry and my throat and tongue were swollen due to the lack of fluids.

As I shuffled my numb legs in a vain attempt to ease the agony of cramp, I heard rather than felt my foot kick against a loose floorboard and it moved to one side. I could feel a vague breeze coming up through the floor cavity and I inched painfully towards the void, my hands moving blindly in front of me.

I felt something cold and hard touch the palm of my hand and my fingers closed around a long, metallic object which I carefully removed from the hole in the floor. Carefully running my fingers along the metal object in the pitch darkness, I could feel that it was over a foot long with a handle at one end and a long, straight blade culminating in a sharp point at the other.

Immediately, I recalled seeing such an item in an old film on the television; it was a World War Two bayonet and it must have been hidden there by my grandfather when he returned home from the army, years ago. I thought about how I could best use this weapon; how it would assist me to escape my tiny prison without disturbing *him* and my mother upstairs. I was getting weaker by the day and desperate measures were required and soon.

I had no idea whether they had forgotten me in their drug-induced world. I hadn't heard any sounds from them for hours, and for all I knew, they may well have overdosed during their latest trip into hell.

I gave it what I guessed to be another hour, and when after that I *still* hadn't heard a sound from above, I decided that it was time to at least *try* to escape before I became too weak to do so.

I wedged the point of the bayonet between two lengths of the tongue and grooved boarding which made up the wall of the cupboard, and twisted it slowly from side to side. There was a cracking noise as the wood sprung apart and I immediately stopped and listened carefully to see whether I had made enough racket to disturb their dope-addled brains. But there was nothing; not a sound, so I tried again.

This time, there was a louder crack and one of the flimsy pieces of pine flew to one side, allowing a little light to flood into my prison. There was just enough room to allow me to peer through the opening and I could see that a heavy sideboard had been dragged across the doorway, completely blocking it. There would be no escape that way, for certain.

I cursed silently and sat back to think. At least there was now a little fading light in the cupboard, which I found comforting.

Then I noticed how the stairs above my head were constructed. If I could just somehow lever the under stair supports away, I might be able to open up the actual tread and escape. Fortunately, my mother had never been what you might even remotely call house proud, and she had never thought that the expense of stair carpet was worth the cost. Hopefully, her meanness would make my escape possible.

The creaking as the nails were eased out by the tip of the bayonet was horrendous and I felt certain that the noise must rouse them this time. But there was no sound at all. No hurried footsteps descending the stairs, no angry shouts. Not even so much as a disturbed snort in their sleep, so I tried again and the first step support came loose with screech.

I waited a full five minutes, just in case, and then set to work on the other side and, within fifteen minutes, I had a gap which was just about large enough for me to wriggle through and escape my prison of the last few days.

I felt almost dizzy with the smell of fresher air and I was elated that I had escaped my confinement. I sat on the bottom step, gulping in air and thinking what I should do next.

My first priority was to get some food and water to slake my hunger and terrible thirst. But what if they came down now and caught me? And after all the damage I had done to the staircase?

No…it would be better to pad quietly upstairs and see what kind of a state they were in first. Then I would know whether it was safe or not and I could then feed myself without the constant terror of being discovered. There was nothing else for it. I would *have* to go upstairs and take my chances. Either way, I would be in serious trouble.

I still had the bayonet, though I had no idea what I would do with the thing. At least it would keep *him* at arm's length for a bit if I was caught…give me chance to escape maybe?

The weight of the steel blade felt comforting in my hand as I inched my way slowly up the stairs, towards their bedroom. Every time a stair creaked, I froze, held my breath and listened for any sounds of movement, but there were none and I carried on.

At last I arrived on the landing outside their room and I pressed my ear up against the door, listening with every fibre of my being.

Not a sound.

Could they have gone away somewhere? Was it possible that they had just left me there, under the stairs, leaving me to die in that stinking cupboard? *Surely*, my mother still had *some* feeling of love for me, however vague or remote it might be?

Anger welled up inside me.

I grasped the bedroom door handle and turned it as quietly as possible, inching the door open very slowly.

The curtains were open, and I could clearly see from the light of a nearby street lamp, two figures huddled together in the centre of the bed, covered by a filthy, stained sheet. They were *cuddling* one another! My mother and *him*, that creature who had ruined our lives and brought nothing but misery and pain to us, and chronic drug addiction to my mother.

Yes, she was cuddling *him*, while her only son had been locked in a stinking cupboard without food or water?

I took a step closer to the bed and stared down at them as they slept. I could see that my mother actually had a *smile* on her face as she slept. That fucking, drug-sodden *whore* was *smiling*, without a care in the world or a single thought for me. I could have been *dead* in that tiny cupboard for all she cared, as here she was, lying next to *him...smiling*!

I stood right beside the bed now, looking down at the two of them, hoping, *praying* that one or other of them would wake up and find me there, bayonet in hand, silently watching them. I hoped that for just one second, *they* could feel a fraction of the terror which I had endured at their hands, for such a long time.

But they slept on.

I realised that even in *his* drugged-up state, he would still probably be able to put up a good enough fight to fend me off, so I decided to start with him. It was only fair anyway, as he had been the main cause of all this misery.

I eased back the disgusting sheet so as to better see what I was about to do, then I placed the point of the bayonet just above his right eye, before sweeping it down, through the eye socket and deep into his brain.

I stabbed again and again and again, until his head was a crimson mush of blood, shattered bone and bits of brain and destroyed eyeball, yet he never made a sound. Not even so much as a groan. Had he really been that far gone?

Worse still, my mother hadn't woken or moved a muscle as I had hoped she would, and she now lay there spattered with blood and gore from her lover's destroyed head, yet still she slept on, with that stupid happy smile on her smug fucking face!

Even when I started to hack off her head, sawing at her neck with the rusty blade of the bayonet, a great geyser of blood arcing across the room as I severed the arteries, cutting through the soft cartilage in her throat and finally hacking my way through her vertebrae and thick muscles at the back of her neck, even *then*, she didn't move or try to cry out.

They were clearly so *evil*, so vile and depraved, that they were beyond all human feelings; even as they died, deservedly so, they were incapable of any sensations from this world.

I prayed that they would feel things in the next world, for people like them would surely be bound for the fiery pits of hell? I hoped with all my heart that they would suffer every minute of every day, for the rest of eternity, for what they had done to me!

*

So, that is how I remember it all. That is the story of my horrific childhood and of the inhuman people who raised me and made me what I am today.

As I lay in my cell each night, with the thick padding lining the walls, blocking out most of the sounds from the outside world, reminding me once more of being back *there*, safe inside my mother's womb, I think of all the insane garbage those doctors keep telling me.

As if *they* would know. As if *they* were there and went through all the horrible things which I'd experienced. Stupid bastards!

They've been trying to convince me that it was all in my head.

They try to brainwash me into believing that I was raised by a loving and devoted Christian couple, my father a brilliant doctor and my mother a nurse.

Doctor? Nurse? Fucking drug-taking, drug-dealing junky bastards, was what they were!

These *imbeciles* tell me that we all lived in a beautiful house in the country. They say that I was privately educated at an expensive school. They say that I wanted for nothing. They know *nothing* of my suffering!

They have tried to convince me that I fell into drug abuse while still at that school and that I was eventually kicked out for beating another boy so badly that I almost killed him.

They are crazy enough to accuse me of murdering my so-called loving parents as they slept peacefully in their bed one night, hacking them to pieces and spreading their body parts around the house as I laughed insanely.

They tell me that I was still laughing like a maniac when the police broke down the front door and shot me in the leg as I wielded a large, blood stained kitchen knife at them, threatening to kill them all.

But *they* are the mad ones!

There is *nothing* wrong with my memory...*nothing*!

I can still remember being safe in my mother's womb.

I remember my grandfather,

I remember being locked in that cupboard under the stairs.

I remember everything. EVERYTHING!

A PROBLEM SHARED...

(Inspired by Michelle O'Neill)

"He never says no to a tea."

"And your point is?"

"Just that...he never says no to a tea."

"So what are you saying...exactly?"

"That he never says no to a tea...maybe we could put something in it...?"

"'Put something in it'...like what, for instance?"

"Poison...we slip some poison in his tea."

"Oh...we slip some *poison* in his tea, do we? And where, pray tell, do we get this poison from?"

"Well, I dunno...from somewhere..."

"Somewhere like...? Oh, I know...we pop into Poisons R Us and buy some...of course...simple when you think about it!"

"Well there's no need to be sarcastic! I'm only trying to be helpful...!"

"Slipping poison in his tea is an idea, I'll grant you that...but which *type* of poison? Will it just make him ill or will it kill him off? And where do we bloody well get it from?"

"I thought the aim was to kill him. So, a poison that kills, naturally. There must be *loads* of poisons which'll do the job."

"Brilliant; name three. I believe that you're thinking back to Dickensian times when doctors knew very little and you could actually poison someone and get away with it! These days, they probably have a bloody phone app to tell them which poisons do what and all the symptoms they should look out for! Tea or no tea...it's a shitty idea!"

"Well, I don't know...it was just a thought...a suggestion..."

"If you can't think of something better than that, don't bloody bother! This is supposed to be a serious business. He has to go and *we* have to get rid of him. Think, man...*think!*"

"Okay...how about electrocuting him, then?"

"Oh yeah...while he's drinking his tea, I suppose?"

"Why not...what's wrong with *that*?"

"It's better than the poison, I'll give you that. Keep thinking..."

Three days later, their father was dead.

Their mother walked in on the latest planning meeting, which was being held in the garage.

"Your father is dead."

The boys looked at one another in surprise and then turned back to their mother.

"How?" they asked in unison.

"Don't know. He suddenly developed these dreadful stomach pains. He must've eaten something that disagreed with him. Not sure that was what killed him, though..."

"Then what *did* kill him?"

"It could have been the loose cable on his bedside light. Gave him a *really* nasty electric shock, for sure..."

"So, he was electrocuted then?"

"Oh yes...but I still don't think that that was what killed him, though."

"Then what *did* kill him?"

"Well, it was most likely the carving knife that I stuck in his back a dozen times while he was unconscious after the shock. I think *that* finished him off...probably."

The boys looked at one another for a few moments and then smiled.

All their scheming had been for nothing. Their mother had sorted the problem for them. As mothers invariably do.

"Well done, Mum. We'll help you bury him in the vegetable garden."

"Thanks, boys...but I was thinking more like having a great big bonfire to burn all the old rubbish."

"We'll get the matches."

"Good boys."

Also available from
Parallel Universe Publications

A PLACE OF SKULLS by David Ludford
ISBN: 978-0-9935742-6-9

HAUNTED GRAVE by Ezeiyoke Chukwunonso
ISBN: 978-0-9935742-3-8

INTO THE DARK by Andrew Jennings
ISBN: 978-0-9935742-5-2

TOUGH GUYS by Adrian Cole
ISBN: 978-0-9935742-2-1

CLASSIC WEIRD 2 selected by David A. Riley
ISBN: 978-0-9932888-4-5

OTHER VISIONS OF HEAVEN AND HELL by Jessica Palmer
ISBN: 978-0-9935742-1-4

A SAUCERFUL OF SECRETS by Andrew Darlington
ISBN: 978-0-9935742-0-7

THE WINTER HUNT AND OTHER STORIES
by Steve Lockley & Paul Lewis
ISBN: 978-0-9932888-9-0

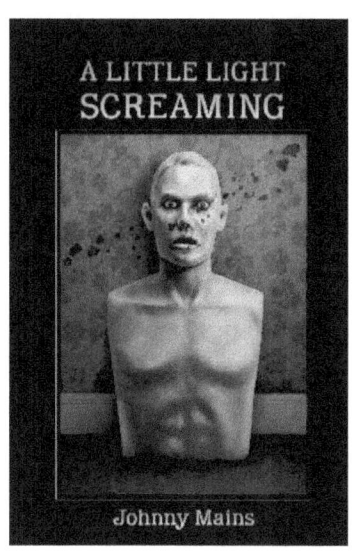

A LITTLE LIGHT SCREAMING by Johnny Mains
ISBN: 978-0-9932888-5-2

ENGLAND 'B': 90 MINUTES OF HELL by Richard Staines
ISBN: 978-0-9932888-7-6

AND NOBODY LIVED HAPPILY EVER AFTER by Kate Farrell
ISBN: 978-0-9932888-8-3

FISHHEAD: THE DARKER TALES OF IRVIN S. COBB
ISBN: 978-0-9935742-4-5

KITCHEN SINK GOTHIC: Selected by David and Linden Riley
ISBN: 978-0-9932888-3-8

WILL ANYONE FIGURE OUT THAT THIS IS A REPACKAGED FIRST
COLLECTION? by Johnny Mains
ISBN: 978-0-9574535-7-9

BLACK CEREMONIES by Charles Black
ISBN: 978-0-9574535-5-5

HIS OWN MAD DEMONS:
DARK TALES FROM DAVID A. RILEY
ISBN: 978-0-9574535-8-6

THEIR CRAMPED DARK WORLD by David A. Riley
ISBN: 978-0-9574535-9-3

THE HEAVEN MAKER AND OTHER GRUESOME TALES
by Craig Herbertson
ISBN: 978-0-9932888-2-1

GOBLIN MIRE by David A. Riley
ISBN: 978-0-9574535-4-8

THINGS THAT GO BUMP IN THE NIGHT
selected by Douglas Draa and David A. Riley
ISBN: 978-0-9574535-6-2

CLASSIC WEIRD selected David A. Riley
ISBN: 978-0-9574535-3-1

MOLOCH'S CHILDREN by David A. Riley
ISBN: 978-0-9932888-1-4

Check our website:

http://paralleluniversepublications.blogspot.co.uk/

www.ingramcontent.com/pod-product-compliance
Lightning Source LLC
Chambersburg PA
CBHW070030260626
47159CB00005B/2006